MEREDITH OUT OF THE DARKNESS

SECOND EDITION

THE MEREDITH SERIES
BOOK ONE

AMANDA GALE

We can only appreciate the miracle of a sunrise if we have waited in the darkness.

— UNKNOWN

CONTENTS

Chapter One   1

Chapter Two   18

Chapter Three   45

Chapter Four   69

Chapter Five   84

Chapter Six   97

Chapter Seven   113

Chapter Eight   136

Chapter Nine   149

Chapter Ten   160

Chapter Eleven   184

Chapter Twelve   193

Chapter Thirteen   206

Chapter Fourteen   224

Chapter Fifteen   251

Chapter Sixteen   281

Meredith Against the Wind   295

Also by Amanda Gale   297

Acknowledgments   299

CHAPTER ONE

SIX YEARS AGO

*M*eredith peeked cautiously around the doorway, her brow raised with attention. She heard footsteps and soft chatter downstairs, but upstairs she appeared to be alone. Quietly she tiptoed from her old bedroom, across the hall to her parents' room. She tapped the door until it opened enough for her to slip through. Once inside she hurried to her mother's jewelry box, an ornate antique of cherry wood, bestowed upon her mother by Meredith's grandmother Josephine.

Her heart beating double time, she opened the lid and gazed inside. She fingered through diamonds and rubies, considering for a moment changing her mind—but then she discovered what she had been looking for. She smiled as she gingerly took the pearl earrings in her fingers and held them up to her ears, then studied herself in the mirror. These earrings always had been her favorites, but Patricia never let Meredith borrow them. Tonight Meredith was feeling bold. She would risk incurring her mother's anger, for once grateful that her weapon of choice was frigidity. It meant there would be no confrontation.

Upon closing the box Meredith caught sight of another favorite. She brought her hand to the antique ring before she could stop herself. She twiddled it in her fingers and was just about to slip it on for size when a shadow fell on her from the doorway. Her head snapped toward the door, her already wide green eyes even wider with guilt, and she suddenly lost the momentum it had taken her twenty minutes to build.

"I didn't realize you were such a thrill seeker," said her brother, one hand on the doorframe, his weight resting casually on one leg. Like Meredith, he was dressed in his evening best, and his tuxedo showcased the sleekness of his build and the dark sultriness of his face. "I guess I get it. Some people skydive or swim with sharks; you tempt fate by stealing from our parents."

Meredith's heart returned to her chest, and she sighed with relief. "Maybe I am living a little dangerously," she replied, chuckling.

"I'll say. Mom's cold shoulder would freeze you to death, though Dad's more likely to murder you violently. Your odds don't look good either way." His playful expression turned even more mischievous. "Come on, you've been in this family for twenty-six years. You should know this."

She returned her gaze to the jewelry box, which she closed carefully, the pearl earrings and the antique ring in hand. She placed the earrings on her mother's dresser and slipped the ring on her finger. She cocked her head back as she held out her hand to examine the view. "What do you think, Vince?" she asked, her face bright with excitement. "Is it me?"

"No," Vince replied, entering the room and looking cross-eyed at her finger as she held it very close to his face. He waved her hand away. "Apparently, it's me. You know Mom wants me to have it."

"It's not your color," Meredith said slyly, with a crooked grin. She sighed and replaced the ring in the jewelry box. The ring, like the jewelry box, had belonged to her mother's mother, Meredith and Vince's beloved grandmother Josephine. Patricia inherited the ring when Josephine passed away, and it was intended for Vince, the older child, so he could present it to his future wife.

"You're not kidding. If Mom really gives me that ring, I might as well be the one wearing it. I'm not getting married."

"Don't say that," Meredith said dreamily as she closed the lid and faced him. "You never know where life will take you. You could meet the love of your life tomorrow. Then you'll want that ring."

"Your starry-eyed optimism is getting old, Merry," said Vince, rolling his chocolate-colored eyes and heading toward the door with a cool swagger. He stuck his hands in the pockets of his slacks and turned to face her once more. "You and Adam have been on only two dates and already you're trying on rings."

"Well, you never know. There's such a strong connection, and we have so much in common."

Vince looked amused. "Oh, yeah? Like what?"

"Like we're both teachers, and we both love the theater. In fact, he runs the drama club at his school. Right now he's working on a production of *Romeo and Juliet*."

"Very romantic."

"It is, isn't it? But it's more than that. We understand each other." Her eyes twinkled. "I can really see a future with him."

Vince rolled his eyes again.

"Oh, what do you know," said Meredith, shaking her head. "You never even make it to the second date. You're the last person I should be listening to when it comes to relationships."

"Why would I go on a second date when I can have another first date?"

"You never give anyone a chance. You could have been with the perfect woman last night, and you'd never know it."

"I'm just trying to spread it around, Merry. I'm trying to give as many women as possible the chance to go out with the perfect man."

It was Meredith's turn to roll her eyes, but she couldn't

suppress a grin. Vince's self-confidence and nonchalance were part of his charm.

The sound of soft footsteps reached them from the staircase, and they scurried from the room. Meredith returned quickly to the bedroom she had occupied as a girl. It was now a tastefully decorated guest room; none of the remnants of her childhood remained. Meredith's flowery bedspread had been replaced with an embroidered white quilt, and an expensive Persian rug of black and gold lay on the hardwood floor. White linen curtains hung from the tall windows. Original oil paintings by well-known local artists hung on all four walls.

Meredith stood before the cherry cheval mirror that sat heavily in the corner. She examined herself once more before joining her brother and parents downstairs. She had spent weeks looking for this dress and now twisted and twirled as she admired herself with glee. It was a little black cocktail dress of silk and taffeta, the knee-length skirt pleating at the waist and showing off her form. It was sleeveless, with a deep v-neck in front and back that accentuated the graceful curves of her shoulders and neck, and made the subtle mounds of her breasts look pleasingly delicate rather than small. Her tall, strappy black heels elongated her legs, adding what was, in her opinion, much-needed height to her petite frame. She had carefully tucked her chestnut hair into a neat, elegant coif, and as she turned her head and studied herself out of the corner of her eye, she observed her high cheekbones and dainty features. She had spent the better part of an hour dressing, and it had been worth the effort. With a nod of approval, she slipped the earrings onto her ears, then stood back to take in the final image. She wished Adam could see her now. It was a shame that all this care and attention should be devoted to an evening spent with her parents and not with him. Grabbing a small round purse from the dresser, she vowed to wear this exact outfit again on a date with Adam; she then turned out the light and walked into the hallway.

The light was on in her parents' room. Meredith could see her mother slipping into her shoes. She descended the curving staircase and encountered her father, who glanced up at her, did a quick double take as he took in her appearance, and returned his attention to the note cards in his hands.

"Is your mother ready?" Harold Beck asked tersely, concentrating on memorizing the speech he was to give that night.

"I think so," said Meredith, dropping a couple of mints into her purse. "She was putting on her shoes when I left my room."

"Go light a fire under her, will you? I'm jumpy enough as it is without worrying about being late."

"I'm sure she'll be right down, Dad. It doesn't take long to put on a pair of shoes."

"With you women, everything takes longer than it should."

Meredith rolled her eyes for the second time that night. She turned in place, just preparing to go back upstairs to fetch her mother when Patricia glided down the staircase, her wispy hand on the banister and her entire willowy body seeming to float into the air with each step. Meredith forgot her anxiety regarding having raided her mother's jewelry box and took a moment to admire her. Patricia Beck was delicate-looking in spite of her cold demeanor. Tonight she wore a stunning sleeveless dress of lavender, which sparkled with beading and moved fluidly with her as she descended the steps. Like Meredith, she wore her chestnut hair up, and the effect was to make her appear even slimmer than she already was. Suddenly to Meredith she looked fragile.

Patricia's gaze did not fall on Meredith right away. With a stony face she walked into the entryway to retrieve her gold shawl. It was only when she lifted her eyes to search for her husband that she noticed Meredith; she said nothing at first, her gaze moving onward, as had Harold's, when abruptly her head snapped back in Meredith's direction.

"What are you doing with those?" she asked, indicating with the sharpness of her eyes the pearl earrings.

"Forgive me, Mom, but I couldn't resist," Meredith said gaily, trying to cover her nervousness with exaggerated confidence. "I thought they looked so pretty with my dress that I just had to borrow them. I hope that's all right."

Patricia's jaw was tight. She looked downward at her hands, where her fingers clutched her purse, fidgeting with the clasp. "Of course it's all right," she said, her eyes directed on a tissue she was now withdrawing from the purse. "You know my feelings on this subject, but you've decided to ignore them. What's done is done."

Meredith's face fell. "I'll put them back, if you'd like," she said, bringing her fingers to her ear to remove the first earring.

"No, no," said Patricia with a sigh, holding up one hand in protest but now looking at her reflection in a compact mirror. "Clearly those earrings are more important to you than my opinion. You might as well wear them."

Meredith's heart was pounding, but she decided not to let Patricia bother her tonight. She was in too good a mood; the future looked too bright. Removing her own jacket from the coat rack in the hallway, she withdrew once again to the living room, making an effort to mentally escape her parents' cold, formal house in suburban Philadelphia and fly toward happier places, eagerly looking forward to going back to her apartment in New York City and exploring all the glorious possibilities of her new relationship with Adam. She told herself she had only one more night she was required to spend here; tomorrow morning she could resume her own life, free from their chastisements, safe in Adam's arms.

She met Vince as he bounded down the steps, his feet pounding and his tuxedo jacket billowing behind him. He buttoned it swiftly as he approached. Together they entered the living room to wait. Meredith glanced around. Her father had disappeared; she could hear him puttering around in the kitchen.

"Hey," Vince said, holding his arms out at his sides and standing straight. "How do I look?"

"Very nice. What about me?"

"Fantastic," he said as she twirled. "Too bad we're only going to Dad's retirement banquet. Not a whole lot of excitement to be had."

"No," Meredith agreed, straightening the skirt of her dress, "but I'm proud of him. It's not every newspaper columnist who is honored like this upon his retirement. Dad was a great columnist. You have to give him credit for having the gumption to stand up for what he believes in." She leaned against the back of the couch and folded her hands in front of her waist, thinking of her father's illustrious career: he'd established himself not only as one of the boldest, most trusted names in editorial writing but also as a revered Ivy League professor, highly sought-after public speaker, and beloved author of countless political books. "It's too bad he doesn't want to continue teaching, though. He probably could get a job anywhere he wanted."

"Dad's sick of working. He wants the freedom to bitch and moan on his own time, not on anyone else's."

Meredith shushed her brother as her father walked into the room, his diminutive stature made slightly more imposing by the sternness of his expression and the straightness of his posture. His tuxedo made him appear even stiffer and more austere than usual, and his dark hair had been slicked backward, the effect being that Meredith was reminded of a small but formidable bird of prey. He strode with brisk steps toward Meredith and handed her a note card.

"I'd like you to read this, Meredith," he said, pointing. "I need you to tell me if the language should be stronger. I want to talk about higher standards in education, but without offending anyone."

Vince snickered. "Since when are you worried about offending people?"

Harold stared at his son, his expression quite serious. "This isn't a game, Vince," he said, glaring for a moment before squaring his shoulders and looking back to his note cards. "I made my name defending educators. I myself was an educator for forty years. Now that I'm on my way out, I need to make sure I play all sides. It's all about politics." He raised his eyebrows and glanced back up at Vince. "You're next, by the way. Meredith's not the only teacher in this room. I want to know what you think about this, too."

"Actually, Dad," Vince said, and cleared his throat, "as long as we're talking about that, I have something I've been meaning to tell you."

Her head lowered toward the note card, Meredith heard her brother take a deep breath. She looked up at him expectantly. His eyes were wide, his face flushed. He was working hard to appear confident.

"Well, I certainly don't like the sound of that," said Harold. "What is it?"

"I've decided to stop kidding myself. I don't like teaching and never have. The only reason I became a teacher in the first place is because you told me to. I'm going to be thirty. It's about time I take control over my own life, so I'm quitting my job." When nobody said anything, he continued. "I'm going to be a painter."

Meredith's heart had stopped beating. She braved a glance at her father. He was staring at Vince, his eyebrows raised.

"A painter. What kind of bullshit job is that?"

Meredith forced herself to direct her attention to her brother, who was now shifting where he stood and lifting his chin into the air. She regarded him with interest: she'd had no idea he was thinking of leaving education. Part of her was proud of him for taking this risk, for deciding to do something with his talent and his passion, but she knew her father, and she understood what was coming.

"It's not bullshit, Dad. You know it's something I've always wanted to do. And I'm good. I'm really good. I've been networking a little, and I've gotten some great feedback. In fact, I spoke with a gallery owner who told me that I—"

"Vince, do you have any idea how hard it is to make it as an artist? Do you have any idea how lucky you have to be? Get your head out of the clouds. You don't have what it takes."

Harold's words sucked the air from Meredith's lungs. Her lips parted with disbelief; she closed them and swallowed.

Vince's face had turned red, and his eyes had darkened. He stood up straighter. "You haven't even seen my work. You just want me to be a teacher because it fits your personal narrative. Maybe you should stop thinking about yourself for once and be happy for me."

"You expect me to be happy when you tell me you're throwing your life away? Listen, Vince, your mother and I didn't pay an obscene amount of money for you to go to college just so you could flit a paintbrush around. And by the way," he added, and shook his head, "I don't appreciate receiving this news tonight of all nights. It wasn't enough for you to abandon your career—you had to save it for a time when it would hurt me the most?"

"Dad," Meredith interjected warily, before she could stop herself. Her heart had recommenced beating and now was thumping against her chest—out of compassion for her brother or fear of her father, she wasn't certain. "I'm sure he's not trying to hurt you."

"Hush, Meredith. Shame on you. You're a teacher. You should be just as disappointed in him as I am."

Meredith cast her eyes at her brother, her soft lips now turned downward into a sympathetic frown; however, her brother was flicking some dust off the arm of his jacket and did not meet her gaze.

"Teaching isn't for everyone," Meredith said, trying to affect a casual attitude by shrugging, though her nervousness showed in the flush that had crept onto her face. "Under different circumstances I might have pursued my own interests and chosen to go to culinary school instead of teachers' college."

"What's gotten into you?" Harold asked, leaning back to examine her. "You usually have more sense. One doesn't get ahead by throwing away opportunities. Now no more of this talk. Vince, when you decide to start making some smart decisions, then talk to me. I don't need this kind of aggravation on one of the biggest nights of my career." He squared his shoulders again and stuck his neck out as he straightened his bow tie. He resumed his stance looking over Meredith's shoulder at the note card in her hand. "Come on now," he said, pointing once more. "Let's get serious."

Meredith shot Vince a final look of commiseration. The gentle expression on his face told her that he understood that there was nothing she could do.

But there was a little something. On an impulse, she turned her head slightly so as to hide her face from her father. *Josephine*, she mouthed, her blood pulsing: it was the code word they'd used as children. Their grandmother Josephine was always kind to them; she'd supported them in all their endeavors, praising Vince's art, even hanging it on her walls, and cheering on Meredith's early attempts at cooking. Growing up, brother and sister would whisper the word to show sympathy under their parents' criticism; its meaning had expanded, becoming a discreet signal of encouragement.

Vince nodded in acknowledgment. The knot of her anxiety loosened.

"Okay, Dad," she said, surrendering and bringing her attention to the note card. "You're right. Let's see what you have to say here."

THAT EVENING as she lay in bed thinking about the events of the evening, Meredith abandoned her show of indifference and let the self-reproach, brought on by her parents' undisguised displeasure, wash over her. Meredith was proud of herself. She had studied hard and graduated from college. She had secured a teaching position and recently had begun to study for her master's. She was living in the city and taking care of herself, without her parents' help. She was pleased with her life; it was all she could ask for, and more. She had a job she loved, and she was good at it. She was self-sufficient and had taken steps to better herself. In doing so she had been thrown into the path of a man who was perfect for her: she had met Adam in graduate school. She had proven to herself that she was competent, that she could make her way in the world and be successful. Why did she still let her parents get to her as if she were a little girl?

It was the house, she decided. When she was in New York, she felt free of their watchful, critical eyes. Something about the stone exterior, dark woods, marble fireplaces, and stately furniture opened the old wounds and made her vulnerable. Here her parents always reigned, always pushed her harder and faster and let her know that as much as she was doing, she always could be doing more. When she was away she could bear it; she was surrounded by evidence of the contrary. But in her parents' house, her parents controlled her, reminded her of all the insecurities she had had to overcome in order to fight for where she was today.

Meredith was startled by the sound of soft knocking at her door. She sat up in bed and folded her legs.

"Come in," she called.

Vince's brawny silhouette appeared in the doorway, his expression indiscernible as he stepped into the room and closed the door.

"Hey," he whispered, and sat down on her bed. "I thought you'd still be up. Some night."

"Yes," Meredith agreed, nodding. She recalled the bombastic speech her father had given. Having thanked *The Philadelphia*

Times and his loyal readers for a two-decade run of weekly political columns, Harold had resigned his position with a bang. He
was as apt to speak his mind in public as he was at home, and in
spite of his efforts to "play both sides" tonight, he had elicited
quite a few shocked exclamations from the audience. Meredith
and Vince had been approached by many bewildered guests
asking what it was like to live with Harold Beck, the question
asked jokingly but with a serious undertone that always made
Meredith bristle. As contentious was her relationship with her
father, she respected him for his beliefs and felt he had every right
to express them. And she resented strangers suggesting otherwise. "At least we won't have to do this anymore," she told her
brother. "Now that he's retired, he and Mom are going to spend
most of their time traveling and visiting friends. Maybe he'll relax
a little now."

"Not a chance," said Vince. "Now he'll have even more time
than ever to breathe down our throats. Dad's brutal. Nothing is
ever good enough for him. He is one brutal bastard."

"Don't talk like that. Dad's not a bad person. Just look at how
much money he donates to education charities. Look at how
many adoring students he's had over the years."

"Yeah, what about that, anyway? Why is it that he's so chari-
table with students and total strangers, but not with his own
kids?"

"He just has certain expectations. Maybe he pushes too hard,
but he means well."

Vince snorted and muttered something under his breath.

"What did you say?"

He sighed. "It's nothing."

"No, tell me."

He looked at her frankly. "I said I guess I shouldn't expect you
to understand."

She straightened, taken aback. "What do you mean?"

Vince smiled solemnly. "Come on, Merry. You're the best sister in the world. But you're the golden child, always have been."

"The golden child?" Meredith repeated. She was dumbfounded. "But they criticize me, too."

"Sure, because it's their nature. But it's different with you. You have more promise, in their eyes." Vince patted her hand. "It's not your fault. But you were always the one who was going to fulfill Dad's dreams. It's why you never can stand up to him."

Meredith blinked a few times as Vince's words sank in. "Yes I can," she said weakly, but his words rang true, and tugged at her.

"I'm not blaming you, Merry. It's just who you are. You don't like people to be upset with you. You avoid confrontation. You like to accommodate."

"I like for people to be happy." She regarded him coolly, trying not to be hurt. "I just think things can be resolved without the drama."

"Of course you do. It's because you're a nice person." Vince smiled more warmly now, and she was comforted somewhat. "It's not a criticism. Being nice isn't a bad thing. I'm just saying, if you were less easy on Dad, you wouldn't be wrong for it."

"His heart is in the right place. He's tough because he cares."

"Well, whatever the reason, I can't take it anymore. I'll never get Mom and Dad off my back as long as I'm not doing what they tell me to do. I'm never going to meet with their approval." He patted her knee. "That's why I'm moving, Merry. I'm getting out. I've been trying to find the right time to tell you."

Meredith's eyebrows rose with surprise. "You're moving? Where are you going?"

"Do you remember Heather?"

Meredith's brow crinkled. "Who?"

"That woman I dated a couple of years ago. You know, with the short hair. I met her at that New Year's party."

"Oh." Meredith didn't remember; there had been so many women. "What about her?"

"So she found me on social media. She lives in Maine now. She was telling me about this company that sends painters all over the country to work on power plants, factories, and that sort of thing. It'll help pay the bills while I try to do some real painting on my own, and I'll get to travel. I think it could be fun."

"You're going to sell your paintings?"

"That's the plan."

"I'm so happy to hear that." The encroaching heartache brought on by the news that he was moving away was tempered somewhat by the thought of him doing what he really loved. "I know how important it is to you."

"Thanks, Merry. And hey, I almost forgot. I have something for you."

Meredith waited, reeling and bewildered, while Vince stood and hurried back to his room. When he returned, he was holding a piece of paper. It was warped in places, as if it had been wet and then dried.

"What's this?" she asked as he handed it to her, sitting beside her once more. She lowered her gaze and looked at it, then gasped at its stunning beauty.

"I've been dabbling in watercolor," he told her, as her hand traced the delicate lines. "It's my first attempt. I'll get better at it."

"It's gorgeous." Indeed, it was breathtaking. It was a sunrise, in luscious gold and blue, the colors swirling and fading into each other, deepening in interesting and unexpected places. She lifted her eyes to his. "You are so incredibly gifted."

"Thank you." He said the words casually, with a small smile, but there was latent pride beneath. "You were always so supportive. That's why I wanted you to have it."

"I appreciate it." Her face fell. "Then is this a goodbye gift?"

"Not goodbye. More like, 'Catch you later.'"

"I wish you weren't leaving. I really, really do."

"I know. I just have to."

"But why Maine?"

Vince shrugged. "Why not? It's no worse than any other place."

"But it's so far away."

"The farther away the better."

Meredith frowned. She didn't like the idea of her brother trying to escape.

"But I'll never see you."

Vince put his hand on hers and squeezed. "I'm sorry, Merry," he said, his voice heavy with emotion. "I don't want to leave you, either. You're like my best friend. You've always been." He attempted a weak smile. "But you're the only thing keeping me here. And you're so busy all the time that I hardly ever get to see you anyway."

Meredith felt tears rushing to the corners of her eyes; she swallowed hard, trying to hold them back. "At least we had the chance, though. When you were living in Philadelphia, you were only a couple of hours away. I could come down and see you whenever I wanted. But I'll never get up to Maine," she lamented, her voice shaking. "And once you get away, you'll never want to come back."

"Of course I will. I'll always want to see you."

"I don't know, Vince. Don't you think you're being a little too rash about this? What about Heather? Do you see a future with her?"

"Does it matter? I'm living for today, Merry. I'm not worried about the future." He smiled and nudged her playfully hard, making her lean over and laugh. "You're the one with romantic notions about love. I like to see where the day takes me."

Meredith righted herself and turned serious once more. "I'm just worried, Vince. Maybe Dad is right. What you're doing is so uncertain. Don't you want a more stable life? Don't you want to know where you're going?"

He sighed then and removed his hand from hers, now leaning

forward and resting his elbows on his knees, and clasping his hands together. "I know it's fast, but I have to do this. There's nothing for me here. I need a new life, a change of pace." He laughed once, nervously. "I feel a little lost."

Meredith thought of how she at least had school and work to keep her occupied and distracted, and friends. She thought of Adam, and of Tara, her best friend from high school with whom she had always remained close. Vince had nothing keeping him there, no ties and nothing to look forward to.

"I guess I understand. I hope you find what you're looking for."

"I don't know what I'm looking for. But I know it's not here. Unlike you," he said with a warm smile, his voice becoming more upbeat as he attempted to lighten the mood. "You seem to have it all together. New school, new plans, new man—your life is just the picture of perfection."

Meredith sensed a bit of teasing in his tone. "Don't make fun of me just because I'm happy," she said with playful chastisement. "Not everyone has to move as far north as possible to escape."

"I'm not making fun of you. You're happy playing the game. Good for you."

"There's nothing wrong with playing the game," she responded, her voice laden with naive authority that made Vince laugh. "So far I've been pretty good at it."

"I'm not telling you not to play the game," Vince said, and stood. He stretched, sticking out his chest as his arms folded behind his back. He straightened, then leaned down to kiss his sister's forehead. He turned and began walking toward the door. He opened it a crack; the light from the hallway seeped into the room and once again turned his frame into a dark outline. "I just hope you're not disappointed. I just hope your optimism pays off."

"Why wouldn't it pay off?" she asked brightly, lifting her hands to her sides in a gesture that suggested the answer was just that simple. "I'm only twenty-six years old; I have my entire life in front of me. I have a good head on my shoulders, and I know what I want from life. No," she said, shaking her head, "I won't be disappointed. I know how to get what I want. I'm not going to settle. I'm going to make my life perfect."

CHAPTER TWO

PRESENT DAY

"Where are the songs of spring? Ay, where are they? Think not of them, thou hast thy music too, while barred clouds bloom the soft-dying day, and touch the stubble-plains with rosy hue."

Meredith's voice sang from the front of the classroom. It was seemingly propelled by her hand, which was extended toward her smiling students as they sat with pens in hand, eagerly anticipating the questions they knew would follow their teacher's recitation.

"So where are the songs of spring?" Meredith asked, now bringing her hand to her chin and holding it between her fingers. "According to Keats, what has its own music too?"

From the sea of raised hands before her, Meredith chose the hand belonging to a particularly gregarious boy, and said his name.

"Autumn," he responded, and grinned. "Hence the title, 'To Autumn.'"

Delighted giggles resounded from throughout the room.

Meredith smiled. "That's correct. Now expand on that. Why does Keats say autumn should not think of the songs of spring?"

The boy nodded confidently. "He means that spring isn't the

only beautiful season, just because it's full of green grass and flowers. Autumn is beautiful, too."

"And what about autumn does he find beautiful?"

The boy frowned. "I'm not sure."

Instantly the air was once again full of waving hands. Meredith called on a shy girl who sat toward the side of the room.

"It's the soft-dying day and the stubble-plains," she said tentatively.

"And the rosy hue," added a boy sitting next to her, noting the girl's crimson face. He poked his friend in the shoulder with his pencil. "Don't forget that rosy hue."

The room erupted in good-natured laughter.

Meredith's face softened as she watched the girl who had bravely answered her question. "Very nice. Now what is it about those things that Keats finds so beautiful?"

The hands returned to the air, but Meredith was still looking at the shy girl and nodding encouragement.

The shy girl sat up a little straighter in her chair and returned her gaze. "It's because they aren't loud about their beauty, like the beauty of spring. He likes that those things are humble."

"Excellent," Meredith said. "Keats is finding virtue in quietude and modesty."

The girl returned her smile and relaxed in her chair.

"I don't understand that," interrupted another girl, without raising her hand. "What's a stubble-plain?"

Meredith's eyebrows rose. "Well, what do you think it is?"

The room was silent as the students cast cautious glances at each other.

"What do you think of when you think of stubble?"

Her question was immediately followed by more laughter.

"You're right," Meredith replied, joining in their laughter. "A stubbly plain is like a stubbly face. It's shaven and bare, only the remnants of the harvest remaining."

"But why would Keats find that beautiful?"

Meredith looked around the classroom at her students, their eyes wide with expectation, and thought about the amazing array of personalities it contained.

"I think Keats is saying that something doesn't have to be flashy to be beautiful. Spring is lovely with all its blooms and bright colors, but the barrenness of autumn is no less so. In fact, its peacefulness is its greatest strength."

"I like that," mused a girl as she raised her hand into the air. "It's like the soft-dying day. It may be past the excitement of the rest of the day, but its calmness is kind of nice. Everyone can slow down and relax then."

"That's right," Meredith responded with a smile. "I think you said it perfectly."

The brash ringing of the bell startled them out of their conversation, and Meredith closed her book.

"We have a few more lines to discuss tomorrow," she said. "In the meantime, tonight, please read the rest of the poem and find other words and phrases that tell you what Keats is admiring about autumn. Enjoy the rest of your day."

With that, the students packed up their books and papers, then shuffled speedily from the room. Meredith watched them with a smile, warmth encircling her heart. No matter how many discussions she led, their earnestness never failed to move her; no matter how many students trickled through her classes, they never failed to endear themselves to her. Despite their teenage bluster, they were so innocent—they were kids. They were good-natured and eager to please; they were finding themselves and looking forward to their futures. They represented infinite promise.

The door banged behind the final straggler, and Meredith's smile melted. She faced forward. A familiar agitation rose faintly in her gut; recognizing it instantly, she directed her gaze inward.

It's a pointless feeling, she told herself. *It doesn't do you any good.*

She envisioned herself pushing the feeling away, and waited.

The quivering subsided. She closed her eyes and took in a long, deep breath, pausing to feel the air enter and fill her lungs and then holding it steady before releasing it, deliberately focusing on the gradual lightening of her chest.

She'd made it through another day.

She gave herself a minute before opening her eyes. In this time, she let it all consume her: the stillness of the room, the steady slowing of her heartbeat. *It's okay,* she reprimanded herself, but gently. *You knew it would be okay.* She opened her eyes and looked about her, grounding herself in reality, in the present: it was her classroom, a room she held dear. Here was her desk. Here were her books. There were her students' desks.

She laughed to herself. She was so silly. There was nothing, absolutely nothing wrong.

Recentered, putting her lapse of strength immediately out of her mind, she turned toward her desk and organized her materials into her messenger bag, pleased with the day's classes but ready to go home and to have some quiet time to herself. She had slipped into her coat and scarf and was digging her keys out of her purse when the door to her classroom opened.

Meredith suppressed a sigh. It was Ned Mallard, the math teacher. About her age, he frequently paid her unsolicited attention. He too was wearing his coat and scarf, and he had his own work bag in one hand and keys in the other. Evidently he was prepared to escort her to her car again.

She made herself smile. "Hello, Ned."

From the doorway, he waved his hand in an exaggerated gesture that seemed full of forced confidence. "Howdy, Miss Beck. Headed for the parking lot?"

"Indeed I am, Mr. Mallard."

"What a coincidence—so am I! I'll walk with you."

"Thank you, Ned. That's very nice of you."

Ned was encouraged, and he held the door for her as she shut off the lights and exited her classroom.

"Do you know anything about the new art teacher?" he asked her.

"Mrs. Nguyen, yes. She seems fantastic. She moved here from Boston, where she was a docent at the MFA."

"I hear she was a docent at the MFA. That's the art museum in Boston. Such experience! What an addition to the team!"

Meredith did not respond. They meandered around students rushing to their lockers.

"I see there are some scuff marks on your bag," Ned noted, pointing to the brown leather strap that was slung over her shoulder. "I can totally help you with that problem."

"I'm not sure it's a problem," said Meredith. "It—"

"I bought this stuff for my own bag. It's called Scuff-Away. Great stuff! Took those marks right out. I'll bring it in for you."

"Thanks, but I don't—"

"No need to thank me. I'm happy to do it."

"Okay. Well, I appreciate it."

A mob of students rushed toward them. They momentarily separated as the students pushed by.

"Oh look, it's a flyer for the drama club." Ned pointed to a bulletin board as they passed. "They're looking for teachers to help, you know."

"Yes." Meredith had seen the flyer and for a quick moment had considered volunteering, but she'd put it out of her mind. She had no experience with drama.

Ned gave the peace sign to a passing student who'd wished him goodnight. "I heard through the grapevine they're modernizing *Romeo and Juliet*," he told her.

Meredith stopped walking, her heart missing a beat.

"Oh," she muttered, recovering, and regaining her stride. "Isn't that nice."

A group of choir students who had gathered for an impromptu doo-wop song forced Meredith and Ned to separate once more. As he passed around the side of them, Ned snapped his fingers and pretended to sing along. The surrounding students clapped and laughed good-naturedly.

"The kids were rather peppy for a Thursday, didn't you find?" he asked when they were once again side by side.

Meredith was already mentally in her car and had no interest in making more small talk, much less with Ned, whose persistence felt demanding, for reasons she could not quite explain. His need to know her opinions somehow always seemed more about him than about her, and she wasn't in a space to accommodate him today. She wished she hadn't taken those extra moments in her classroom; if she'd left a minute earlier, she'd have made it out before he saw her. *That isn't nice*, she scolded herself, ashamed. *He's only trying to be friendly. He's doing the best he can.*

She tried to be generous with him; he meant well. She forced some cheer into her voice. "Yes, we had some very lively discussions."

"Oh? What on?"

Meredith hesitated, knowing he wouldn't have the vaguest idea what she was talking about. "Well, my sophomores discussed Keats's 'To Autumn.'"

"Indeed? Fascinating!"

Meredith hid the distaste she felt at his insincerity. "And my seniors compared and contrasted *King Lear* and *Antigone*."

"*King Lear*—Shakespeare, right?"

"Right."

Ned felt he had scored. His tone brightened even further, though Meredith hadn't thought it was possible. "I've always loved Shakespeare. The Old English doesn't bother me one bit."

"Actually, it's not Old English. It's—"

"If it were done when 'tis done," Ned pontificated loudly, and lowered himself down to one knee as he threw his hand into the air, ignoring the snickers of departing students, "then 'twere well if it were done quickly." He resumed his normal stance and looked at her expectantly. "Eh?"

She was both amused and horrified. She tried not to see the students pausing on their way out the door to point and whisper. "Quite impressive. But that's *Macbeth*."

He smoothed his hair and shrugged. "Same difference. Everyone dies in the end, right?"

She smiled in spite of herself. "I can't argue with you there."

He was pleased to have scored again.

"Say, Meredith," he said as he made a dramatic point of holding open the door of the school for her to step through, "there's a great new restaurant downtown. It's called Antoinette. Have you heard of it?"

"Yes, it's French fusion."

"It's a French fusion place. That's when French cuisine and another cuisine are combined. Antoinette is supposed to be amazing. I actually know the host there, and he says he can get me a table any time. All I have to do is ask."

Meredith knew where this was going and instantly began fabricating excuses. As they approached her car, she was grateful to remember that she actually had one.

Ned stood in front of her and looked at her square on. "I was hoping that if you didn't have any plans this weekend, maybe you'd want to, you know, join me for dinner one night."

Meredith desperately wanted to avoid his eyes but knew that would be rude, so she looked at him. He was on the tall and gangly side, with a friendly-looking appearance. His black hair was thick and professionally cut, his smile was bright, and his dark eyelashes drew one's attention to the clarity of his eyes. He made a gallant attempt at fashion, wearing only designer clothes and choosing glasses that were stylish and bold—but somehow the attempt only made more painfully obvious the fact that he was trying too hard. She knew, however, that his approachability made him likable and relatable to his students, and she respected him for that.

"I'm sorry, Ned, but I can't. My brother is coming into town tonight, and we're planning on spending the weekend together."

Ned looked disappointed but was undeterred. "Well, maybe next weekend."

Meredith wondered if she should spare his feelings or put him out of his misery. Feeling bold, and frantic to escape, she chose the latter. "I'm afraid not, Ned. Honestly, I'm just not..." A wave of sympathy overtook her. "I'm just not looking for that kind of thing. Just yet." She felt that was sufficiently vague to put him off without injuring his ego.

Ever optimistic, however, Ned persisted.

"Well..." he said, and stuck his pointer fingers outward at her, "you're not ready now, but maybe soon you will be!" When she said nothing in response, he straightened and sighed with resignation. "Sorry, Meredith. I should probably back off. I just think we'd be really good together. You know?"

Abruptly, a feeling began gnawing deep within her, something subtly corrosive. It was like the faint nagging of a thorn inside her stomach. She didn't know what it was, but she knew she had to make it stop.

"Ned, I said no."

Ned sighed again. "All right, all right. I get it. If you change your mind, you let me know."

Giving up, she said she would.

Backing away, he stuck out his pointer fingers again. "Great." He turned and walked through the parking lot, bellowing, "If it were done when 'tis done, then 'twere well if it were done quickly!..."

She watched him go in silence, then turned to her car and quickly stepped inside.

∼

MEREDITH WALKED through the front door of her parents' stone colonial and into the wide entryway. She leaned her messenger bag against the white wainscot panels and sifted through the mail, but as usual there was nothing of interest for her, only bills she was to take care of now that she was caretaker of the house in her parents' absence. Depositing her coat on the coat rack, she rubbed her arms with her hands and shivered, then ascended the staircase to change out of her suit before the cold of the big empty house could consume her.

Flipping on every light she could, hoping to create the effect of cheerfulness, she headed toward the kitchen to prepare dinner. With its elegant cabinets and ample granite counters, the well-equipped kitchen was a haven for her, the room in which she was most comfortable.

She felt herself relaxing even as she collected her ingredients. The motion of her hands as they reached for this spice and that drew her thoughts away from her day, the rhythmic sounds of pouring and measuring lulling her into safe, familiar space.

As she reached for a mixing bowl, a familiar object caught her eye. After the night of her father's retirement dinner, Meredith framed the watercolor her brother had given her. She'd brought it with her to her parents' house and had placed it in the kitchen, where she spent her most peaceful time. Despite the turmoil of the last year, it always made her swell with pride. Looking at it now brought a tingle of anticipation to her blood, and she hopped a little more quickly about the room, working off a hum of anxiousness.

When her phone buzzed from the back pocket of her jeans, she withdrew it and answered the call without pause.

"You're four minutes late," she said. "I was beginning to worry."

"I have two kids," answered Tara. "Cut me a break."

"I can't believe you still call me every day at the same time. It's been a year."

"You're my best friend. I'll call you for a hundred years if I have to."

Meredith smiled and grew more serious. "I know. Thank you."

"It's nothing. Now," said Tara, "on to more interesting topics. What time is Vince supposed to be there?"

"He said seven o'clock," Meredith said as she held the phone between her chin and shoulder and peeked outside the kitchen window, "but we both know how reliable he is."

"You should have told him you'd have a woman waiting for him. That would get him there in no time."

Both women laughed.

"Speaking of which," said Tara, "I take it things fell apart with Hannah?"

"Heather," Meredith corrected. "And yes. That's ancient history. It lasted about five minutes."

"The job stuck but the woman didn't."

"Exactly." Meredith looked out the window again, parting the curtain with her fingers. "The snow has already started falling. I hope it doesn't delay him."

"Honey, it's been years since you've seen him. Another couple of hours won't make much difference."

Meredith licked her lips nervously; she'd avoided thinking too hard about the recent disconnect between her and Vince, instead choosing to focus on the underlying affection and their shared history. "I hope it isn't too awkward," she said. "He's been keeping his distance ever since he had that falling out with my parents when he quit teaching. This last year has made it even worse."

"I'm sure as soon as you two are together again, you'll pick up right where you left off. He's going to be there for at least three months while he works on that job. That's plenty of time to catch up."

"Still," said Meredith as she began removing pots and pans from the cabinets, "I'm anxious about it. I want this visit to go well."

"It'll be great. You've been alienating yourself for too long, and it isn't like you. You need some company now, especially through the holidays. You just worry too much. By the way, speaking of worrying, how was your trip to the Poconos? I always worry about you driving all that distance by yourself."

"Oh, it was wonderful," Meredith said with a smile as she recalled the crisp blueness of the open sky and the smoky smell of the forest through which she had hiked. "I needed that time for quiet self-reflection. I feel most like myself during those times."

"But why the mountains? Why not just self-reflect back here at home?"

"I like the way I feel dizzy when I look at them. I like the way I feel overwhelmed and happy."

"The same effect can be reached by drinking. The next time you feel the urge to self-reflect, just call me and I'll take you to a bar downtown."

Both women laughed once more.

"Well," said Meredith, her fingers deftly rocking her knife as she sliced into her garlic, "hopefully it won't be needed any time soon."

"Hopefully. Hey, Merry."

Meredith knew what Tara was going to say even before she said it—there was something about her tone. "No."

"You don't even know what I—"

"Tara." Meredith's voice was soft and patient; she knew her friend was worried about her. "I'm not going back to the therapist."

"I just think it would help you so much."

"But I don't need the help. Really. I'm doing so well."

"It definitely can't hurt."

"But it did. That's the thing. All it did was make me depressed. I can do this on my own, without the help. And I think it'll be better for me. It'll make me even stronger."

"I disagree, but I can't make you do it if you're set on not doing it. In any case, you know I'm always here for you." Tara paused. "How are you doing today?" she asked then, more gently.

"I'm great today! Feeling good. Feeling really good, actually."

"Are you sure?"

"Of course I'm sure. Why?"

"I don't know. You sound a little too perky, I guess."

"Well, that just shows you how well I'm doing."

Tara began to answer, but she was interrupted by boisterous shouting in the background. Meredith smiled. She loved Tara's little daughters, who were sweet and loving and endlessly full of life.

"So what are you making your guests for dinner?" Tara asked when the noise had subsided.

"Beef bourguignon," said Meredith as she tossed some carrots and potatoes into a heavy copper pot. "After the long drive from Maine, Vince and his friend probably will want something substantial. I was going to make pâté en croûte, but it's a very difficult dish, and I've never tried it before. I don't know if I can pull it off. I thought it better to go with a sure thing."

"Honey, I don't know how you cook like that every night."

Meredith shrugged. "It keeps me busy, and it's something I enjoy. Plus I'm good at it."

"You just like to show off your skills. Admit it."

"Well, I'm usually cooking only for myself, but I won't deny that I like pleasing company, too."

"Don't get me wrong, I'm not complaining. I've been reaping the benefits of your cooking since high school. You can self-reflect in my kitchen anytime."

Meredith chuckled. "You say that, but you wouldn't let me bake Evelyn's birthday cake."

"I wasn't going to put that on you the weekend your brother's coming into town. But that reminds me. Be here around ten o'clock on Sunday so we can pick up the cake from the bakery. The party doesn't start until noon, so you can help me set up."

"Okay. That sounds fun." Meredith glanced toward a little table in the corner, where a wrapped present sat waiting. "I need to put some more thought into her gift. I have one, but it doesn't seem right. It has to be perfect."

"I'm sure it's fine. She'll love whatever you give her, because it's from you."

"I usually have these things taken care of well in advance. It's not like me."

"You've been distracted."

Meredith and Tara chatted a few more minutes as Meredith prepared dinner. Meredith had just turned toward the stove and taken the tea kettle in her hand, intending to relax with a cup of tea and her schoolwork, when the sound of tires slowing in front of the house interrupted her reveries.

With an excited little start, she hopped from her spot, removed her apron, and ran to the front of the house to greet her brother. She drew in a deep breath and steadied herself, firmly pushing down the sudden tumbling in her belly.

She flung open the front door. Vince was just stepping out of the driver's side, his friend the passenger's side. The two shadowy figures lumbered up the walkway, her brother in front and his friend behind. They pulled their suitcases behind them as they walked with their heads lowered toward the ground, avoiding the snow that was sticking to their coats and hair. Her face melted into a wide smile as with one strong heave Vince lifted his suitcase off the ground and over the steps, then scooped her up and engulfed her in an enthusiastic embrace.

"Well, if it isn't my baby sister," he said as he placed her back on her feet. He threw his hands in the air and grinned. "How the hell have you been?"

Meredith stood back to look at her brother for the first time in years. A rush of tenderness overtook her, warming her blood and sparking the beginnings of tears behind her eyes. Ever in vogue, he was wearing his dark hair modestly spiked and fashionably messy, and yet he still managed to look well-groomed and slick. She studied him a moment, cherishing the safety in his familiarity—and noticing the subtle changes the passage of time will bring. Though the gleam in his eyes was youthful, the lines in his face were more pronounced; the years showed on him, but faintly, maybe something in his stance or in his smile. But he was her brother, and he was here; their time together had begun. She shook her head, amazed: how had they let all this time pass?

"Oh, I'm great!" she said with a laugh. "You know, couldn't be better. Although I'm much better now that you're here."

"That's what they all say."

Meredith laughed, bringing him in for another hug. "I am so, so happy to see you."

Another figure appeared in the doorway. He entered the house quietly and gently stomped his feet on the rug, then stood in silence as if waiting to be addressed.

Meredith pulled away from her brother to greet her second guest. "You must be Nick," she said with a smile, and extended her hand. "It's nice to meet you. Make yourself at home."

"Thank you," he said softly, with a little appreciative nod.

The gentleness of his voice surprised her. "Have you ever been to Pennsylvania?" she asked.

"No, first time here."

Meredith waited for him to say more, but he didn't.

"I guess you and my brother travel together a lot," she added, when he continued to remain silent.

"Yes."

His succinct answers seemed the result of shyness, not lack of interest; his voice was quiet, but his eyes held a subdued smile.

Meredith cocked her head curiously. She had expected him to be like Vince, brash and boisterous, and ready for a good time. But he appeared reticent and reserved, inclined to fade into the background. The contrast with her brother was stark. Meredith tactfully took in his appearance. His features were sharp and angular, his eyes crisp, earnest, and blue. His figure was tall, slender, and strong, and he stood straight and firm. He was dressed ruggedly in a black parka, faded jeans, and scuffed carpenters' boots. His hair was golden blond, thick and almost too long as it fell in folds over the sides of his face, which was expressionless but not unkind.

"You'll have to excuse Nick," Vince told her, his booming voice something of a shock after Nick's hushed one. He stepped toward his friend and clapped him on the back. "He's not much of a talker. Hell of a painter, though."

Nick smiled, but was silent, letting Vince pull him in.

"That's okay," said Meredith. "Come as you are, in my opinion. The world needs both talkers and listeners, right?"

Nick's eyes creased genially in the corners. "Right."

Meredith smiled, strangely warmed by the unlikeliness of this friendship.

Vince and Nick took off their coats and went upstairs to deposit their suitcases, and Meredith checked on dinner. She was just peeking into the oven when she sensed a presence behind her. She turned to find her brother standing over her, his nose extended, sniffing.

"So thanks for letting us stay here and intrude upon your life," he said.

"It's not an intrusion at all. I'm very grateful your job brought you to Pennsylvania."

"Me too. As long as I have to travel, I might as well reunite with my sister while I do it." He smiled as he picked a crouton out of a bowl of salad and popped it into his mouth. He was looking about the room; he gestured with his finger toward his watercolor. "I've gotten so much better since then."

"Don't be silly. It's beautiful."

He shrugged and shoved his hands into his pockets. "Speaking of jobs, tell me about yours. Pretty posh position you landed yourself. Dover Academy's one of the best private schools around."

"Oh, it's fantastic! It's a great job. I'm loving it."

Watching her with a furrowed brow, Vince grabbed a hot roll from a hand-painted bowl. He took a bite, and his eyes promptly opened wide with pain. He spit the roll into a towel, grabbed the open bottle of wine Meredith had been using for her beef, and chugged it.

"Glad to hear that," he mumbled, coughing, and wiped his lips. "It sounds like you're living the life."

Meredith said nothing as she stirred her sauce.

"So are you also loving being back at Mom and Dad's house?"

The gnawing of the thorn in her gut returned. She brought her hand to her stomach, and it subsided.

A dark smile crossed her face. "Yes, it's exactly where I want to be at this point in my life."

They stood in silence for a few moments.

"Why did you come back, anyway?"

Meredith slowly turned to face him.

"Look, I'm not going to lie to you," she said. "It isn't the dream situation. Being in this house again, I can almost hear them criticizing me." She turned back to the counter, where she began scooping vegetables into a bowl. "But they needed someone to look after the house while they took their next round of vacations, and I didn't have anywhere else to go. I'm living here for free. It makes the unpleasantries worth it."

"What about Adam?"

The gentleness left her face, and her heart beat a little faster. "What about him? That part of my life is over."

"I know, but maybe you're running away. Maybe you came back here to escape."

Meredith took one wine glass in one hand and two in the other and started making her way into the dining room. She forced a smile and held out her arms. "That's ridiculous. If I were going to escape, why would I come back here?" She made herself laugh, but it sounded maniacal.

When she returned to the kitchen, Vince was staring at the floor. She put on a bright smile to lighten the mood. "Tell me all about your life in Maine," she said. "How is your painting going?"

Vince snorted a little, and his face darkened. "What painting?" he muttered.

Meredith turned toward her brother and frowned. "Oh, no. You're not working on your own painting anymore? But you quit your teaching job so you could work on your own paintings. You told Dad—"

"You don't have to remind me what I told Dad," Vince interrupted tersely. "Believe me, he's made his feelings known."

"I'm sorry," she said, and approached him. She placed her hand on his arm. "I don't want to make you upset." She sighed, removed her hand, and resumed preparing dinner. "I just feel awful that you're not doing what you want to do when it was so hard for you to make the choice to do it."

"Don't feel awful. As you said, it was my choice. I've got only myself to blame."

"I didn't mean it that way," she said, nervous now by the tension in his voice. "I just want you to be happy."

Vince's expression softened. "I know." He leaned toward her and patted her on the back. "Don't worry about me. It just didn't work out. It's not that big a deal."

Meredith looked at him. His expression was unreadable.

"You're right," she said. "I'm sorry."

He watched her for a moment. "Listen, Merry," he said, "I want to apologize to you."

"What for?"

"For not being there for you."

Meredith grew uncomfortable. She shook her head. "Please, Vince. Don't do this."

"After my big fight with Mom and Dad, I didn't want to visit for a while, and eventually time just got away from me. But I should have put that aside and been more supportive last year. I know how much pain you were in. Not that you can't handle it on your own," he added as he noticed her opening her mouth in protest. "But everyone needs a little help sometimes—even you," he said, and smiled.

"You have nothing to feel guilty about. I've always known you've been there, even when you haven't actually been there." She slid oven mitts onto her hands. "And besides, I'm fine. Let's just not talk about it anymore. Okay?"

Vince watched her as she removed the beef from the oven. "All right. Whatever you say."

Meredith straightened, beef in hand. "Dinner's ready," she announced cheerfully.

"Great. It's been too long since I've indulged in your cooking."

"Well, I'll tell you what," she said, turning to him on her way to the dining room. "This time, let's not let years go by before you get another chance."

"It's a deal."

THEY PASSED a leisurely dinner in the dignified dining room, Meredith and Vince exchanging gossipy family tidbits, Nick sitting quietly listening and contributing to the conversation when asked for his opinion. After, when they had gone their separate ways for the night, Meredith went to her bedroom, where she changed into light blue cotton pajamas, washed her face, and studied herself in the mirror. Running her fingers through her hair, she was slightly dismayed to find a few more grays. She was thirty-two, still young but too old, in her parents' opinion, to be shifting around, as they felt she had been doing for too long. For good measure she rubbed some cream on her face, then threw on her white bathrobe and headed back toward the kitchen to make herself a cup of tea.

She stood in the dark kitchen, the only light that which crept in through the window from the streetlight outside. She closed her eyes. The teacup in her hand began shaking, and she placed it on the countertop before the tears arrived. They rushed her all at once, in an instant. The sound came, too, in sharp, loud bursts, and she let them, too overcome to fight.

"Adam," she sighed, her face in her hands. She was just bringing her hands to her thighs to dry them when a shadow fell on her from the doorway.

She turned. Nick was standing there, backlit by the light in the hallway.

"Oh," she said, startled, as she quickly wiped her eyes with the back of her hand. "I'm sorry, I—"

"Are you okay?" he asked.

"Yes," she said, and he took a step backward to let her through the doorway as she hurried past him. She returned upstairs and crawled into bed, where her tears stained her cheek and wet her pillow.

MEREDITH PASSED an uneventful day in school Friday and rushed home to prepare a nice dinner for her guests. That night at the table they enjoyed lighthearted banter until the conversation turned to the weekend.

Vince leaned back in his chair and sighed, rubbing his belly.

"Hey," he said. "Let's do something fun tomorrow. Let's all go out."

Meredith clapped her hands. "A day out sounds wonderful. What do you want to do?"

"I don't know. Why don't you surprise us?"

"Okay. Don't worry. I'll think of something fun."

"Great. Just please don't take us to the library."

"You're in luck," she said, patting his arm. "I was just there earlier this week. I won't need to go back for a few more days."

"Shucks." Vince smiled and snapped his fingers with mock disappointment.

Meredith slumped a little as she pondered. Through the doorway that led into the kitchen, she spied Vince's framed watercolor painting sitting on the counter. Her back straightened. "How about the art museum downtown? We could walk around the museum and then grab some lunch."

The idea seemed to appeal to Vince, who raised his eyebrows. He turned to Nick. "What do you think?"

"That sounds great."

"Then it's settled," said Vince. "What do you want to do Sunday?"

"Sunday afternoon is Tara's daughter's birthday party," Meredith said. "Hey, you should come!"

"How old is Tara's daughter?"

"She'll be four."

"As fun as that sounds, I'd have to say no thanks." Vince leaned back in his chair and folded his arms across his chest. "On second thought, I'll be there. I'd like to see Tara again. I always thought she was sexy."

"Back off, Vince," Meredith said with a crooked grin. "She's married with two children."

"That doesn't mean she can't be sexy. Don't worry about me, Merry. I don't involve myself with married women." He stifled a belch. "Even I'm not that bad."

Meredith looked at her brother. She felt a warm rush of affection for the man with whom she had grown up, in whose arms she had found respite from her parents' harsh criticisms. When she was a little girl she had looked up to her big brother, had seen him as an infallible caregiver who could heal all wounds. Being older now, and wiser, Meredith saw him for who he truly was, with his faults and insecurities and earnest attempts to find himself. His good-natured honesty was perhaps what she loved most about him. She was overwhelmed with gratitude that he had come back into her life.

She took her plate in her hand and headed toward the kitchen, but before she did so she kissed her brother on the top of the head. "I love you, Vince," she told him. "I hope you know that."

As she crossed from the dining room into the kitchen, she turned her head back toward the table. Vince was holding his phone and appeared to be sending a text message. Nick was watching her, his long lips pulled into a straight, serious line, but his eyes soft, a gentle smile crinkling them at the corners.

WHEN THE LIGHTS were out and silence sat heavily in the air, Meredith peered outside her bedroom door. Finding the hallway empty, she tiptoed down the stairs and scurried toward the kitchen, where in the darkness she put up her little tea kettle and stood waiting, steadying herself for the tears.

They rose quickly and urgently, and she had no choice but to submit to them, allowing the jarring convulsions to overwhelm her. Minutes passed. Still she stood there quivering, until she wiped her eyes with her hands and, aching and exhausted, with a weary sigh, she trudged toward the stairs, her tea untouched.

MEREDITH CREPT BACK UPSTAIRS and into her bedroom, where she stood standing before the mirror for several moments, watching her own face as she indulged in a few deep breaths. She closed her eyes, relishing the calm.

She was startled by the sound of soft knocking at her door, and she turned in that direction. She could see the outline of feet in the small empty space between the door and the floor. She drifted toward the entrance of the room and paused, then cautiously turned the doorknob.

He met her gaze immediately.

"I'm sorry," he said. "I don't want to bother you."

Meredith expected him to say more, but he was silent. They stared at each other from opposite sides of the door until Meredith grew uncomfortable and shifted where she stood.

"It's just that..." he began, and stopped. Abruptly he ran his fingers through his hair. "I heard you crying," he said.

Something about his obvious discomfort at having knocked on her bedroom door moved her, and she suffered another rush of tears. She turned away and picked a tissue from her nightstand, dabbing at her eyes.

Nick took a small step into the room and stood there patiently in silence. He glanced around, then down at the floor.

"Thank you for checking on me," she told him. She sat down on the bed, still sniffling. "It's very kind of you. I'm okay, really. Please don't worry about me."

"Is it about Adam?"

Immediately the smile fell from Meredith's face. He was looking fully at her now, his chin slightly lifted with contrived confidence, his chest rising and falling as he recovered from his act of boldness.

"I just...I don't know who he is." He shrugged, clearly losing courage; he was avoiding her gaze, and he seemed undecided over whether to fold or unfold his arms. "You said that name, so I thought..."

Her surprise had left her speechless. At her hesitation, he faltered. "I don't want to pry," he said, and waved his hand in parting as he started toward the door.

Then, she surprised herself.

"Adam and I were together for five years," she said in a rush, without really knowing why; he was practically a stranger, and she knew almost nothing about him. But he was there, and he was asking, and the calm composure about him somehow made him trustworthy. As she spoke, he stepped back inside and carefully shut the door. "I met him while I was in graduate school. We were supposed to get married this spring." He stood waiting as she took a deep breath. "Last year he was diagnosed with leukemia. It happened very quickly. He passed away just before Christmas."

Nick said nothing, and Meredith braved a glance at his face. It was expressionless except for his eyes, which had widened.

"I'm sorry."

She was touched by the tenderness in his voice. Her view of him was clouded by tears, and she buried her face in her hands.

She did not see him approach, but before she knew it he was sitting beside her, and his hand was resting on her shoulder as she wept. She looked back toward the floor, mindlessly fidgeting with the tissue in her hand. "We were both teachers in New York while he completed his doctorate at NYU. I finished out the year and moved back here this past summer."

"You must be very brave."

"I'm really not. I'm only here because I had nowhere else to go. I've had to reevaluate the direction of my life and postpone my plans for a family. I thought moving home would give me time to think of how to get my life back on track." She blew her nose into her tissue. "But I still feel just as lost as ever."

Nick was silent, his gaze directed at the space between their knees.

"You hold it together during the day." He paused a thoughtful moment. "But it's hard on you."

Meredith sucked in a shaky breath. She cried into her hands, violently, unprepared for the intense relief the acknowledgment of this realization would bring. He rubbed her back, the pressure of his hand light and hesitant. She calmed somewhat, breathless.

"Yes," she gasped, wiping her eyes with the backs of her hands. "Yes, I suppose it is."

Neither said anything for some time. The motion of his hand had slowed and ceased. He withdrew it once she had recovered.

"It's exhausting, actually," she went on, her voice more or less returned. "I hadn't thought about how exhausting it is. I don't think I even knew that it was happening. I don't talk about it a lot." She paused. "Not even with myself."

He didn't respond right away.

"When you're just trying to survive," he said then, "you don't really have time to think about how you're doing it."

It wasn't the kind of response she'd been expecting. But there was simplicity to it, and truth. She sat with it for a moment. She felt a little better.

"It's a strange thing," she said; the succinctness with which he described thoughts she hadn't even known she'd been having compelled her to tell him more. "I know I have to move on, and I am. But part of me doesn't want to." She fought back another rush of tears. "But I know he would want me to be happy."

"And so you act happy. For his sake."

Meredith stared at him. This hadn't occurred to her. "Yes," she said, a bit astonished.

His eyes crinkled kindly. "I can understand that."

She returned her gaze to the floor. She couldn't believe the personal things she had said to him. They were things she hadn't said to anyone, not even to Tara. She wasn't sure why she was so inclined to open up like this.

They were silent for a minute or two before he spoke again.

"You must have a picture of him."

Meredith's eyes met his. "Yes."

"Can I see it?"

It was no small question, but somehow it did not feel intrusive. She watched him a moment, then rose slowly and walked to the dresser. She opened the bottom drawer and removed some spare blankets, then reached to the back and withdrew a small photo album. She handed it to him and sat beside him.

He opened it to the first photo, which showed Adam and Meredith in caps and gowns, smiling and holding diplomas.

"Graduation ceremony," she said. "We had just earned our master's degrees."

Nick stared at the photo. Meredith looked much younger, though the photo hadn't been taken so many years before. Her hair was longer then, her smile livelier. Meredith looked at Adam. He stood only a couple of inches taller than she did. He was leaning toward her, a wide smile on his boyish face. His auburn hair was neatly parted on the side under his cap. Khaki slacks and a plaid shirt peeked out from under his gown.

Silently, Nick flipped to the next photo. This one showed Adam and Meredith on lounge chairs on what appeared to be the porch of someone's house.

"His parents' house in Connecticut."

This picture had been taken at closer range. Meredith was reminded of Adam's brown eyes and high cheekbones. They were leaning toward each other, their heads touching.

Meredith looked away.

There were about half a dozen photos in the entire album. Nick examined each one. Meredith noticed, with curiosity, the studiousness of his expression, the way his eyebrows creased with thought and the way his fingers toyed a little with his lower lip.

Finally, he closed the album and handed it back to her.

"Thank you," he said.

She smiled soberly.

"It must be hard for you to see these pictures."

"It's bittersweet. Looking at them reminds me of the perfect life I used to have. But then I think of where I am now." She swallowed hard, holding back tears. "I miss him. And I miss who I was back then, too."

Meredith stole a glance at him as he sat beside her. His hands were once again folded in his lap, his knees spread before him.

Abruptly he looked at her.

"My mother died of cancer ten years ago," he said.

Meredith was taken aback by his candidness, and said nothing.

"So I can imagine how you feel."

Her eyes grew misty as she was warmed by a rush of sympathy. "I'm sorry," she said, and rubbed her eyes with her fingers. "It isn't a feeling I would wish on anyone. It's very hard to watch someone you love go through that."

"It makes the world seem a much scarier place, doesn't it?"

She looked at him. The harshness of his words was at odds with the softness of his expression.

"How do you handle it?" she asked.

He shrugged. "I just look around me at all the good things in life. And I see that the world has more beauty than pain."

Tears welled in her eyes once more. When she turned to him again, he was staring at her. His eyes were somber and warm, and she couldn't look away from them. His good-naturedness was evident in the gentle creases in the corners. And she was struck by their pure blue depth as he studied her, just as she was studying him. Something shifted inside her. She noticed more attentively now the way his hair curved around his temples, the sharp lines of his face. Her heart ached in her chest as she was forced to acknowledge that he was, in fact, painfully handsome.

She lowered her gaze, all at once realizing how close his knee was to hers.

"Thank you for sharing that with me," she said. "I'm sure it isn't easy for you to talk about."

"I just want you to know that it does get easier."

Meredith nodded numbly.

"And that you're not alone."

"Thank you," she said again, surprised by the sound of her voice, which was barely more than a whisper.

His eyes met hers. "You're welcome."

The earnestness in his face helped ground her. It was nice to connect with someone who understood.

A soft smile touched her lips. "You seem a nice person, and a sage one."

His eyebrows rose slightly. "Thank you."

As he and Meredith looked at each other his eyes grew kinder, the corners crinkling with a smile even though his lips remained long, straight, and serious. All at once the smile left his eyes, and Meredith felt the intensity of their gaze as tangibly as if he were physically touching her. Inexplicably her pulse began racing. Her lips parted as her breath left her; startled, she turned away from him and stood.

"Thank you for making me feel better," she said, a little too quickly.

Nick stood and said nothing.

"It really means a lot to me."

His voice was hushed, even more so than usual.

"You're welcome."

She cautiously lifted her gaze to his face. Without thinking, she placed her hand on his shoulder and kissed his cheek, horrified at her boldness even as she was doing it.

Her heart was pounding mercilessly in her chest. His arm was tight and powerful under her fingers. His skin was soft against her lips. Slowly she pulled away, lingering long enough to absorb the thick, masculine scent of him. He took a breath, and she felt its warmth on her neck.

She brought her face around to his. His eyes were wide, his lips parted. She backed away, stunned.

Nick closed his lips and swallowed, then turned toward the door.

"Goodnight," he whispered, and left.

Meredith stood frozen until she heard the door of Nick's bedroom shut. Then she climbed into bed in a daze. As she drifted toward oblivion, her mind pleasantly blank, she didn't even realize that it was the first night in a year she didn't cry herself to sleep.

CHAPTER THREE

BEAUTIFUL THINGS

"And we're off!" Vince called with hearty enthusiasm as Meredith backed out of the driveway and pulled onto the street.

They drove through the snowy neighborhood toward the art museum, observing people clearing off sport utility vehicles while their children built snowmen and threw snowballs at each other, laughing.

"I haven't been to the art museum in ages," said Vince. "Not since school."

Meredith smiled. "We used to hide in the cloisters and pretend we were a prince and princess, locked away by an evil queen."

Vince shook his head and smirked. "Little did we know," he mumbled.

"Know what?"

"That we weren't really pretending."

"Vince, stop," Meredith chastised. "She tried her hardest."

"How soon you forget the violin incident." He was looking out the passenger window, watching the houses go by. He faced forward then and relaxed in his seat. "You wanted a dollhouse for your birthday. She got you violin lessons. She said the dollhouse was a waste of time. You were six."

Meredith laughed. "Classic Mom."

"You didn't think it was so funny back then. You cried for days." He shook his head, his expression grave. "She told you to be mature about it. What the hell?"

"I don't remember that. But I do remember how you built a pillow fort and played board games with me for hours." She smiled warmly and turned to him. "It really made me feel better."

She patted his hand. He patted hers back, his gaze directed forward.

Vince was silent for several moments. Then, making an effort to be lighthearted, he said, "It'll be good to go back and see some of my favorite paintings. Maybe I can learn a thing or two, in case by some miracle I paint anything other than walls ever again."

"It's never too late to follow your dreams."

Meredith and Vince chatted as they passed the Victorian manor homes and stone cottages of their childhood. A few times Meredith stole a glance at Nick. He sat silently in the backseat, gazing out the window, his legs spread and his hands folded in his lap.

"Hey, look," said Vince, pointing out his window to a large stone farmhouse with tall brick chimneys and gabled dormer windows. "It's Mrs. Gallagher's old place. I used to sneak into the stables in the back and mess around with her granddaughter."

"Of course. You made me lie to Mom about where you were. None of your shenanigans would have been possible without my help. I was your very first wingman."

Meredith registered silent laughter coming from the backseat and caught a glimpse of Nick in the rearview mirror. He was grinning.

"What's so funny?" she asked, a shy smile on her face.

Nick cleared his throat and straightened in his seat. "Nothing," he said. "It's just that some things never change, I guess."

"I take it you've had to help Vince out of a scrape or two, as well."

"My buddy Nick's got my back," said Vince. "We travel together a lot. He's my wingman now. He's my shotgun on long road trips and my designated driver on short ones. I think every man needs a Nick."

"Maybe I'll have my own Nick one day," said Nick, and everyone laughed.

"Hey Nick," said Vince, leaning over the back of his seat, "my sister is a pretty savvy woman. She knows a lot about almost everything. We're lucky to have her as a tour guide."

Meredith chuckled. "You forget I've only been back here a few months, and I haven't exactly been living it up. And besides, we're only in the suburbs. I probably don't remember much more about Philadelphia than you do."

"No worries. Nick isn't much of a city guy anyway. Isn't that right, Nick?"

A little smile crossed Nick's lips. "I don't mind cities."

"You can be honest. It's okay. I know you're just a country boy at heart."

"The country is home, but I like to see new things."

"Merry, you might have noticed that Nick isn't a man of many words. But when he does talk, you get a lot of bang for your buck. That's why we get along so well, because he's too quiet and I'm too loud. We even each other out."

Meredith had woken up that morning thinking about how she'd so openly talked to Nick about Adam and how his responses had been short, but sensitive and incisive. She glanced again in the mirror at him. This time, she caught his eye. They locked gazes for a second, then both looked away.

They drove on into the city, and finally the museum came into view.

"What do you want to see first, Vince?" Meredith asked.

Vince did not respond. He had his phone out and was texting someone.

She glanced briefly at him. "What are you doing?"

"Nothing," he said, returning the phone to his pocket. Then he answered, "I don't care. Whatever you want to see. Although I have to say, I always have liked those Tibetan sculptures."

"You and I will be on opposite ends of the museum, then. I'll be headed for the Impressionist painters."

"That's fine. We can start together and then split up."

Suspicious, Meredith raised her eyebrows. They arrived at the museum, parked the car, and walked up the famous "Rocky staircase," Vince coercing Nick into taking a picture with him running with their arms in the air like Sylvester Stallone. Sure enough, when they reached the entrance of the museum, a stylish, carefully made-up woman who had been looking around searchingly recognized Vince and, a little too warmly, moved in to embrace him.

Meredith stopped short. "Sandy," she said, taking a few steps forward, having recovered from her shock.

The woman turned and, spotting Meredith, squealed loudly and rushed toward her, arms extended.

"Hi, Meredith!" Meredith instinctively stiffened as Sandy wrapped her arms around her and squeezed her tight, muffling her breath with her face and hair. Meredith returned the hug politely, and put on a friendly smile when Sandy pulled away. "It's so good to see you again!"

Meredith cast a glance at her brother; unsurprisingly, he was avoiding her gaze. "You too, Sandy."

"How long has it been? Three, four years?"

"It's been about six."

"Wow, time sure flies! I can't wait to catch up. We are going to have *such* fun today."

"For sure."

"Well, now that you two are reacquainted," said Vince,

slinking his arm around Sandy's back, "let's go see some paintings."

Meredith rolled her eyes: some things never did change. Sandy was an old high school girlfriend of Vince's, one he'd taken to stringing along and igniting false hope in every time he was in town. A year above Meredith in school, Sandy had always been friendly enough—but it was always the same. She and Vince hung out and hooked up for a couple of months, partying and bar hopping, filling every second with flirtation and fun. Vince always made it sound like he was into it long-term, flattering Sandy and making plans as if they had all the time in the world. When Vince's attention was inevitably diverted elsewhere, Sandy would stick around for a while, texting Meredith about her brother's whereabouts or picking her brain about how to win him back, occasionally inviting her out for coffee under the flimsy pretext of wanting to remain friends. Ultimately, Sandy would vanish for a time, until the cycle began again. Meredith tried to cut her some slack: she didn't mean any harm.

"So what have you been up to, Sandy?" she asked her, in an attempt to reciprocate her enthusiasm. "Last I heard, you were in event planning."

Sandy wasn't paying attention anyway; she had turned back to Vince and had his coat lapel in her hands. "Vince, it is so good to see you again." She tilted her head. "I can't wait to catch up."

Vince said, "You know, I haven't forgotten you after all these years. I see your face in my dreams."

Meredith had to turn away lest the two of them see her disgust. She glanced at Nick. His eyes met hers. His face wore an amused grin.

"Let's go in, shall we?" Meredith chirped, a little too brightly.

"Sure," Vince said, and held his arm out to escort Sandy inside.

Sandy excused herself to take a call on her cell phone. When she had turned her back and walked away, Meredith slapped Vince's arm. He winced and frowned at her.

"What the hell was that for?" he whined.

"You know what that was for. I thought this day was for us to hang out and spend time together, not for you to try to score with your on-again, off-again."

"Sorry," he said, but it was clear he was not sorry at all. "I had told her I was coming into town, and she kept harassing me to get together. I figured this way there would be an even four of us. I didn't think you'd mind. Don't be mad," he said, and opened his puppy dog eyes widely with pleading.

Meredith sighed. She shook her head with disapproval but couldn't keep the momentum of her anger. "You sure don't waste any time."

"I'm efficient like that."

They walked toward Sandy, who was talking animatedly into her phone.

Vince turned to Meredith. "I hope you aren't mad," he said again, putting his arm around her shoulder. "I know it's not right. It's just..."

"It's okay, Vince. We have plenty of time to spend together."

Sandy hung up the phone and rolled her eyes, indicating her irritation at whomever she had been talking to. "Sorry about that," she said, and took Vince's arm.

"All right, let's move," Vince said jovially. He and Sandy walked ahead, Nick and Meredith following behind.

They turned to the right and walked into Meredith's favorite galleries, 19th-century European art. Meredith stood pensively taking in the luscious swirling colors of the works of Cassatt, Renoir, and Cezanne, moving from frame to frame and allowing herself to become lost in her thoughts. Before entering the next gallery, she glanced around the room. Vince and Sandy were arm in arm, chatting and blithely strolling past each work without barely a glimpse. Casting her eyes to the other side of the room, Meredith spotted Nick. His eyes were already on her. She left her place in front of a Courbet and headed toward him.

"I love the play on shadows in this one," she observed with deliberate pretension, indicating the painting to which he had turned.

"Hmm," he murmured with mock gravity, cupping his chin in his thumb and index finger, and nodding, as if deep in thought.

"The artist is said to have influenced Monet," she replied, continuing the game.

"Is that so."

Serious now, she turned toward him. "Thank you again for last night. It was good of you to make that effort."

"It was no effort," he said, and a smile touched the corners of his eyes. "I hope I helped."

"You did." She returned his smile.

They passed a few moments in silence, avoiding each other's gaze.

"I was sorry to hear about your mother," she said, her eyes now meeting his. "I'm sure she was a very special woman."

"She was a good woman, and a good mother."

"Was she?" Meredith asked, her face brightening with interest.

"She told me all sorts of stories," he said, "and made me think about things. She taught me not to take anything for granted." His eyes were intent on hers. Meredith couldn't believe how blue they were, and how clear. She recalled a poem by Keats. *"Blue! —'Tis the life of heaven...'Tis the life of waters...What strange powers hast thou, as a mere shadow!—But how great, when in an Eye thou art alive with fate!"*

She straightened and swallowed. "That's beautiful."

They said nothing for some time, looking at the floor.

"Do you like roses?" he asked.

She blinked. "What?"

"Look over here," he said, and walked away. She followed, mystified.

He stopped in front of a medium-sized painting in an ornate gold frame. It was an Impressionist piece of red and yellow swirls, at the center of which was a young woman holding a bouquet of roses.

"I think she looks like you," he said when she came to a halt just behind him.

She stared at the painting. The woman was delicate-looking and pretty. Her chestnut hair fell straight to her shoulders, and her large green eyes drifted thoughtfully toward something or someone out of view.

He faced her.

"I hope you're feeling better today."

Meredith felt her eyes soften. "Much better. Thank you."

He looked about the room. "I'll bet all the beautiful things here make it easy to feel better." He turned to her and smiled. "I'm glad you suggested this."

Meredith was beginning to feel lulled by the reticence of his voice. "Me too," she managed to utter.

"Would you walk around with me?"

She experienced a light fluttering in her chest. "I'd love to."

Together they walked around the room, stopping frequently to discuss each painting. After nearly an hour, Meredith paused to try to reach her brother on his cell phone, but he didn't answer. She and Nick continued to roam the museum on their own.

"You seem to know a lot about art," said Meredith, looking up at him with a smile.

Nick shrugged. "Not really. I just think it's interesting."

"Have you studied art at all?"

"No. Art is just how people feel about the world. I think it's pretty simple, actually."

Meredith thought about this. "Is that why you became a painter? Because you like art?"

"I got into it because my father was a carpenter. So was his father. When I was a kid, he used to let me help him build houses. I've done carpentry and paint work on and off for years."

"I can see the connection. I think you need to appreciate art to be a carpenter."

"There is a lot of art in carpentry. You have to have an eye for detail and symmetry. I love carpentry. I love working with wood and making it fit my vision. There's not a lot of art to my job, though. I just came across it when I was looking for steady pay."

They passed through the Grand Stair Hall. Nick stopped suddenly and turned, his eyes wide.

"Wow."

Meredith was delighted: she knew what he was looking at and had been excited to see it, too. Standing beside him, she faced Diana, the gleaming golden giant that was the beating heart of the museum. The goddess rested in a massive alcove at the top of the staircase. She stood on a golden ball, arm extended, ready to fire an arrow from her impossibly mighty bow.

They studied Diana in silence for quite a long time. Eventually, Meredith turned to Nick.

"She's pretty incredible, isn't she?"

"Mmm." He furrowed his brow with thought. "The way she's standing on the ball. On one toe." He crossed his arms. "It's like it defies gravity."

"That's my favorite part about it." She gazed at the statue once more. "To me it means possibility, and the ingenuity of humankind." She pivoted to face him. "How about you?"

Nick thought about it, his jaw tight with contemplation. "Isn't Diana the same as Aphrodite?"

"Close." Meredith smiled. "Diana is the Roman version of Artemis, but you aren't that far off."

"Artemis was the goddess of the hunt." It was said as a statement, but he turned to her tentatively, with questioning eyes, as if to verify its truth.

Her eyes brightened as she watched him. "Yes. So how do you think it relates?"

He looked at the statue once more. "I think it's about balance, between the natural world and the divine."

Meredith turned toward the statue. She had seen this statue a number of times and had never thought of it quite like that.

"Who sculpted her?" Nick asked then. "How old is she?"

"Augustus Saint-Gaudens," she answered, "sometime in the late nineteenth century. She has an interesting history, actually." She turned to him again. "If you'd like to hear it."

"I'd love to."

Meredith faced the statue and told him how it had come to be at the museum, keeping the facts tactfully short—she wanted to be helpful, not tedious.

They were jostled by a passing crowd of children. Their hips brushed against each other. Nick's arm found its way around her shoulder, maneuvering them away from the chaos. Meredith's heart quickened at this intimate contact with him, the warmth of feeling protected. She leaned against him a few seconds longer than necessary. A twinge of guilt twisted in her chest. She gave him a wide berth to compensate.

They climbed the sprawling staircase toward Diana, who towered over them, commanding all the space around her, just as a goddess would.

"Stand in front of her," said Nick, when they reached the top. "I'll take your picture."

There was an awkward moment when Meredith didn't know if she should pass him her phone or let him take the picture with his own. Abruptly, she stuck her hand out, and he removed her phone from her fingers. She stood before the statue, as straight and tall as she could. He backed up a few paces, holding the phone out. He moved it around a little, brow wrinkled.

"The statue's so tall. It won't even fit in the photo."

The corners of Meredith's lips turned upward into a little smile. "I know, it's amazing. I've tried to get this picture before."

He tried a number of positions. Meredith chuckled at his

dedication. Finally, he approached her, his face, usually so composed, broken into a wide grin of triumph.

"How about that?"

He held the phone out so she could see. He'd turned the phone diagonally to accommodate Diana's height. Meredith raised her eyebrows, impressed by his ingenuity.

"You have quite an artistic vision."

He shrugged. "I just kind of figured it out."

"She really is impressive. Look how small I look in comparison."

"But at this angle, you're like an extension of her. It's like you're supposed to be there."

"Do you want us to take one of the two of you?"

This, from a friendly-looking passerby in a tweed coat and glasses. Beside him, a smiling woman, probably his wife, stood by nodding. Neither Meredith nor Nick responded at first, the unsaid words—"We're not together"—lingering tensely in the air.

Finally, Meredith smiled. "Sure," she told the man, leaning forward toward his outstretched hand to pass along her phone. "Thank you so much."

Nick and Meredith stood side by side before the statue.

"Oh come on," the man said, "look like you like each other."

Nick and Meredith laughed awkwardly, then wrapped their arms around each other's backs. The act felt tender, like she was letting him into her world, like he was letting her into his. Meredith was taken aback by the way her blood raced, the way her nerves alighted all over. She stole a quick glance up at him, his angular nose and chin, his blond hair curving around his temples and down around his ear. He was facing forward with a serene, closed-lipped smile.

The man tried to maneuver the phone to fit the entire statue into the photo, just as Nick had, but unlike Nick, he couldn't figure out how to do it. The resulting photo was like the photos

Meredith had taken before: all statue and no pillar, or all pillar and no statue.

"Sorry," the man said genially. "I did the best I could!"

But Meredith liked the photos. They captured a content little moment in time, a thoughtful conversation with someone interesting and new. She thanked the man, and the couple moved on. As they walked away, she stared at the photos for a second or two. They gave her an unexpected little thrill.

She glanced up from her phone to find Nick quietly watching her. When she looked at him, he flushed.

"Shall we?" she asked jovially, extending her arm, willfully ignoring the strange warm sensation that had tried to swell in her chest.

Meredith and Nick meandered along, strolling through galleries, eighteenth-century drawing rooms, and medieval cloisters. Nick seemed particularly interested in the frescos; he was impressed with their size and scope, and he spent many minutes examining them closely, then standing farther away to take them all in at once. Meredith took strange pleasure in watching him. His seriousness, his almost innocent wonder, was heartbreakingly charming. But also, try as she might, she couldn't help but notice his own beauty, made only more fascinating by the contrast between his rugged, unpretentious appearance and the grandeur of the art's subjects. Leaning forward to study details, his eyes sharp and his lips straight with thought, or standing straight and tall as he regarded the masterpiece as a whole, he was almost like a work of art himself. Meredith took advantage of his distraction, studying him as he studied the art, noting well-constructed details, just as he did the same. She looked away, scolding herself, feeling shameful, like a voyeur.

They had already passed the most popular galleries and often found themselves alone. The sound of their footsteps resonated in the stillness. Their hushed voices hummed in the enclosed spaces, intermingling in the air above their heads. It was serene, peaceful, and contemplative. It mirrored perfectly his quiet, pensive manner, the understated depth of their conversation.

At one point as they were leaving a gallery containing Asian art, they were accosted by a traffic jam of people passing each other. Nick's hand found Meredith's lower back, and he guided her out of the room.

The first people they saw when they emerged were Vince and Sandy. They were holding hands and walking quickly, as if they had been trying to find their companions. Upon seeing them, Nick swiftly removed his hand from Meredith's back, but he was a split second too slow. Vince dropped Sandy's hand and glared at them.

"Hi," Meredith said, ignoring her brother's sneer. "Where have you been?"

Vince was staring at Nick. "We went to find the Tibetan sculptures."

"Did you find them?"

"Yes."

Everyone stood in silence.

Sandy looked around at them, puzzled. She said, "Why don't we go grab a bite to eat?"

"Okay," Vince said dryly. "Let's do that."

Meredith risked a quick glance at Nick, but he was looking straight ahead as the four of them walked toward the front of the museum.

Sandy said, "Why don't we eat at the museum's restaurant?"

Everyone looked at each other, but no one said anything. Finally Meredith clapped her hands together and smiled. "That's a great idea, Sandy."

They made their way to the restaurant in silence. Once seated at a table, soup and sandwiches in front of them, Vince, having shaken off his foul mood as easily as he had fallen victim to it, said, "That was fun. Great idea, Merry." He smiled amiably.

"I'm glad you had a good time," she replied, "and that you had a chance to see your sculptures."

"They weren't as impressive as I remembered," he said as he folded his napkin onto his lap. "When I was a kid, they looked big and scary."

"Now you're big and scary," Meredith said, chuckling.

"You mean big and sexy!" Sandy corrected loudly, pulling on Vince's arm and kissing his cheek. Vince's face turned red, and he pushed her away, embarrassed.

As they tucked into lunch, they made polite conversation about the works of art they had seen that day.

"That first room we were in," Sandy said with a sour look on her face. "All the paintings were so...smudged," she spat, indicating her displeasure by shuddering her shoulders.

"The 'smudging' is intentional," Meredith commented. "The painters wanted to recreate the effect of light."

"Light doesn't look like that," Sandy retorted authoritatively.

Meredith said, "It represents the changeable nature of light, like the changeable nature of time. It's all about capturing the essence rather than—"

She stopped short when she caught sight of Vince out of the corner of her eye. His elbow on the table, he had his hand to his face as if scratching his head, but the effect was that his hand blocked the view of his face from Sandy. His eyes were pleading, and he was shaking his head.

Meredith shrugged and gave up. "Oh well," she said as she brushed a crumb off her hand and smiled around the table. "It was a fun day, anyway."

She turned to Nick, who was watching her. She didn't realize she had let her gaze rest on him until she felt Vince's eyes on her. Turning her attention to her brother, she saw a look of impatience cross his face; then his expression cleared, and he slapped his hands on the table. "All right, folks—let's get out of here."

As they left the restaurant and made their way toward the entrance of the museum, Meredith spotted the gift shop. "Just give me a minute," she said, and walked away. She thought it might be a good place to find the perfect birthday present for Tara's older daughter Evelyn.

Inside, she browsed the shelves full of posters, paper weights, pens, clothing, and books. She was just getting ready to leave empty-handed when she noticed a wooden box with beautiful carvings on top. She opened the box. A miniature ballerina—clearly modeled after a Degas ballerina—began dancing, spinning around with her hand and leg perpetually raised. A song with a sweet, pleasing melody tinkled from inside, but Meredith didn't recognize it.

With a smile, Meredith took the music box in both hands and brought it to the register to pay. Evelyn was four and recently had thrown herself into an obsession with ballerinas. This music box would be the perfect "big girl" gift.

She joined the others back in the museum's entrance. Nick and Meredith stood back as Sandy gave Vince a warm goodbye, telling him she'd see him soon and whispering something in his ear, and giggling coquettishly. Vince grinned back at her and patted her rear end as she strutted away. He watched her for a moment and then turned to the others.

"What?" he asked, holding his hands in the air with exaggerated innocence.

Meredith shook her head at him, but there was no malice in her expression. They headed outside into light wisps of falling snow.

Back at the house, Vince didn't take off his coat as Meredith and Nick peeled off their shoes, scarves, and gloves. He bounded upstairs without a word, leaving them in awkward silence as they hung up their coats. When he came back downstairs, he smelled heavily of cologne.

"Hey, listen," he began, "I was thinking of going out for a bit."

"Oh?"

"Sandy invited me to a thing," he said, not looking at her. "I won't be long." After patting his pockets to make sure he had all he needed, he faced her. "Is that okay?"

"You're an adult, Vince. You don't need my permission."

"Thanks, Merry. I know how this looks."

"Vince, it's okay, really," she assured him, with an earnest smile.

He kissed her forehead. "You're the best," he told her, and clapped Nick on the back on his way out the door.

Nick and Meredith stood there looking at each other.

"What is it?" she asked, growing uncomfortable in his intense gaze.

"Nothing," he said.

She glanced around the house nervously. "Well, it's too early for dinner."

"Let's go for a walk."

She stared at him. "In the snow?"

He shrugged. "Why not?"

She couldn't think of a reason.

They put their winter things back on and went outside. At the bottom of the steps, he looked at her expectantly.

She pointed toward the left. "Let's go this way," she said. There was a walking park with a little playground a few streets down.

They walked in silence for a minute, the only sound that of the snow crunching under their boots. Snowflakes drifted downward all around them, daintily, like dancers on tiptoe leaping onto stage. Across the street, two children were pulling each other in a sled. A bird flew by. Meredith wondered how he had missed the message that it was time to fly south.

"So," she began, trying to make conversation, "how do you think you'll like the job here?"

Nick considered. "It's pretty much the same job I do every-where. I'm largely left alone. I have lots of time to think. I'm good at it." He shrugged. "I'm sure I'll like it well enough."

They continued walking along in silence.

"And you?" he said after some time, turning to her. He smiled pleasantly. Her heart lurched as his eyes met hers. "I gather you're a teacher. A very noble profession."

Meredith laughed. "Thank you," she said. "I like my job. I enjoy being in front of the classroom talking about books I love. Plus, seeing the improvement in my students' writing is very rewarding. It makes me feel like I'm making a contribution somehow."

"You are."

She turned to him and smiled. "Thanks."

He took her hand. She held her breath as her heart quickened. They walked in silence for another minute, then turned down a street toward the park. Meredith shivered in the cold, and Nick put his arm around her shoulder. Taking a chance, she wrapped hers around his waist, and they pulled each other close. Melting in this comfort, she lay her head on the side of his chest. He kissed the top of her head.

They walked like this for a couple of blocks until they reached the park. Here the snow looked like a shimmery blanket, for no one had ventured to come here since the snow had begun falling. They entered the park and walked along the trail for several minutes, still holding each other in silence.

"I had a nice time at the museum," she said. "I went to art museums frequently when I lived in New York. But I hadn't been to our museum in years."

"I had a nice time, too," he replied, with an unexpected hint of enthusiasm in his quiet voice. "I never do things like that."

"Oh? Why not?"

"We go to cities a lot for work, but nobody goes to museums."

"No, I imagine not." She watched her feet as they made brief impressions in the snow, then moved on. "What *do* people do?"

"There's a lot of hanging out, just going to bars and all that. It gets old. I like the museum much better."

"That's nice." Meredith smiled. "You had a lot of interesting things to say. I enjoyed hearing your perspective."

He was silent at first. "It was interesting to think about," he said finally. "I'd never had conversation like that before."

"I'm glad you got to do something different."

"Me too."

They continued on. It was overcast, and the bright luminescence of the snow was muted into a soft glow. Meredith indulged in a deep calming breath, letting the brisk air cleanse her.

"Are you originally from Maine?" she asked.

"No, I was born in Vermont. I grew up there."

"What brought you to Maine?"

Nick said nothing for a moment. "I guess I just like the memories I have there. My father used to take me fishing there. I still like to fish whenever I can."

Meredith was delighted by this response. "Does your father still live in Vermont?"

"Yes." They took a few more steps before he spoke again. "He lives in an assisted living facility there."

Meredith turned toward him; he was watching the ground as he walked.

"Is he ill?" she asked, her voice soft with hesitation.

"He had a stroke a number of years ago."

Meredith felt a deep ache in her chest. "I'm sorry."

She listened to the steady sound of their footsteps in the snow as she waited for him to respond.

"He's also been fighting depression. He has a lot of regrets about his life."

"What kind of regrets?"

"Regrets about leaving my mother," he answered, but then said no more.

They walked on in silence. Worried that she was prying, Meredith decided not to ask any more questions. She was surprised when he continued.

"He went back to her right around the time she got sick, and they were together until she died. I wanted to move home to take care of him after his stroke, but he wouldn't hear of it. So I stayed in Maine." He furrowed his brow with thought. "I don't see him as often as I'd like. But at least I get to live somewhere that reminds me of happy times."

Meredith felt a sudden rush of an emotion she couldn't identify. She didn't know what to say next. She directed her eyes downward toward the snow.

"It snowed a lot last night," she said. "I imagine even more so in Maine."

"It's one of the things I love most about Maine," Nick said, and instantly his face brightened. "Some people complain about the winters, but I never mind them. There's nothing as beautiful as the rocky shoreline when it's covered in snow. I don't know what looks whiter, the snow or the waves."

Meredith watched him as he spoke. The simplicity of this comment warmed her, and she couldn't help but smile.

"My town always has winter walks and wildlife watches," he went on. "Some nights people gather to stargaze. The stars always seem brighter during winter."

"It sounds like a very peaceful place," she said, and paused to imagine this. She faced forward once more. "I like the winter, too. I love being snowed in, just sitting in front of the fire with a good book and a cup of tea."

"That's the best thing about winter."

They continued walking, the snow heavy under their feet.

Finally he withdrew his arm and bent down to the ground to

scoop up some snow with his gloved hand. Continuing to walk, he patted it into a ball. "I wonder where Vince went," he said.

Meredith snickered. "I think I can guess."

Nick did not respond. He was packing his snowball tightly.

Meredith said, "Does he cavort like this with women in Maine?"

Nick's mouth contorted into a crooked grin. "You could say that."

"My darling brother," Meredith said pleasantly. "A new woman every week. That's how he's always been."

They continued walking, Nick moving the snowball from hand to hand. Meredith said tentatively, with her heart in her throat, "What about you? I'm sure women fall all over you."

"Why do you say that?"

"Well, look at you." Without looking at him herself, she said, trying to assume a lighthearted, joking tone, "You can't tell me you don't know what women see when they look at you."

"What do you see?"

The question caught her off guard. After a brief moment of thought, she said, "I see a man whose quiet voice seems to reflect the quietude of his soul."

He chuckled once, silently. "That's poetry. You must be a writer, too."

Neither of them spoke. Then she said, "So? Do they?"

"Does who what?"

"Do women knock down your door." *And do you answer*, she thought but did not say.

He said nothing for a moment, then said flatly, looking at the snowball in his hand, "It's complicated." He paused. "I don't think they see what you see."

Meredith didn't know how to interpret this comment, but she let it lie. She didn't really want to talk about past relationships, neither his nor hers.

Abruptly his face grew mischievous, his eyes narrowing and

his lips curving into a subtle grin. "Hey," he said, affecting a serious tone. "What's that up there?"

"What?" she asked, looking straight ahead.

A snowball pelted her in the face. The snow fell down into her scarf, chilling her neck and chin. She stared at him, shocked and aghast. He was attempting to keep his face expressionless but was failing miserably. He opened his eyes wide with pretend surprise.

"I'm sorry," he said innocently. "My hand slipped."

"Oh, it did, did it?" she said, simultaneously irritated and delighted. She bent over and grabbed some snow.

Before she could straighten, he tackled her, falling with her into the snow so she fell on her side. He kneeled next to her.

"I'm sorry," he said again. "I don't know what came over me."

Leaning on her arm to sit up, she said, "I'll tell you what's coming over you." With that, she pushed him into the snowy ground and lay on top of him. They stared at each other, neither knowing what to do next. Suddenly he kissed her. Meredith kissed him back, her pulse racing. She brought her hands to his face and tilted her chin; his hands drifted to her back, and he sighed softly. She pulled away, rubbing his cold nose with hers.

Breathless, they didn't say anything for a few moments. Then he said, "You know, it's cold here in the snow."

"I'm sure it is," she said, and stood. She held out her hand. "Let's go back home and warm up."

THEY PEELED OFF THEIR BOOTS, coats, hats, and gloves in the entryway and walked inside. Meredith went to the kitchen to put on a pot of tea, out of the corner of her eye noticing Nick tentatively following her as she filled the kettle. When she turned from the sink, she saw that he had been watching her. His face flushed when their eyes met, and he stood a little straighter as, possessed by a force of unknown origin, she placed the kettle down and drifted toward him, stopping only when she was close enough to observe him taking a deep breath.

Her eyes rested on his chest; they rose to his throat, but her bravery ended there, and she could look no higher. Mere inches from him now, she witnessed every little detail of him—the gentle depression at the base of his neck, the swelling of the muscles of his arms beneath his sweater, the knobs and crevices of his hands and fingers, which were dotted with remnants of paint.

His hand slowly rose as she studied it, and she registered its movement as if from a distant cloud; then he was brushing the delicate skin beneath her ear, the pressure so faint she could almost feel the roughness of the paint upon his fingers. A hushed breath escaped her. She was still unable to look at his face, but she felt his breath in her hair, sensed his eyes close as his lips met her forehead and rested there softly.

Her chin rose a fraction of an inch, and she lifted her gaze to his jaw. Feeling above herself, spurred and mesmerized by the pounding rhythm of her heart, she brought her hand forward and stroked him, the tips of her fingers tracing the hard, rugged angles of his face. He leaned in farther and kissed her temple. She felt his hair on her face, and inhaled. It smelled like fire.

There they stood, in a strange place that was nowhere, for many moments. She didn't know the next step, didn't remember where to go from here. She was frightened of mistakes. She was nervous she would make the wrong movement or sound. She was nervous about tomorrow. She could almost see the words that formed her frantic questions as they rose into the forefront of her consciousness. But she wanted to be closer to him, craving the comfort of his gentleness against the harshness of the house and of the world. She tried to think, but her mind was spinning. Her breath now sounded immodestly in her ears, but she was power-less to tame it. She closed her eyes.

She didn't know how it happened, but suddenly she was taking his hand and leading him upstairs. He followed her passively and stood still as she shut the door of her bedroom and turned to him. He closed his eyes as she once again approached him, bringing her lips into the space between his neck and his ear. She didn't know what was moving faster now, her hands or her heartbeat; she didn't know why she wasn't self-conscious or afraid. All she knew was the warm support of his hands as they pressed to her back and hips, and pushed her toward her bed.

Without a word they threw their cold, wet clothes to the floor. Before she knew it she was lying underneath him and he was moving not with bewildered hesitation but decidedly, and with vigor, with loving desire in the kisses he pressed onto her lips and into her throat. Meredith felt herself unfurling, her worries dissipating with every movement, with every steady breath. She held tighter to him, and he pulled her closer, and she lifted her chin in bliss. Their heartbeats now in perfect time, she gave herself over to trust and instinct, and as his warm, hard body writhed rhythmically on top of hers, she readily surrendered.

AFTER, they lay motionless together for a long time. Meredith was lulled by the steady sound of his breathing as he slept. Her head on his chest, she delighted in feeling the light thumping of his heart. She smiled as she relished the quiet of the room and the quiet of her mind. For the first time in a year, she saw peace and promise in the days ahead; for the first time in a year, she felt alive.

She drifted into a restful sleep. She and Nick awoke occasionally only to share a kiss or sigh contentedly. Soon daylight began peeking through the curtains. Still they lay there, his arm around her, her head on his shoulder and her face buried in his neck. He gently stroked her arm with his fingers as they enjoyed the silence and the cozy warmth of the bed. When the harsh glare of headlights in the driveway intruded on the serenity of the delicate light of breaking day, he took her neck in his hand and lifted her lips to meet his, taking her in a deliciously deep kiss. He peeled himself from her and slid out of bed, and his sudden absence made her feel cold. Having collected his clothes from the floor, he took one more look at her from the doorway, his face expressionless except for the kind crinkles so familiar to her now. Then he crept from the room, leaving her alone.

CHAPTER FOUR

*W*hen she awoke and went downstairs for breakfast, Meredith was surprised to find Vince at the dining room table eating a bowl of cereal.

"Hey," she said, making a feeble attempt at perkiness as she headed toward the kitchen for some coffee. "How was your night?"

"Good," he said through a mouthful of cereal. "I just got back a little while ago, but I couldn't sleep. There's coffee in there," he called over his shoulder as she walked by.

Armed with her coffee, she reentered the dining room and sat down.

"You look rough," he said as he examined her. "Didn't you sleep well?"

She was trying her best not to blush. Rubbing her face with her hands to hide the redness she was sure was suspiciously visible now, she said, "I tossed and turned all night," and snickered to herself.

Vince cracked his knuckles and returned to his cereal.

"How about you?" she asked, shooting him a sly smile as she

sipped her coffee. "Didn't Sandy let you get a wink of rest last night?"

"No comment."

They sat in silence.

After a minute or two, Vince spoke.

"So what did you and Nick do last night?"

She had been expecting this question. "Nothing much. We just talked for a while, then went to sleep." It wasn't really a lie. She'd just left out the most important part.

"Sounds exciting."

If you only knew, she thought, suppressing a grin.

Vince looked dazed. "I need a nap," he said. He stood and began walking from the table.

"Say, listen," she said, stopping him before he went up the stairs. "I was thinking that it's time to get a tree."

Vince looked at her blankly. "A tree?"

"A Christmas tree." The inspiration had struck her that morning. She hadn't planned on getting a tree, but suddenly, she was feeling a little festive. "Christmas is two weeks away."

Vince ran his hands through his hair. "Oh, right. Do you want Nick and me to pick it up while you're at the party?"

She smiled. "That's exactly what I was thinking."

"Great," he said, beginning to ascend the stairs. "We'll drop you off at the party and get the tree, and then we'll pick you up when the party is over."

"Okay," she said, happy to cross the task off her list.

After breakfast, Meredith showered and dressed in her room. Returning downstairs and heading for the entryway to grab her coat and purse, she found Nick standing there alone. He turned upon hearing her descend the staircase, and followed her with his eyes.

"Where's Vince?" she asked, trying to sound nonchalant.

"He's clearing the snow off your car."

Meredith reached for her camel-colored pea coat, ignoring the sound of her heart thumping ruthlessly in her chest and ears. Nick stepped forward and held one arm of her coat for her to slip into.

The heat from his nearness and the earthy scent of him melted her. She smiled nervously as she slid her arms into her coat. "Thanks," she said, but it came out as a whisper.

She faced him.

He was quite tall, and as he looked down at her she longed to wrap her arms around his waist and lift her chin to meet him in a kiss. He remained silent. His lips were turned down in a frown of concentration, but his eyes were warm.

"Um," she stammered, trying to find something to say.

He lifted his hand and brought it to her ear, behind which he lovingly tucked a lock of hair. As he lowered his hand, he let his finger drift over the soft skin of her neck and down her throat, ending at the gentle swelling of her breast just beneath her heart. He exhaled deeply.

After a moment of silence in which she caught her breath, she said, "Last night..." and trailed off.

"Yes?"

She didn't know. She wanted to talk about what had happened but didn't know where to start, didn't know him well enough to know what he'd want to hear. She couldn't even wrap her head around her own feelings.

His bottomless blue eyes were intimately connected with hers. "Was there a problem with last night?" he asked suggestively with a coy, sly smile.

She nearly choked on her breath as she remembered how he had felt on top of her, the silkiness of his hair as it had trickled between her fingers and the pressure of his body against hers. "No," she gasped.

Seconds of silence passed.

"You're beautiful," he said tenderly.

Meredith felt a warm haze overtake her and had trouble keeping her eyes fully open. In a daze, she reached to retrieve her scarf from the coat rack. Nick took it from her and carefully wrapped it around her neck. His fingers drifted to her chin, lifting it toward his. She closed her eyes as he kissed her once, then retracted his hand.

Not knowing what else to say, Meredith said nothing. Nick stepped toward the door and opened it for her to pass through, then helped her down the icy steps as they met Vince outside.

When they dropped her off at Tara's, Meredith wondered what her friend would think about the events of the last few days and how she would respond to Nick, who would be with Vince later to pick her up after the party. She rang the bell and waited, grinning as she anticipated shocking Tara with what she had to say.

The sound of many feet grew louder from inside the house. Then the door opened, and Tara and her two daughters greeted her with wide smiles. The two little girls were wearing matching pink and white spotted dresses. Tara wore black leggings and knee-high black boots, and a pink sweater. All three of them had the same auburn hair and amber freckles.

"Hi, Aunt Merry," beamed Evelyn. Her wide-eyed expression suggested that she was waiting for something.

Astutely, Meredith noticed a badge on Evelyn's dress. "Hi, Evelyn. What's that on your dress?"

Evelyn beamed. "It says I'm the birthday girl. I got it at school. I was line leader and I got to pick the book for circle time. And also I brought cupcakes. They were pink, and all my friends liked them."

Meredith bent at the waist to look into Evelyn's large brown eyes. She put her hand on her shoulder. "That sounds like so much fun, Evelyn. You are the luckiest birthday girl ever."

"She sure is," sounded Tara's tired voice behind her. "She also got a dollhouse. It took Daddy and me five hours to put the thing together. Here, take the munchkin." She handed Ginger, her younger daughter, to Meredith, who gladly took her.

Evelyn was eyeing the present in Meredith's hand. Meredith handed it to her. "Do you want to ask Mommy if you can open this present before your party? It's a special present."

The little girl's eyes grew wide with the kind of excitement only a child can feel when told she is about to receive a special present. "Mommy?" she pleaded.

"Go ahead, honey. What do you say?"

"Thank you, Aunt Merry."

Meredith and Tara watched as Evelyn removed the pink and green paper, letting it float to the floor as she attempted to discern what was inside. When all the paper was gone, she stared at the box with wonder.

"It's a music box," Meredith said. "Open it."

Evelyn opened the box. The tiny ballerina began her delicate dance, her eternally raised hand leading the way, her dainty foot trailing behind. Evelyn's face wore a look of concentration and awe.

"Evelyn," Tara said, bending down and placing her hand on her daughter's back, "that's a very grown-up present. It's beautiful, isn't it?"

"Mmm," Evelyn agreed, nodding. "Mommy, what song is that?"

Tara looked to Meredith for an answer. Meredith shrugged. "I don't know what the song is. It's pretty, though."

Tara turned back to Evelyn. "You'll have to be very careful so you don't break it."

"I will, Mommy. Can I bring it to my room?"

"Sure, honey. First go tell Daddy that Aunt Merry is here and that we're going to get your cake." Tara grabbed her coat as Evelyn ran off.

Into the room walked Tara's husband, wearing torn jeans and a tie-dyed t-shirt. His dark curly hair was disheveled and full of knots. He was covered with oatmeal, from head to foot.

"Hi, Merry," he said pleasantly as he reached out to take Ginger from Meredith's arms.

Meredith waved. "Hi, Tom." Meredith adored Tara's husband, a kindly, even-tempered scientist Tara often referred to as "the absentminded professor."

"Remember to change your clothes before I get back," Tara said as she picked up her purse. "And don't let the girls get their dresses dirty."

"Sure thing."

They waved goodbye and walked out the door.

"So what's up?" Tara asked as they climbed into her minivan and drove off. "How has Vince's visit been so far?"

"Great. We had a nice time at the art museum yesterday."

"That sounds fun. What did you do last night?"

Meredith suppressed a grin. "Well, Vince spent the night with his woman of the day and didn't return until this morning."

"Of course he did. Anyone I know? Wait, don't tell me. Sandy."

"You got it."

"Surprise, surprise. So what did you do while he was gallivanting about town?"

"Um," Meredith said, and swallowed. "I spent some time with his friend."

Tara's eyebrows rose. She turned to Meredith. "Oh?"

Meredith said nothing more, and there were several moments of weighty silence.

"You slept with him, didn't you."

"Yes."

"You naughty girl! I can't believe you," Tara reprimanded, but her voice was jubilant. "I want details."

Meredith talked all the way to the bakery about the night Nick had comforted her in her room, how they had enjoyed the art together at the museum, how they had discussed the beauty of Maine, and how they had kissed in the snow. Tara nodded, shook her head, clicked her tongue, and gasped, seemingly in rotation. They pulled into a parking spot in the shopping center as Meredith was telling Tara about the previous night and her conversation with Nick that day. Tara listened attentively. They sat in the car until Meredith finished her story, exhausted.

"Wow," Tara said, turning to face Meredith. "I have got to meet this guy."

"Good news. You'll meet him later when he and Vince come by to pick me up."

"Perfect. I'll need to talk to him before I give him my approval. Does Vince know what happened last night?"

"No. I'll get around to telling him, but first I want a couple of days to see where this is going."

Tara sat looking thoughtfully forward before turning to Meredith once more. "Well, I'm glad you're going to have some fun before this year is over. You deserve it. Although, I have to admit that I'm a little jealous."

"What are you jealous of? You have a husband."

"Exactly."

Both women laughed heartily.

"So what happens now?" asked Tara.

"I don't know. I'm still a little in shock that this happened. I've only known him a few days. There's something I really like about him, though. He's so quiet, but he seems to think very deeply. There's a peacefulness about him that's hard to explain. I can't put my finger on it."

"I'll bet you can."

They laughed once more.

Tara thought for a moment before speaking. "Seriously, Merry. I'm really happy for you. You need some excitement in your life."

Meredith nodded.

"I thought you'd never be interested in a man again after Adam," Tara continued.

Meredith was silent.

Tara's voice grew soft. She placed her hand on Meredith's, which was on the armrest of her seat. "Does it upset you to talk about him?"

Meredith shrugged. "A little," she said. "I just try not to talk about him too much."

"Well, I'm glad you told Nick about him. Best to be honest from the start."

Meredith turned to face Tara. "I feel a little guilty," she whispered shakily, "like it hasn't been enough time. I feel like—"

"Stop. You've been very respectful, Merry. Adam was everything to you, and you've honored him completely. The last year of your life has been total darkness. There's got to be something special about Nick if he's making you even think about moving forward. Do you know anything about his past relationships?"

Meredith shook her head. "We haven't gotten around to talking about that yet."

"That's okay," Tara said brightly, attempting to lighten the mood. "You don't have to know everything about him." She grinned. "You already know all the important things."

Meredith grinned in return. "I certainly like what I know so far."

"I'll bet you do. I already like him, and I haven't even met him."

They passed a few moments in silence.

Finally Tara sighed.

"Well," Meredith said, "shall we?"

The bakery was empty except for the white-haired baker and two teenagers standing by the window eating cupcakes. As they waited for the baker to retrieve Tara's cake order, Tara turned to Meredith and whispered conspiratorially, with a piercing grin, "So do you like being so free?"

Meredith didn't respond for a moment. "What do you mean?"

"You know what I mean," Tara nudged her. "You follow your heart without worrying about the rules. You trust your gut without knowing what's going to happen. You take up with a good-looking man you barely even know. What do you think? Do you like being so free?" She inched her way closer to Meredith, prepared to hear the whispered response.

Meredith smiled. "I don't know. I hadn't thought about it."

"Well, think about it now."

"Um," Meredith began. "Now that you mention it, it is nice to just follow my instincts and not think so hard. For once."

"Oh yeah!" Tara teased. Delighted by Meredith's response, she did a saucy little dance. "Here comes Miss Meredith on Nick's wild ride!" Her voice increased in volume with each word. Meredith frantically shushed her and blushed with mortification as the two teenagers by the window stopped, stared, and erupted with laughter.

The baker looked their way with an indeterminable expression. "Here's your cake," she said, examining them with caution as they approached the counter.

"Wow, it looks great, Louise!" Tara exclaimed as her eyes took in the sight of the pink cake with the ballerina painted on top. "Here you go," she said, handing her payment. "I'll see you again real soon!"

Meredith nodded her embarrassed goodbye and followed Tara out the door.

"I don't know, Tara," she said as they climbed into the car. "I've never done anything like this before. Part of me worries that I dove into it too quickly."

"It's pointless to fret over it," Tara said, putting her hand on Meredith's headrest while she backed out of her parking spot. "No offense, honey, but that ship has sailed."

"But what if I'm wrong?"

"You already did it, so you might as well enjoy it."

"I just can't believe I did this," she mumbled, blushing.

"You're a grown woman, Merry. You didn't do anything to be ashamed of. There's nothing to regret."

Meredith grinned. "I didn't say I regret it."

"Good," said Tara. "That's what I wanted to hear."

As they drove back to Tara's house to prepare for the party, Meredith felt deeply appreciative of Tara, whom she always could count on to be honest and supportive. A warm rush of gratitude overcame her as she thought about how fortunate she was to have this special friend in her life.

Tara pulled into her driveway and turned off the ignition. Unbuckling her seatbelt, she made to get out of the car.

"Tara," Meredith said, turning to face her fully.

Tara stopped and looked at her. "Yeah?"

Meredith put her hand on Tara's. "Thank you."

"For what?"

"For always being there for me, no matter what."

"Don't be silly."

"I'm serious. You're the only one who has always stood by me. The only one." Her face turned serious, and she swallowed. "I love you."

Tara's eyes grew tearful. She put her other hand on top of Meredith's. "Oh, sweetie. I love you too. And don't you ever forget it."

Meredith smiled through her own tears. "I won't. You won't let me."

"I want you to be happy."

Meredith nodded. "I know."

Tara smiled. Then she withdrew her hands from Meredith's and dabbed at her eyes. Looking at Meredith once more, she said, "Okay now? Let's go."

❧

WITHIN THE HOUR, ten little four-year-olds, all dressed in pink and purple, were giggling and galloping through the Spanglers' small house. Delighted squeals could be heard in every room as the little girls danced, sang, and played make believe. Finally it was time for the cake. Tara sent Tom—who had changed into fresh clothes that looked remarkably like the old clothes, minus the oatmeal—to the kitchen to light the candles. She herself dimmed the lights and grabbed her camera.

Above the din of laughter and amusement, Tara bellowed, "All right, everyone! Time to sing 'Happy Birthday' to our birthday girl!"

As the song began, Tom emerged from the kitchen, gingerly carrying the cake. Four pink candles gleamed as he placed the cake in front of his beaming daughter at the head of the table. At the end of the song, Evelyn closed her eyes, smiled as she thought of her wish, and blew out the candles. Everyone clapped, and Tara turned the lights back on.

Meredith's clapping and laughing stopped when she glanced over to the front door, only to find it wide open, Vince and Nick halfway inside. They were bundled in their winter gear, their cheeks and noses rosy from standing out in the cold choosing a Christmas tree. Their dark clothing and broad statures were at odds with the all the pink, miniature things in the room. As the scene calmed down, everyone stopped to stare at them.

"Hey," Vince said blithely to the room at large. "What's up?"

The clamor resumed. Instantly they were surrounded by the little girls, who interrogated them with chaotic enthusiasm.

Amidst the little girls and the chaos, Vince and Nick spotted Meredith and Tara. Politely extracting themselves from the cluster of girls, leaving them to their own entertainments, they made their way clumsily, stepping over little girls left and right.

"Well, gorgeous," Vince said to Tara as they approached, "it's been way too long."

"I know!" Tara said, and kissed his cheek. "And who is your friend?" she drawled with too much interest.

"Tara Spangler, this is Nick Kelly. Nick, Tara."

Tara scooped up Ginger, who had stumbled into the center of their little circle, and extended her hand toward Nick.

"It's a pleasure to meet you, Nick." Her voice contained a touch of mischief that made Meredith nervous. "Ginger, honey, no no," she gently reprimanded as she dislodged her daughter's fingers from the inside of Nick's ear. She turned to Nick. "I'm sorry."

"Not at all," Nick said, and smiled.

"So," Tara said, replacing Ginger on the floor and watching her scamper away. "How long are you in town for?"

"At least three months," Vince answered.

"That's a good long time. Do you have any big plans?"

"I'm psyched to catch up with old friends, see the old sights, you know," Vince responded. "The usual. Mostly we'll be working."

"And how about you, Nick? What do you like doing in your spare time?"

It was subtle, but Meredith could sense the teasing in Tara's voice. She felt the color drain from her face, and then it returned as she stifled laughter.

"I like to be outdoors," Nick told her. "I love camping and climbing, anything that puts me closer to nature. In cold weather I usually head up to the mountains somewhere, or hike through the woods."

"Meredith can show you all those places," Tara replied. "That's right up her alley. I can't keep that girl out of the woods. She knows where to do all those things."

Nick turned his head in her direction. "That would be great."

The heat wouldn't leave Meredith's face. "Sure, there's lots to do around here. I'd be happy to show you."

"Well," said Tara, "no matter what you do, I certainly hope you enjoy your time here in Pennsylvania."

"Thank you."

"You are most welcome," she said, and smiled coyly.

"So," Vince asked cheerfully. "What are you folks doing for Christmas?"

"We always go to Washington, DC," Tara responded. "My aunt and uncle live just outside the city, in northern Virginia. My parents and sisters join us. It's sort of a family tradition."

"Sounds nice," said Vince.

"What about your family? What exotic location are your parents visiting this year?"

"Thailand," said Vince. "No, Greenland. No, Scotland."

"Iceland," said Meredith, laughing. "They're touring the fjords with some old journalism friends."

"Wow," said Tara. "How long are they staying?"

"Through the summer, I think. It always changes."

"How's the trip so far?"

"I have no idea." Meredith instinctively pulled her phone from her pocket and checked her email, even though she knew they hadn't messaged her. "They haven't been very forthcoming with their communication. I tried to reach them last week, but I haven't heard back."

Vince sniffed. "I am shocked, *shocked* that Mom and Dad are unresponsive. It's so unlike them."

"Enough, Vince," said Meredith, but one side of her mouth had ticked up with amusement. She returned her phone to her pocket. "They are who they are, and it's okay."

"So what are your Christmas plans?" asked Tara. "Just hanging out this year, enjoying each other's company?"

"Pretty much," Vince said. Then, turning to Meredith, he said, "That is, unless you have other plans for us."

"No other plans," she said. "I'm looking forward to an uneventful Christmas this year."

Meredith and Tara exchanged quick, meaningful glances.

The party seemed to be winding down; the little girls were now forming discarded wrapping paper into balls and throwing them across the room, bubbling with laughter.

"Well, Merry," Vince said, "ready to head home?"

"Sure," Meredith replied. "Let me just say goodbye to the birthday girl."

On her way out the door, Meredith was stopped by Tara, who pulled her back by the arm.

Tara leaned in and whispered in her ear. "He's nice. Just stop worrying and have some fun," she told her, and nudged her with her elbow. "It doesn't have to be like anything you've done before. Maybe you're due for a change."

THE TREE they had chosen was big. Meredith worried that they wouldn't be able to get it into the house and that once they did there wouldn't be room for it. However, with some maneuvering, they set it up in a corner of the living room, where it stood regally, making the room feel cozy and full of cheer. All three of them stood back to admire it.

Meredith took a deep breath. "It smells wonderful!"

"Sure does," said Vince, rubbing his hands together. "Now where are those ornaments?"

Vince, Nick, and Meredith spent the rest of the day decorating the tree and reading by the fire. Meredith welcomed the chance to relax, cheered beyond measure by the company. That night Nick crept to Meredith's room, where he was welcomed eagerly by Meredith, who was already in bed.

He hurried over to the bed and slid beneath the blankets. Bunching the back of her nightgown in his hand, he engulfed her in a needy kiss, his foot rubbing playfully against hers, his breath warming her lips and his soft sighs making her blood tingle. Her hand rising to the side of his face, she let her fingertips drift across the bristly skin of his cheek until they reached the back of his neck, where they combed through his hair as it fell to the pillow. His hand had now abandoned the nightgown; she felt its electrifying heat as it glided over her hip and sensuously rubbed the small of her back. Their legs intertwined, and she sighed as all cares were pushed from her mind. Once again she was surprised by how easy it was to let go. *How does he do that?* she asked herself dreamily as he rolled her onto her back. It was the last thought she had that night.

CHAPTER FIVE

SERIOUS

*M*eredith jumped right out of bed with her alarm the next morning. Having showered and dressed, she bounded downstairs toward the kitchen only to find Nick already seated at the dining room table.

Standing behind him, she placed her hand on his shoulder and leaned forward to kiss his cheek.

"Good morning," she whispered.

"Good morning," he repeated as he lifted his chin to kiss her, his hand cupping her face.

She sat beside him as he sipped his coffee.

"How are you?" she asked.

"Tired."

There was silence as she nodded in agreement.

"But happy," he said, and smiled.

"Me too," she responded, also smiling. "This was the best weekend I've had in a long time. I've enjoyed talking to you. Thinking about beautiful things has been very refreshing." She took a deep breath. "You've really brought some sunshine into my days," she said, and immediately cursed herself.

"I feel the same way. It's nice to have someone to talk to about those things."

She was encouraged by his comment and decided to be bold. "The nights have been nice, too," she whispered, a little breathlessly.

"No argument here."

He stroked her hand as it rested on the table. A thrill rippled through her. Then footsteps sounded at the top of the stairs. Nick withdrew his fingers.

Meredith turned to see Vince standing at the top of the stairs. He had a strange look on his face, his eyes wide and his lips taut. Nick turned to look at him a second later.

"What's up?" she asked.

"We have to go to work," Vince said as he shuffled down the stairs. His eyes remained sharply focused on Nick until he reached the entryway, where he began pulling on his boots. He threw on his coat and grabbed his keys from the little table, then turned toward the door. "I'm warming up the car," he told them, and walked outside with heavy steps.

"We should tell him," said Nick when the door had shut.

"Okay," she said, and nodded. "I'll tell him tonight."

"You don't think we should talk to him together?"

"No, let me do it. It probably will go more smoothly if it's only one of us."

Meredith wanted to say more, but she didn't have time before Vince returned. The three of them said goodbye and headed to work.

That day Meredith threw herself into her classes with gusto, refreshed, giddy, and feeling grand. During lunch, she sat with her friend and colleague Beth, or Miss Goldberg, as she was known to the students in her biology classes. Over their salads, they chatted about their weekends.

"How are things going with your brother?" Beth asked between bites.

"Great," Meredith said. "We went to the art museum on Saturday. Then yesterday we relaxed at home until my friend's daughter's party."

"Sounds nice."

"They picked up my Christmas tree while I was out. We decorated it when we got home."

"Who's 'they'?"

Meredith gulped. "My brother and his friend. I didn't tell you about that?"

"What kind of 'friend' are we talking about?"

Meredith laughed. "No, just his friend. They work together in Maine. Nick is down here with him working on the same job."

"Uh huh," Beth said, sipping her water with raised eyebrows.

Meredith didn't say anything; she focused on her lunch.

"Am I to assume from your silence that there's more to this story?"

Meredith didn't want to tell Beth about Nick, but she knew her face gave her away. She leaned in. Beth leaned in to meet her, an expectant grin on her face.

"Okay," Meredith began. "I'm going to tell you, but this is strictly between you and me. Only one other person knows about this."

"Yeah, yeah," Beth said impatiently, gesturing with her hand for Meredith to continue.

"Well," she murmured, avoiding Beth's eyes, "it seems that Nick and I are having a bit of a thing."

"What kind of a thing?"

Meredith rolled her eyes and told Beth what had happened.

Beth's eyes opened wide, and she squealed.

"Shh," Meredith admonished with furrowed eyebrows as she looked nervously around the room.

"Well, Miss Beck," Beth said as she leaned back in her chair. "You do surprise me. I had you pegged as the kind who would save herself for the good on paper guy."

The gnawing thorn in Meredith's stomach began eating away at her once more. *What on Earth,* she wondered, annoyed, and forced it to retreat.

She chuckled, putting the thorn out of her mind. "And what of the good at heart guy? I'm not the kind who would save herself for him?"

"A good heart is even better," said Beth, smiling. "He just doesn't seem like your type, is all."

"Why do you say that?"

Beth shrugged. "I guess it's because I know who your father is. You've told me a little about your family. Plus, look at you. You're the epitome of professorial." Beth laughed good-naturedly, eyeing Meredith's gray pencil skirt suit, silk blouse, and scarf; Meredith couldn't help but laugh a little, too. "You look like you'd date another teacher, or something."

Meredith's face fell before she could stop it. Catching herself, she forced herself to smile, despite the anxiety amassing in her chest.

"What's wrong?" asked Beth, noticing the change, and instantly turning serious. "Did I say something?"

"No, no." Meredith sighed—as long as she was confessing, she'd might as well go all the way. "It's not your fault. It's just..." She rubbed her lips together, steadying herself. "My fiancé was a teacher. Adam. He passed away last year." She folded her arms on the table, then leaned her head in her hand, attempting, poorly, to appear casual. "I don't really talk about it. But it's why I'm here."

"Oh, my God." Beth reached across the table and squeezed Meredith's hand. Her eyes were so warm with sympathy, Meredith couldn't regret telling her. "I am so sorry."

"Thanks, Beth."

"What I said must have seemed so insensitive."

"Don't be silly. You didn't know."

"It must be such a struggle every day."

Meredith's breath caught a moment. "It hasn't been easy. But I'm doing okay."

Beth leaned back in her chair and regarded Meredith with somberness. "You've really been through hell. I'm sorry I made you talk about it."

"No, really. It's fine." Truthfully, that she should have told Beth —or anyone—about Adam had actually occurred to her before. She wasn't really sure why she held this information so close. Tara knew, of course, and Vince, and people in her old life, in New York. But it wasn't something she opened up about in this new, evolving chapter. The information was mostly reserved for the people in her most cherished, innermost circle. The only person she'd confided in was her principal, Kevin Williams.

Beth smiled kindly. "So this is the first person you've been with since, I assume." At Meredith's little nod, her smile softened further. "Well, it doesn't matter who he is as long as he makes you happy. I think it's great." Beth's eyebrows rose. "Do you?"

"Yes." The ache subsided, with compliance that surprised her. "Yes, I do think so."

"And hey, forget what I said about your type. I wouldn't have teased you had I known. I was just playing around."

"Oh, I know you were. And you aren't wrong." She returned Beth's smile and shrugged. "Maybe life has always thrown the same type of man my way. I guess I never saw myself going in any other direction, much less jumping into it so quickly. But all I really care about is that he's a nice person. Nick has a gentle soul and a more simple perspective. He's all about slowing down and smelling the roses, not being good on paper. I like that. My best friend says I'm due for a change. Maybe she's right."

"Well, then good for you. I never thought you had it in you."

"Neither did I," said a deeper voice behind them.

They both turned around sharply. Ned Mallard stood behind them, his arms folded and his face so red it was almost purple. He was glaring at Meredith disapprovingly.

"Ned," Meredith breathed, putting a hand to her chest. "You startled me!"

"Yeah, what were you thinking, sneaking up on us like that?" Beth scolded.

Ned ignored Beth. "Are you serious?" he demanded of Meredith, his hands in the air. "I thought the reason you couldn't go out with me was that you wanted to spend time with your brother."

"That was true. It's just that—"

"It's just that you didn't have the guts to tell me you're not interested, so you decided to use your brother as an excuse."

"I tried to tell you," Meredith said meekly. She seemed to choke on air; she coughed and cleared her throat. "I didn't want to hurt your feelings."

"So I've been rejected *and* condescended to. Lovely."

Beth put her hands on her hips and faced Ned squarely, looking up at him with reproach. "That's uncalled for, Ned. This is none of your business. Meredith isn't required to like you."

"Well, it's hard to sit back and watch a friend make a huge mistake."

Meredith looked up from her chair. "Ned, you don't even know him."

"Do you?"

Meredith frowned. She wasn't sure how to answer that question. "It doesn't matter. I don't have to explain myself. This doesn't concern you."

Ned shook his head. "I just can't believe you're messing around with some stranger after one weekend when I've been asking you out for months. I guess I'm glad to know where we stand, Meredith." He sniffed, pressed down the wrinkles in his suit, and stalked off before Meredith could respond.

Beth put her hand on Meredith's back. "Are you okay?"

"Of course." Meredith attempted a smile, but the result was flat and bland. "Why wouldn't I be?"

"What an entitled ass." Beth was glaring angrily at the door from which Ned had just exited. She turned back to Meredith. "He had no right to talk to you like that."

"Yeah, well." Meredith sighed and brushed some nonexistent crumbs off her lap. "His feelings were hurt. We all say things in anger, I guess."

"No, we don't. We all get angry, sure, but we don't all lash out like toddlers."

"It's fine, Beth."

Beth stared at her. "I don't know how you can be so forgiving of him."

"He means well."

"No, he doesn't."

Meredith's brow furrowed. "What do you mean?"

"I mean that if he did, he wouldn't snap at you like that. It just proves it's more about him than you. He's just like every other egotistical guy who yells at women who reject them. He doesn't really care about you. He just wants to get in your pants."

"That's so pessimistic." Meredith frowned, disturbed. "I don't like to think of people like that. I think behind every behavior, there's usually a hurt or a reason." She shrugged. "I try to keep that in mind."

"Some people are just assholes, Meredith."

Meredith straightened, and an uncomfortable twinge pulled in her stomach. "I just think it's important to see where people are coming from. People mostly mean well."

Beth's face softened; she placed her hand on Meredith's. "I can understand why you have to believe that. You've been through a nightmare, and that attitude has probably helped you through it. You are a wonderful, beautiful optimist." She patted her hand. Her face turned stern. "But you're wrong."

~

MEREDITH ARRIVED BACK HOME AND, in the mood for something bold and cheerful for dinner, improvised a lemon chicken piccata. That evening her sobered mood was brightened as the three of them sat around the dinner table, Vince and Nick complimenting her on the meal. They spent the rest of the night chatting in the living room, then stood and stretched for bed. Meredith and Nick exchanged a knowing look, and Nick waved goodnight and headed upstairs, leaving her alone to break their news to Vince. Meredith was just sucking in her breath to begin her confession when Vince approached her.

"I want to talk to you," he said.

Meredith froze. "What about?"

"Why don't you tell me?"

"I don't know what you mean."

"You sure about that?"

She narrowed her eyes warily. "Why don't you just cut to the chase and tell me what's bothering you, Vince?"

He folded his arms, his expression grave.

"There isn't anything you want to tell me?"

"Such as?"

"Such as what's going on between you and Nick?"

Meredith was still. She felt this was the perfect opening for her news, but Vince's confrontational tone made her nervous. She lost her nerve.

"What are you talking about? Why would you even ask me that?"

He seemed to falter with her vehemence, mistaking fear for denial. "Are you saying there's nothing going on with you two?"

"Vince, I'm really not enjoying this interrogation," she said, with more self-assurance than she felt. "Do you want to get to the point?"

Vince looked uncertain. He frowned as he considered. "Maybe I'm overreacting," he said, moderating his tone. "I'll let it lie. Just make sure nothing does happen. Okay?"

"Vince," she said, trying to remain calm, "what business is it of yours, anyway? Even if something was going on, why does it matter to you? We're all adults. I have the right to have a relationship with anyone I choose."

"Just trust me on this. Nick isn't your type."

"Oh?" she asked, somewhat indignant but also amused. "And who is my type, according to you?"

"I don't know. Someone with more direction and more ambition, someone more serious."

"Nick seems pretty serious to me."

"Maybe about trees and mountains, but not about life."

They stared at each other in silence.

Vince placed his hands on her shoulders. "I'm just trying to look out for you. Nick travels, like, six months out of the year. And when he's not traveling, he's living in the middle of nowhere. How would you even do this, Merry? What would you have to give up? Just do me a favor, Merry. Do yourself a favor, and move right along."

"Vince, Nick has been nothing but polite since he's been here. It's clear he doesn't mean anyone any harm. He seems like a very nice person."

"I never said he's not a nice person, Merry. Nick's a good guy. But you deserve more."

The gnawing of the thorn resumed; Meredith grimaced but ignored it. "What more is there than being a nice person?"

Vince snorted, grinning wryly. "Think about it. You'd really want to be with someone who voluntarily hangs out with me? Come on."

Meredith shook her head. "But there's nothing wrong with you."

Vince worked his jaw a little, appearing to have something to say. However, he remained silent.

Meredith studied him, vaguely annoyed. "Vince, it's been so long since we've seen each other." She chose her words carefully.

"How do you even know what's good for me anymore?" she said brightly, affecting a joking tone.

Something flickered in his eyes, a sharpness of some kind. "Well, that's the point now, isn't it?" he asked her; though his intonation matched hers in brightness, there was a darkness underneath. "I wasn't here all that time. I'm making up for it, aren't I?"

"Making up for what?"

"For being your big brother. For making sure you're okay."

Her defensiveness melted away: it seemed his concern was as much about their relationship as it was about Nick, and she couldn't help relenting. She smiled sadly. "You don't have to make up for anything. Things happen. It's fine."

"Hmm."

Neither said anything. Meredith waited a moment, letting him work out whatever he was working out.

"Seriously, though," he said finally. "If something were going on, I just hope you'd trust me enough to tell me about it."

A twinge of anxiety pulled at her chest. "Of course I trust you."

"Okay." He seemed to relax. "I guess I was worried that you thought you couldn't tell me. I mean if you were deliberately keeping it a secret, that would be the only thing it could mean. You know?"

Meredith nodded, forcing onto her face what she hoped looked like agreement. "Right. No, of course." She swallowed. "Right, that's what it would mean, and that's why there's no secret." She didn't know what she was doing. Her heart pounded at the dangerousness of this lie.

"Good," he said, looking relieved. "Because your trust is important to me."

She gave his arm an affectionate tap. "I know you're my big brother and that you care," she told him. "But don't go overboard. That isn't helpful, either."

Vince's anxiousness had passed, and his usual swagger

returned. "As your big brother, Merry, it is my job—nay, my duty —to make sure you don't do anything irresponsible. I am older and wiser, after all."

"Did you just use the word 'nay'?"

"I did. That's how serious I am."

Meredith tried to assure him by softening her face and looking sympathetic. "Don't worry. I'm not about to do anything irresponsible."

Vince attempted a weak smile. "I know. It's not your style." He took a deep breath as he watched her. "I'm sorry, Merry. I shouldn't have given you the third degree."

Guilt swept over her. "It's okay. I know you're just looking out for me, and I appreciate it."

"Thanks."

He held out his arms to embrace her. They hugged for a moment, then parted ways and said goodnight.

❧

"I DIDN'T TELL HIM," Meredith said later that night as she lay next to Nick in her bedroom. "He told me not to get involved with you before I could even begin. He insisted you're not my type."

Nick's eyebrows rose. "What else did he say?"

Meredith hesitated. "He said you're serious about mountains and trees but not about life."

Nick was silent for a moment. "I think those things are a big part of life. I think they're pretty serious," he said. "Don't you?"

She considered. "Yes, I do." She closed her eyes as his lips brushed against her forehead. "Actually, I've retreated to the mountains and trees many times in the last year, since my life has been through so many changes. I wish I could retreat to them more often. They've been my saviors, in a way."

"That makes sense. There is a kind of holiness about those things."

Meredith watched him. "What do you mean?"

Nick closed his eyes and shrugged. "I guess I just mean that that's where you find the answers to the big questions. In the mountains and trees. That's where you see your place in it all. I always go there when I have questions. I understand more the deeper in I go." He opened his eyes. "Funny how the best way to find yourself is to get lost."

Meredith smiled. "You're very wise."

Now Nick smiled. He kissed her once, and his smile turned more sober. "I wouldn't call it wise. I just think it's the truth."

"I completely agree."

She brought her hand to his face and toyed with a lock of his hair between her fingers. Nick's face nudged under her cheek, his lips seeking the soft space at the base of her neck. Meredith closed her eyes and grinned happily as a pleasant tingling sensation rippled across her skin. She tilted her head a little to accommodate. Beneath the covers, their legs entangled.

She opened her eyes. She couldn't get Vince's words out of her mind: it was the second time that day someone had suggested Nick wasn't her type. She wondered why this bothered her so much, why the stinging of the thorn plagued her whenever somebody brought it up. Did she really have "a type"? Should she have one? Why did it matter? What did it even mean?

"I just don't understand why he's so against it."

Nick pulled away to look at her. "I've had a pretty quiet life, Meredith. I don't have any secrets." He brought his fingers to the side of her face and tucked her hair behind her ear. "Why don't we just let him see that it isn't as bad as he thinks?"

"You're probably right."

He took her face in his hands and kissed her slowly as his fingers combed through her hair.

"So when do you want to tell him?" he asked.

"I don't know. Let's give it a few more days."

Nick rubbed his cheek with hers. She said nothing while he playfully kissed her behind her ear. She sighed and smiled, then turned more serious.

She was fearful of hurting his feelings but felt encouraged by his willingness to talk about it. "He also said I should be with someone with more ambition," she said tentatively.

Nick considered. "I guess I've never worried about ambition. I don't want a lot." His eyes turned more thoughtful. "What about you? What do you want?"

Meredith sighed again. "Honestly, I don't even know anymore."

His expression softened. "Well, I just want to feel alive. And I want someone who can enjoy the simple things in life with me."

His blue eyes locked knowingly with hers. Heart fluttering, Meredith was still as she contemplated this response.

He wrapped his arm around her, his hand landing on the small of her back. "I think we should forget about it for now," he said.

She smiled. "You do?"

"Yes." He kissed her once, gently. "I think we should forget about everything."

She closed her eyes as his kiss enveloped her completely.

CHAPTER SIX

IN MY LANE

"Meredith," said a kind voice from the direction of the door.

Meredith smiled: she knew the voice. She put down her pen and looked up, leaning back in her chair and waving in her principal, Kevin Williams.

It was the end of the night; Meredith had stayed late, along with all her colleagues, for parent conferences. She was dressed more formally today, in a black suit and heels, with a cream-colored blouse beneath.

"Hello, Kevin," she said as he stepped inside. "Good to see you."

"Good to see you, too," he said jovially as he took a seat in the first row. "How were your conferences?"

"They were great!" Enthusiasm rang in her voice: she was so pleased by her conferences, which had been positive and productive. One never knew what conferences would look like, whether parents would feel upset or angry, or worst of all, hopeless. It was impossible to predict whether there would be a lot of pushback. But tonight's parents had been eager to listen and willing to help;

they'd asked questions, and thanked her, and told her they were grateful their kids had her. "In fact," she added, remembering the best part of the night, "one family even asked me if I'd consider private tutoring. I told them it's my job to help and that they don't need to hire me; if their daughter is struggling, I can meet with her before or after school. And it gave me an idea."

"What's that?"

"I was thinking of starting a study club, a place where students can get help with the readings or with organizing their papers. I think there are a few other students who would reach out for help if they knew there was a safe space." She paused. "What do you think?"

"That's fantastic. By all means, go for it."

"Thanks." Meredith smiled fondly, pleased. "It'll be great for the kids. And I love working one-on-one with students. I'm excited about it."

"Well, I'm glad. Great idea, Meredith."

"Thank you. And how about you, Kevin? How has your day been?"

"It's been going well, thanks. And you have the opportunity to make it spectacular."

Surprised and curious, she raised her eyebrows. "I do?"

"Yes. Of course you know that every year our drama club puts on a production in the spring."

Meredith froze as a tumult of emotions rushed her. "Of course."

"Yolanda Jones, whose position you filled. She had a brilliant idea, to have the students modernize *Romeo and Juliet*. She was going to supervise the rewrites, as she used to work with the students to help them memorize lines and whatnot. But, as you know, she left us in the spring, leaving us without a supervisor. It also left us without a set builder, since her husband took care of that for us, but that's beside the point."

"I see."

Kevin and Meredith studied each other for a moment or two, in silence. Kevin's face slowly melted into a sly smile. Then he chuckled.

"I guess you're going to make me say it."

Meredith laughed. "I'm going to make you say what?"

"Meredith, I'd love for you to supervise the writing of the school play."

"Oh. How wonderful." Meredith nodded, eyes wide. "Of course, I'd love to."

Kevin raised an eyebrow at her. "Are you sure?"

"Of course I'm sure." She smiled brightly, shaking her head with confusion. "Why do you ask?"

Kevin chuckled again. "You'll be a great supervisor, Meredith, but you're a terrible actress." His expression grew serious. "It doesn't appeal to you?"

"Oh, it does, Kevin. It really does. It's just that—" She paused. She wanted to tell him that she'd love to help with the play, not only for herself but for Adam; that she'd been thinking how satisfying it would be to follow in his footsteps and to help students the way he wanted to help them; that she'd always had an interest in theater and that she'd never had a chance to do anything with it, that taking on this project would prove how well she was doing and how far she had come, that there was poetic justice in all this and that the pieces seemed to be falling into place, right before her very eyes—but she was silent. From the most hidden depths of her heart came a whisper of warning, a suppressed voice of panic that would not accept being silenced. Through the cracks in the wall, it reminded her that *Romeo and Juliet* was the play Adam directed the year they first met; it insisted that following in his footsteps would pull her backward into grief, that it was too risky, that it wasn't worth it, that her answer should be *no*.

"It's just that I'm surprised," Meredith uttered; she cleared her throat and smiled. "I'm so new here. And just so you're aware, I don't have any experience with drama."

"Well, of course I won't force you, and I know it's quite a responsibility, especially now that you're starting a study club. I'd understand if you thought it was too much." Meredith couldn't help but warm at Kevin's sympathetic expression. "But I have faith in you, Meredith. I have ever since you started here." He shrugged. "I thought a special project might be good for you. And I have a hunch you'd be exceptional at it."

Meredith's smile softened as she recalled her interview with Kevin. They'd had an instant amiable connection and had talked for hours about favorite books and art. Kevin had told her all about his grandchildren. He'd seemed to sense her steady hand and competence, and she'd been charmed by his sincerity and kindness. And they had another connection: Kevin lost his wife a few years before Meredith lost Adam. It was partly why she felt safe opening up to him—that, and his genuinely good heart.

"I'll even sweeten the pot," he added. Meredith watched with interest as he opened the folder in his lap and pulled out a few sheets of paper. He stood and reached over, placing them on her desk.

"These are theater tickets," Meredith said, taking them in her fingers as Kevin returned to his seat. She looked up at him. "They're tickets to *Romeo and Juliet*."

"Yes, they are. Four of them, for Friday night. It's showing at the Emerald, downtown."

"These are for me?"

"Yes. We thought it would serve as good inspiration. We bought them for Yolanda months ago, before she put in her resignation. Now they're for whoever takes over, which hopefully will be you. As long as you're up to it."

Meredith ignored the twisting in her stomach; she was fine, she was happy, and she always enjoyed a challenge. "That's so generous of you, Kevin. And it's an offer I can't refuse." She smiled fully now, with earnestness, excited for this new and promising project. "I'd love to help, and I'm definitely up to it. Thank you so much for asking."

THE REST of the week passed quickly for Meredith as they settled into a comfortable routine, Meredith and Nick avoiding eye contact in the mornings before work and getting to know each other at night, when Nick crept into her room so they could begin the best part of their day. Meredith was in a happy fog. She'd forgotten what it was like to have something to look forward to; she'd forgotten what it was like to feel closeness and desire.

As she was getting ready to turn out the lights and leave her classroom Friday, her door opened. Looking up, she caught sight of Ned entering her classroom. He waved grandly. "Greetings, Miss Beck," he chirped, and Meredith wished with all her might that he would stop trying so hard.

"Hi, Ned."

"Do you have a sec?"

"Okay." Meredith glanced at the clock. She had a few minutes to spare. Vince, Nick, and Sandy were picking her up today: they were going into Philadelphia to see *Romeo and Juliet*. Meredith was looking forward to it and had been hoping to scramble from her classroom without delay.

"I've been meaning to talk to you all week." Ned's face was drawn downward into a very grave frown. "I didn't know you lost your fiancé," he said. "I'm so sorry for your loss. Adam must have been very special."

Adam's name on Ned's lips felt discordant and wrong. Meredith grimaced but forced herself to smile. "Thanks."

"If you ever want to talk about it, you know where to find me."

"That's very nice of you. Thank you."

"I'm serious. I'm here for you, and I'm a good listener. You know what Shakespeare said about grief, of course."

"No." Meredith closed her eyes a moment. "What did he say?"

"He said, 'Give sorrow words; the grief that does not speak knits up the o'er wrought heart and bids it break.'" Ned paused, looking at her knowingly. "*Macbeth*."

Meredith had no intention of talking to Ned about grief, or any other personal feeling, and she was annoyed by the implication that she had no one else to talk to, but she suppressed her impatience. He clearly was feeling guilty about his outburst and was trying to make it up to her. It was overkill, certainly, but it was coming from a good place.

"That's wonderful. Well said."

Ned seemed pleased; he relaxed his stance and his expression. "I also wanted to apologize," he went on. "For the other day." He waved his hand in a gesture that Meredith guessed was supposed to refer to the fact that it happened in the past but that somehow seemed dismissive instead. "I guess I kind of yelled at you. I'm sorry."

"Thanks, Ned. I appreciate it."

"Are you sure you don't want to give me a chance?" he said then, and held out his hands. "It makes so much more sense. We're both teachers, and we both can appreciate Shakespeare's dark side," he added, and attempted a grin. He turned serious again, and stuck his hands in his pockets. "What do you see in this guy, anyway?"

"I'm sorry, Ned, but it just doesn't seem like any of your business."

"You're right. My bad." He raised his eyebrows in inquiry. "Are we good?"

Meredith smiled politely. "We're good."

"Great." His own exaggerated smile returned. "In that case...I see you're preparing to head out to your car. Allow me to escort you. I don't know how you manage to walk through the icy parking lot in those heels."

"Sure, Ned. Thanks."

In the hallway, they were jostled by students eager to escape for the weekend. As they squeezed their way through, Ned turned to her.

"So, Miss Beck. Are you aware that performances of *King Lear* were prohibited from the years 1788 to 1820?"

"Yes, that's true. It was because—"

"It was because of the *madness* of King George III," Ned explained, crouching lower and waving his fingers before her in a mysterious manner. "You know, because Lear was mad, too. In my recent studies, I've been fascinated to find that—"

"Ned, Ned," Meredith stopped him as they reached the entrance to the school. She stood before him and looked at him squarely. "Please, don't do this."

"Don't do what?"

Meredith looked at him. She was tired of mincing her words; she decided that honesty was in order. "You try so hard to impress. It isn't necessary. Just be yourself."

Ned's face turned red. "I see."

"I'm sorry, Ned. I'm just trying to help."

"Ah, trying to help. I get it."

Meredith's expression grew more gentle. "I wasn't trying to hurt your feelings."

"My feelings? Nah," he assured her with a wave of his hand. "It's cool."

He held the door for her, and they walked out of the building side by side. Ned attempted to make conversation. "You know, I picked up my copy of *Antigone* this week. Weird stuff."

As he chatted about his literary discoveries, Meredith's eyes drifted longingly toward the parking lot. She was half-listening to

Ned, her mind desperately working out how to escape without having to make introductions. She slowed to a stop before stepping off the sidewalk.

"Actually, Ned, you don't have to walk me to my car today. My brother is picking me up. You go ahead—go home and enjoy your weekend. I'll wait here."

"Perfect, I'd love to meet your brother. Anyway, about *Antigone*—"

Meredith sighed with exasperation, her eyes searching the parking lot for signs of Vince's car. Vaguely she resented Ned's sense that he was entitled to access into her life, but she was too anxious and in too much of a hurry to think about it.

"...So that's when I said, Hey, Creon! Why don't you just let her bury Polynices?" Ned laughed. "Ridiculous."

"It is ridiculous. I think that's the point." Meredith hoped she hadn't sounded as abrupt to Ned's ears as she had to her own; she'd finally spied Vince's car pulling in through the entrance. Her heart pattered with anticipation. Her eyes sought out Nick's face: he was sitting in the passenger's seat. Sandy was leaning forward from the backseat. All three of them were waving at her, wearing wide, excited smiles.

Vince swung the car swiftly beside her. He rolled the window down and leaned his elbow out, his face bright with a charming smile.

"Hey hey, Merry! It's the weekend. Let's have some fun." His eyes shifted to Ned, and he offered a quick, friendly wave. "Hey, how's it going."

"Great!"

Meredith discreetly held up a finger, indicating she'd only be a moment. She turned back to Ned. "Well, thanks for the company and for the chat." She waved. "Have a great weekend."

"Now, hang on, Meredith," said Ned, gesturing widely with his hands. "It would be pretty rude of me not to say hello."

Meredith attempted a casual attitude, but her stomach was in knots: Ned had made her increasingly uncomfortable as the week had progressed, and his presence as she embarked on her weekend, his insistence on inserting himself into her personal life, seemed somehow violating. Once again, she found herself chastising herself for her insensitivity. He'd apologized, after all. If he was awkward about it, it wasn't his fault.

"Okay," she said, extending her hand between them. "Vince, this is Ned. Ned, my brother Vince."

Ned took a few steps forward. "Hello, Meredith's brother Vince. It's a pleasure to meet you!" He bent at the waist to peer into the car. He waved first at Sandy, then took a long moment to glare at Nick, his eyes seeming to take in every detail. Meredith guessed this was why he'd wanted to be introduced to Vince. It made her feel exposed, and she cringed, a creeping unease prickling her skin.

Sandy rolled down the window and called cheerfully to Meredith. "Hey, Merry! I'm so excited for a fun night out with you!"

Meredith bristled at Sandy's addressing her by her nickname, used only by those closest to her. "Hi, Sandy," she said politely, with a wave, keeping her feelings to herself. "I'm excited, too."

"Come on, hop in," said Vince to Meredith, his arm still hanging out the window, patting the outside of the door with his hand. "We don't want to be late."

"Go, have fun, Meredith!" Ned pushed the air with his hands, indicating she should move. "Don't let me stand in your way."

"Okay." Meredith turned to Ned. "Well. Have a nice weekend, Ned."

"Yes. Have a nice weekend."

Meredith had taken a few steps toward the car; at his tone, she spun around.

"Is something wrong?"

He held his hands up and opened his eyes wide, as if taken aback. "What could possibly be wrong?" It was his usual theatrical delivery, but there was something darker about the eyes. He nodded toward Vince's car. "Have fun." He smiled and waved extravagantly, as always, then headed toward his own car.

~

SAFELY IN THE CAR, Sandy next to her and Nick in front of her, Meredith felt glorious as she entered her weekend. All cares left her, the confrontation with Ned already feeling unimportant.

"Hey," Vince said as he pulled out of the parking lot. "What's up with Ned? It seems like he has a bit of a crush on you. Could his 'pleasure' to see us have been any more forced?"

"Poor Ned," Meredith said. "I suppose he means well."

"He looked at Nick like he wanted to kill him, or worse."

"He probably thinks you two are together," Sandy chimed in helpfully.

"I'm sorry about that," Meredith said, trying to distract them from Sandy's comment. "Ned has some things to work out. He'll be okay."

"Any chance there, Merry?" Vince asked, his tone half-joking.

Meredith chuckled. "I'm afraid not."

"Why not? What's the matter with poor Ned?"

Meredith hesitated. Her eyes darted in front of her toward Nick. He was gazing out the passenger side window.

"No, Ned isn't Meredith's type, Vince," said Sandy, leaning forward and playfully slapping his arm. "Meredith needs someone strong to sweep her off her feet."

"Can we change the subject?" Meredith asked desperately; she didn't want to expose her secret relationship with Nick, and she was weary of discussions of her "type." "Let's talk about the play. I'm excited to see *Romeo and Juliet*."

"Me, too!" exclaimed Sandy. "I'm so glad you got these tickets, Merry." She leaned forward and patted Vince's shoulder. "Vince," she said. "Give her the thing."

"The thing?" asked Meredith, as from seemingly out of

nowhere Vince produced a large bouquet of colorful flowers and handed it back for Meredith to take.

Meredith reached for the bouquet, instinctively smelled the flowers, and smiled. "This is for me? What's this for?"

"For being the best sister in the universe," Vince said brightly, looking at her in the mirror, his face wearing a happy smile. "Just a little gesture to thank you for your hospitality."

"This was so unnecessary." She blinked a few times; she was almost overwhelmed. "But thank you, I'm touched."

"Aren't they beautiful?" Sandy put her nose in the flowers and breathed in their scent. "I helped him pick them out."

"Thank you so much, Sandy. They are beautiful."

Sandy leaned back in her seat and relaxed. "The play was a good excuse to buy a new outfit, so thanks for that, Merry."

"It's pretty." Meredith admired Sandy's pumpernickel-colored coat and the shimmery blue dress beneath. She glanced down at her brown pencil skirt and cream-colored cardigan. "I kind of wish I had worn something a little perkier for the theater, though I guess more somber colors are also appropriate, considering the subject matter."

"You look fine, Merry," said Vince, checking his mirrors as he zipped by a few cars. "Don't worry so much."

"I'm not worried." She grinned. "Well, not about that. I am a little worried about your driving, to be honest."

"Speeding around curves has never been your style."

Vince leaned on his horn and slammed on his brakes as a trac-tor-trailer squeezed between him and the car in front of him. Meredith sucked in her breath and leaned back in her seat.

"I don't see the point in it," she said, after the dangerous moment had passed. "We're not running late."

"You know me, Merry. I like to live life like I'm always running late."

"You're in his lane!" Meredith exclaimed suddenly, gripping her seat as Vince weaved too far over the line, nearly side-swiping another vehicle. The other driver leaned on his horn, making them all jump.

"Sorry." Vince checked his mirror and put on his blinker, and switched lanes without any additional drama. "All good." He grinned at her in the mirror. "Not comfortable out of your lane, eh Merry?"

Meredith exhaled; her heartbeat slowed somewhat. "I just enjoy being in one piece, thanks."

"Sorry, Merry. I'll slow down and stay safely in my own lane. I know recklessness isn't your thing."

"Well, I *love* what you're wearing, Merry," Sandy said, and patted Meredith's thigh. "It's so sophisticated!"

The conversation strayed this way and that. Meredith leaned back in her seat to enjoy the ride. They chatted happily about the night ahead, their voices buoyant with excitement. In this frame of mind, even Sandy seemed pleasant company; Meredith appreciated her vibrancy and enthusiasm.

They approached the city, darkness falling around them. The city lights were blazing in front of them as the tall buildings transformed from routine workday offices to beautiful beacons that ushered in the weekend.

Meredith's phone pinged. She looked at the notification, surprised.

"Look at that," she said, reading the email that had just come through. "Dad finally wrote me back."

"Did he?" asked Vince, with a quick glance back at her in the rearview mirror. "What's he pissed off about this time?"

"He says he wasn't expecting my email, we're usually not in touch, etcetera, etcetera." She grinned snidely as she scanned the message. "He says he thought something must be wrong with the house."

"But if something's wrong with one of us, that would have been fine."

"Hey, you should plan a party!" cried Sandy, clapping her hands together and looking at Meredith with wide, excited eyes. "For their return. I could help!"

Meredith laughed. "No, I don't think so."

"They'd love you for it, Merry. And I'd love to plan a party for someone famous like your father."

Meredith bit her lip, refraining from telling Sandy that being famous didn't make someone a nice person, and that her father was a case in point. Truth be told, the idea of impressing her parents was not unappealing; however, planning a party was the last thing Meredith felt like doing. It was just as well: her parents were used to glitz and glamor, and would feel a party back home was simply a waste of their time.

"It's a nice idea, Sandy, but it doesn't feel right."

"Hey, Nick," said Vince, pointing. "Check out that skyline. See those big things? Those are called skyscrapers."

"Vince, stop," said Sandy, leaning forward to slap his shoulder. "Don't make fun."

But Nick was smiling, unfazed. "I didn't know they could make buildings that tall."

Finally they pulled into a parking garage near the theater. As Meredith stepped out of the car and joined the others on their way toward the sidewalk, an uneasiness began gathering in her gut, and her heart rate picked up speed. Despite the frigid December air that slapped their faces and made them hide in their scarves and coat collars, her face flushed, and she was sweating; the hordes of rushing people around her seemed to spin, barely registering in her vision. As they approached the busy theater—*Romeo and Juliet* spelled out in golden script above—Meredith suffered a sick, twisting ache in her stomach. It was as if she were being repelled by the wrong end of a magnet: she was dizzy with panic, and she could not make herself step through that door.

Vince and Sandy hurried through the entryway, away from the

cold. Nick, a few steps behind them, glanced back to make sure she was still there.

He stopped when he saw she hadn't followed.

"What's wrong?"

Meredith was staring at the golden script, mouth agape.

He turned fully and took a few steps toward her.

"Meredith? Is everything okay?"

She lowered her eyes to meet his gaze.

"I..."

His brow furrowed. At the concern in his eyes, her own eyes misted.

"I can't do it."

They regarded each other in silence. Nick's face was serious with thought. Her fingers tingled, as if her blood were drained, but her heart was pounding, making her sweat through her clothes. Though only seconds passed, it seemed to her that time was standing still. She didn't know what was happening to her.

She had no time to ponder it, as Vince and Sandy blew back through the door, hands clasped tight.

Vince raised his eyebrows at her. "What's up?"

Meredith stared at him blankly. She couldn't say the words out loud.

They all turned at the sound of crying. A couple with two distraught young daughters were at the box office, pleading.

"Please," the mother was saying. "It was my mistake. I mixed up the dates."

"I sympathize," said the ticket teller, "but there's nothing I can do."

"There have to be a few more seats."

"I'm sorry, it's a full house."

Nick turned to Vince.

"Meredith doesn't want those girls to miss the play," he told him. "She wants them to have our tickets."

Vince's mouth dropped open, and he stared at her. "What? Are you serious?"

The distraction had helped to pull her back toward reality. She swallowed, the tingling sensation beginning to fade.

"Yes," she croaked; she cleared her throat and managed a weak smile, feeling more herself. "I...The girls...I think we should..."

"What a sweet idea." Sandy stepped toward Meredith and wrapped her arm around her back, gripping her shoulder. "That is so decent of you, Merry."

Meredith was still somewhat dumbfounded. She shot Nick a quick, appreciative look; as usual, his face was without outward expression, but a smile touched the corners of his eyes. Her heart did a little tumble. "I'd just like them to know some wishes come true."

"You're absolutely positive about this?" Vince was looking at her skeptically, brow raised and face crumped a little with surprise. "Isn't your principal going to be mad?"

"Kevin won't be mad." That was one thing Meredith could be sure of: there weren't many people in her life she felt she could be honest with, but she knew Kevin would understand.

"We're already in the city. What else do you want to do?"

"I'm sure you can think of something, Vince." Meredith breathed in the brisk winter air; it filled her lungs, simultaneously chilling and warming her, cooling her flushed face and sharpening her mind to her surroundings. "Let's do it."

Vince shrugged, and Meredith pulled the tickets from her purse. She approached the family and explained that they were unable to use their tickets, then asked if the family would like to use them instead. The joy in their faces was worth missing the show under any circumstances, and Meredith walked away smiling, the vision of the elated little girls one she knew she'd never forget.

"Well," said Vince upon her return, rubbing his hands together against the cold, "what now?"

The four of them stood in silence.

"I know," said Sandy, holding up one finger. "How about we go ice skating at Penn's Landing?"

Meredith turned to her; she couldn't help but smile. "You saved the day again, Sandy," she told her, warmed by an odd swell of gratitude after her moment of crisis. "You always know what we should do next."

Sandy brightened, then blushed. "I'm just happy to be with all of you. Let's go have some fun."

CHAPTER SEVEN

WISHES

*T*hough Meredith was familiar with Penn's Landing, she had never been ice skating there before. Situated along the Delaware River waterfront, it was an expansive open space that boasted fabulous views of the Benjamin Franklin Bridge as well as the New Jersey waterfront across the river. It was usually swarming with people eager to take in not only the views but also the entertainment: it hosted art events and markets, music concerts and restaurants. It was a popular site with all ages, providing a romantic atmosphere for couples, and for children, exciting visions of ships and of the hustle and bustle of sea life.

Around the holidays, it turned into an enchanting winter wonderland, with a chalet-style ski lodge providing warm beverages and cocktails. Strings of white lights stretching above cast the scene in a golden halo, and the resulting silhouettes lent to the air the kind of coziness only possible on a chilly winter's night. A colorful winter garden, complete with a holiday tree, lured visitors into its magic. The rink itself was situated right along the water's edge, affording an unobstructed view of the endless city lights sparkling against the darkness—which, reflected in the shimmering water beneath, made the night feel cheerful and alive.

They donned skates and took some turns around the rink, the lights of Philadelphia and the grandeur of the bridge looming beside them. Vince and Sandy locked arms; Vince occasionally had to stop and help upright Sandy, who would suddenly crumple, a little dramatically, in Meredith's opinion. As for Meredith herself, she had not been on skates in years, and moved gingerly at first, but took to it again quickly, feeling exhilarated as she pushed herself forward and let momentum carry her away. Nick glided easily beside Meredith, taking his time. The air was biting, the scene dazzling, and Meredith yearned to take his hand. The space between them was lonely, after the closeness of their nights. Occasionally, she caught him sneaking glances as she floated along beside him; evidently, he agreed.

After a while, Vince and Sandy disappeared into the crowd. Nick suggested he and Meredith take a break. He bought them a couple of hot chocolates, and they made their way through the glittering garden. They leaned on the railing by the tree, watching the skaters laugh and stumble.

In unsaid understanding, they had positioned themselves far enough away to avoid suspicion, but close enough for their arms to make subtle contact. The air seemed charged with electricity. Meredith's blood was restless, her senses astir. She wanted to turn and look at him but dared not do it. She stared unseeing at the skating rink, her thoughts and heart aflutter.

She turned at gentle pressure on her forearm. Nick's arms were folded over the railing; the hand closer to her had rested just above her wrist, the fingers stroking her skin under her sleeve. His eyes were directed downward, but in response to her movement, he met her gaze.

"What is it?" she whispered.

His eyes moved over her face, taking her in.

"You look pretty," he said. His voice was quiet, as always, but his face was alight with mischief. "Your nose is pink." In a quick, playful motion, he touched the tip of her nose. "So are your cheeks."

For a moment, everything around them disappeared. Meredith leaned in without meaning to, eyes drifting shut just as she registered him leaning in, too.

The spell was broken by a falling skater, who clumsily crashed against the railing right where they were standing. Meredith and Nick jumped back. The skater, laughing, apologized and stumbled on.

They relaxed once more against the railing, this time, without touching.

Meredith knew she had to say something.

"Thank you for what you did back there." She swallowed, preparing to empty her heart to him once more. "It was really nice of you." She patted his arm. "You're a quick thinker."

He smiled. "You're welcome."

"I'm impressed with how easily you came up with that story."

He shrugged, a little bashfully. "I don't like lying. But I knew once I said it, you'd agree with it, so I figured it wasn't actually a lie."

Meredith's smile widened as she looked at him, his earnest expression, the blue clarity of his eyes. She felt warm and tingly all over. *How crushingly decent you are*, she thought, but she didn't say it.

"I'm sorry we went for nothing," she told him instead. "To the theater. I don't know what was the matter with me."

He was silent a moment, looking beyond the skaters and out toward the river.

"You seemed pretty upset," he said finally. He turned his head slightly toward her, but did not meet her eyes. "You don't have to tell me."

At those words, she knew she wanted to. She took a deep

breath and sighed. "I have a history with *Romeo and Juliet*. Adam directed it. We used to go to the theater together."

He looked back out toward the rink, saying nothing.

Meredith went on. "It's a funny thing. I think I'm fine, all day. I mean, I know I'm fine. And then something sneaks up out of nowhere. It takes me by surprise."

He nodded but still didn't speak. He was watching the skaters, his eyes serious with thought.

She rubbed her lips together nervously. "It doesn't mean I shouldn't be with you. Or that I'm not ready." She hesitated. "If that's what you were thinking."

He turned slowly then, and faced her.

"That isn't what I was thinking."

She started a little at the conviction in his soft voice. "Oh."

"I was thinking that that's how it works. That things sneak up on you. It happens with my mother, too."

"Oh," she said again, in a whisper. She cleared her throat. "That's good to know. Thank you."

"I don't expect you to be over it. You'll never be over it. It's like a scar. You carry it with you. I think of my mother every day."

"I know." Her eyes softened with sympathy. "And I know living my life is natural and necessary. It makes me happy to know I'm at the point where I can do it. It's just sometimes, the little things..."

She didn't finish the sentence; saying it was admitting it, not just to him but to herself. She'd worked so hard to be okay, to feel enthusiastic about the future. She had to move forward to survive. She didn't like to talk about the things that were holding her back.

"Anyway," she concluded, too loudly, in an attempt to sound natural. "I'm sorry it affected everyone's evening."

"You don't have to apologize. You shouldn't apologize. And look." He spread his hands, indicating the cheerful scene around them. "It worked out great."

Meredith's eyes misted; she took a breath to steady herself. "Okay."

"You shouldn't do things you don't want to do. And it wasn't for nothing. You just..." He shrugged. "You just have to take it and make something better of it." His forehead wrinkled with thought. "If that makes sense."

"It makes sense. It makes perfect sense." The knot in her chest began relaxing: she understood what he was saying. She smiled. The tears had receded, but her eyes still glimmered. "You are amazing." She shook her head, watching him with wonder. "You're incredible. I've never met anyone like you. I..." She was suddenly choked up. She swallowed, and recovered. "I appreciate you, Nick."

His expression, as always, remained straight, but a smile touched the corners of his eyes. Meredith focused on them, on the joy it gave her to please him; it distracted her from the guilt she felt at having said these words.

He was still watching her, his blue eyes alert and clear.

"I appreciate you, too."

He seemed to be standing a little taller. Meredith took him in, his broad shoulders, the sharp features of his face and his blond, wind-swept hair. Her lips parted, but no words came out. She closed them, smiling awkwardly. She looked around at the crowd.

"Vince and Sandy are around here somewhere." She looked at him once more. Her heart thumped painfully, warmth emanating from her pores. Her eyes drifted to his lips; she lowered her voice. "I wish I could kiss you."

His jaw firmed, as if he were stifling a smile, and his chest rose, as if with a breath. The change was nearly imperceptible. It felt like a secret that only she knew.

"Some wishes come true," he whispered, in a tone that weakened her knees. They surrendered their place by the railing, walking side by side back toward the rink, Meredith quite incapable of suppressing a wide grin.

THEY HAD EXITED Penn's Landing, lungs full of brisk winter air, refreshed from the physical exertion. They were walking along Market Street, assessing restaurants, when something interesting happened, something that would impact Meredith's life in ways she could not, at the time, possibly foresee.

"You," said an official-looking woman in a sleek black outfit and headset; she was carrying a clipboard and pointing to people in the crowd. "You, and you."

As people were identified, they watched in confusion as she approached them, spoke with them in a quick, confidential manner, and pointed into a restaurant. Those singled out looked surprised at first, and then excited; then they hurried, with the help of her hand on their backs, into the restaurant, as the woman turned to the crowd once more.

"What's going on here?" asked Vince.

The woman heard him and looked up at him with interest. "You." She looked at the rest of them. "All of you. It's your lucky day."

She ushered them aside. They all leaned in to hear what she had to say.

"How would you like to be in the audience for the pilot of a new show for *Gourmet*?"

Meredith raised her eyebrows. She adored *The Gourmet Channel* and often tested recipes from its many celebrity chefs, sometimes taking it upon herself to make improvements. "Where? When?"

"Here. Right now."

The woman gestured behind her at Sydney's, a much talked about new restaurant that was fully booked for months. Meredith had heard of it but had never been inside. She'd been curious about it: it was said to have a daring menu, and its owner was a known philanthropist who donated large portions of their restaurant's proceeds to charities around the city.

"Wow. You mean we get to eat at Sydney's?"

"Well, no," said the woman. "Dinner isn't part of it. But you do get to witness the birth of a new food empire. Chef Shane Thayer is the star and judge of 'Gladiator Gourmet,' an exciting new show that pits the most accomplished chefs against each other in a heart-pumping, nail-biting competition of imagination and skill. May the best chef win!"

Meredith couldn't conceal an amused grin at the woman's elevator pitch. "Gladiator Gourmet?"

The woman didn't have time for pithy commentary. "This is the opportunity of a lifetime. Are you coming or not?"

Meredith looked at her companions, eyes bright. "Should we?"

"Abso-fucking-lutely," said Vince. He held his hand out to the woman. "After you."

They shuffled hurriedly inside, the woman turning them over to the care of a harried usher. As they were led to their seats in a dimly lit room with smoke-colored wood and modern decor, Meredith's heart quickened with excitement. She didn't know much about Shane Thayer; she knew only that he was executive chef at a restaurant in Washington, DC and that he had served as a judge in one or two competitions on *The Gourmet Channel*. She was delighted to be part of this experience and to learn what she could from such well-known chefs.

As they chatted, Meredith took a moment to gaze about the room. At the front sat two elaborate chef's stations, between which was a smaller table with a candle and a wine glass. Cameras were focused on the scene in front; a flurry of important-looking people rushed around barking orders and making preparations. The urgency was exciting. Meredith couldn't wait for the show to start.

Although dinner was not included, a Sydney's cocktail was. Meredith selected what turned out to be a misty-looking concoction in a martini glass. It contained Crème de Violette and tasted of fairy gardens.

"This is spectacular," she murmured, her lips just parting around the edge of the glass to let the cool liquid pass down her throat. "I might actually finish it."

"You should finish it," said Vince, downing an impressive sip of his Manhattan with shocking ease. In response, he puckered his lips and nodded appreciatively, swirling his glass. "Let your hair down. Have fun."

"I don't know." Meredith set her glass down, already feeling a mellow spinning sensation. "I still have to get up and navigate the city."

"No, I mean literally let your hair down." Glass in hand, he gestured toward her head, where her hair was piled into a loose, wispy bun. "The librarian look is nice, but we're out for a night on the town."

"Leave Merry alone, Vince," said Sandy, squeezing Meredith's arm. "She doesn't have to let her hair down if she doesn't want to!"

The audience was quieted, and the two competing chefs were introduced, one of whom was the executive chef of Sydney's. Before long, the chefs were busily preparing their meals, and the room smelled of tomatoes, garlic, and oregano. The audience looked on with interest, pointing and whispering as various dishes were plated before their eyes. Everyone gasped and clapped as one as the Sydney's chef lit his flambé on fire, threw it up into the air, and spun it around theatrically.

"Wow!" cried Sandy, leaning in to look at Meredith. "That was amazing, Merry! Can you do that?"

Meredith laughed. "I'm not sure, but I don't think I'm ready to find out."

They watched as the other chef removed meat and dough from the refrigerator. Meredith sat up straighter to see the action.

She gasped when she took stock of the ingredients and realized what was going on.

"He's making pâté en croûte," she breathed, remembering how she hadn't dared attempt this dish for Vince's first dinner back home. "I can't believe it."

Vince was less impressed. "He's cheating. He just took half the dish out of the fridge."

"I guess they had time to prepare beforehand. It's an incredibly difficult dish. It'll still be a challenge."

Meredith studied the chef's movements, taking mental notes of everything he was doing.

At one point, she nearly jumped out of her seat.

"He turned it upside down!"

Sure enough, the chef had unhinged the mold and removed the plate, placing it on top and then turning the whole thing upside down.

"Genius."

Beside her, Nick leaned in.

"Why did he do that?" he whispered.

"He's ensuring there are no seams." Meredith paused a moment, appreciating this little trick. "The thing about pâté en croûte is that the crust can't have any seams. Seams let liquid leak out, including the aspic." She turned to him. "Aspic is gelatin. It holds it all together."

She continued watching, in awe. Flipping the pâté over also meant the ingredients would put pressure on the seams below.

"Marvelous."

The chef slid the dish into the oven. Meredith leaned back in her seat with a smile, inspired. Why had she thought she couldn't cook this dish? It was just a matter of thinking ahead, of anticipating the problems and coming up with out-of-the-box solutions. It was a matter of getting outside your head, of doing things that were a little unconventional, of taking risks. There was no reason to be afraid. *I could do this, if I wanted to*, she told herself. *I'll have to give it a try.*

She heard excited buzzing from the crowd. She redirected her attention to the front of the room, where the chefs were shaking hands and walking to their corners to await judgment as Chef Thayer strode right past them. With thick chestnut hair parted neatly on the side, he was much taller and burlier than he appeared on TV, and he walked with a swinging gait that drew attention to his brawny frame. After a brief introduction, in which he thanked everyone for joining him and explained how he would judge the meals, he took his seat at the center table and waited to be served. Each chef humbly presented each course, hanging onto Chef Thayer's every word and scrutinizing his expressions as he took his first bites. After the presentation, each chef stood on either side of Chef Thayer, awaiting the results. Chef Thayer favored the Sydney's chef, and the crowd burst into applause. The two chefs shook hands, the Sydney's chef wiping his brow and embracing his staff, finally shaking Chef Thayer's hand and thanking him.

Meredith wasn't sure what made Chef Thayer a more qualified judge than the competing chefs, each of whom was great in his own way; she respected the chefs for their hard work and courage, and she bristled a little in their defense at the cool, rehearsed manner with which Chef Thayer spoke to them. In spite of her misgivings, however, Meredith had enjoyed herself and felt grateful to have witnessed these two great chefs at work.

Exhilarated, she walked with the others to a more casual restaurant for dinner. Sandy and Vince took full advantage of the romantic atmosphere, feeding each other bread and kissing over the corner of the table. Over coffee, they all leaned back, full and satisfied, and settled in for a bit of light chatter.

"How's school, Merry?" asked Vince, taking a break from Sandy's affections, and turning toward her. "Anything interesting going on?"

"School is going well," she answered. "I really love my classes. And I start my study club next week."

"That's cool." Vince smiled kindly. "Glad you're having a good year. You deserve it."

"And you're helping with the play." Sandy gestured with her hand, encouraging Meredith to say more about it. "You're going to be amazing!"

"Yes." Meredith sipped her coffee, shifting in her seat. "That will be a fun challenge."

Later, Vince and Nick stood and walked to the back of the restaurant to settle the bill. Meredith looked around happily contemplating the exquisite evening.

"Has he said anything about me?" Sandy asked suddenly, interrupting Meredith's thoughts.

Meredith turned to her, not liking the direction in which this was going. "Excuse me?" she asked, buying time; Vince never talked about her.

Sandy sighed. "I know it's a silly question. But I was just wondering if Vince has said anything about me."

Meredith turned thoughtful. "I know he likes you, Sandy," she said, not wanting to lie but hating to hurt her feelings.

"He does?" Sandy asked, her voice full of hope. "How do you know?"

Meredith felt sorry for Sandy. She didn't know how to tell her that Vince knew how to use his good looks and charm to get what he wanted and that most women fell for it, that he never stuck with any woman for too long, that Sandy was probably one of several he'd see while he was in town, that she'd been through this before and that it would never change, that she would be no different from any other woman Vince had used until he had had his fill, and then discarded.

She bit her lip, not knowing how to respond. "Well," she said, "I think it's obvious by the way he invites you to hang out with us."

"Oh," Sandy said, her back straightening and her face growing serious. "I didn't want to impose."

"No, Sandy," Meredith assured her, placing her hand on hers. "That's not what I meant. I just mean that he clearly wants to be with you; otherwise he wouldn't ask you out all the time. Right?"

"I guess," Sandy responded dejectedly.

Meredith glanced toward the back of the restaurant, wondering how long it would be before Vince and Nick returned. She was relieved to see them standing at the counter. She was about to turn back to Sandy when something caught her eye, and she focused her gaze on them once again. Vince and an attractive woman were engaged in animated conversation, the woman's face lifted with interest as Vince spoke. Nick stood waiting in silence.

Not wanting to alarm Sandy, Meredith turned to smile at her; however, Sandy had noticed them by now and was staring piercingly in their direction. She looked away, and Meredith, turning, saw that they were on their way back. Her heart sinking, she braced herself for a scene she'd witnessed too many times before.

"Who was that?" Sandy shot at Vince as he and Nick removed their coats from the backs of their chairs.

"Who was who?" Vince asked, looking downward.

Sandy clicked her tongue disapprovingly, her face contorted with disgust.

Vince looked at her, irritation and impatience on his face. "What's your problem?"

Sandy looked away.

Meredith felt inclined to intervene. "Seriously, Vince," she said, trying to make her voice calm, hoping she sounded nothing more than curious. She and Sandy stood and slipped into their coats. "We saw you talking to a woman back there. Who was that?"

"Oh," Vince said, brushing his hand in the air to suggest it was too insignificant even to remember. "Just this woman I used to know. She worked at the diner when I did, that summer when I was off from school."

"You two seemed to have a lot to catch up on," Sandy inserted bitingly.

Vince glared at her. "Come on, Sandy. You're not really going to do that, are you? She's just some random person I knew a million years ago. I was talking to her for less than five minutes. Lighten up."

"Vince," Meredith said, and shook her head.

He regained his control and smiled diplomatically at Sandy. "I'm sorry, baby. But it's nothing. Let's just get past it, okay?"

They walked back to the car in silence. Meredith tried to come up with a topic that would jumpstart the conversation, but she couldn't think; the mood had darkened significantly.

Vince tried to make small talk on the way home, but Sandy was intent on giving him the silent treatment, her gaze fixed out her window and her arms crossed. Meredith did her best to lighten the mood, but failed. Eventually everyone gave up and drove to Meredith's school in silence.

Meredith had forgotten all about her car and groaned at the thought of having to climb into a cold car and drive home alone. However, that problem was solved for her as soon as Vince pulled up in the spot next to hers.

"So listen," said Vince, turning around to look at her. "I want some time to try to appease Miss Grumpy over here. You and Nick can drive your car home. Is that okay with you, Merry?"

"Of course," she responded, hoping her excitement wasn't obvious. "Go ahead and have fun. Nick and I will go home together."

Vince hesitated at these words, and Meredith inwardly kicked herself; however, when he spoke again, he seemed to have put his worry aside. "Great. I won't be long."

Nick and Meredith got out of the car, followed by Sandy, who took Nick's seat up front. Vince rolled down his window to wish them goodnight.

"Don't wait up," he said. "I'm sure you're both pretty tired."

"Okay. Have a good time."

"Thanks," he said to Meredith. He stuck his hand out of the open window and waved once to Nick before driving off.

Nick and Meredith stood in the dark, deserted parking lot, once again confronted with the prospect of a night to themselves. They faced each other.

Nick spoke. "Let's go for a drive."

Meredith smiled. "Okay," she said, and unlocked her car.

Meredith didn't know where she was going; she just put the car in gear and drove. It didn't much matter to her. She relished the fact that they could speak and act as they pleased. She mindlessly drove north toward the more open spaces of Bucks County, somehow drawn away from the bustle of the city, away from the commotion and noise. The darkness around them was soothing, especially after the frenetic energy of the city. They passed very few cars. Large farmhouses sped by them, the only lights those shining from the front porches. Meredith felt they were truly alone, and truly at peace.

"Did you enjoy the show?" he asked.

"Yes, it was fun. I like seeing great chefs in action." A grin crept onto her face. "I used to delude myself into thinking I'd be a great chef one day."

He looked at her and smiled. "You are a great chef."

Meredith turned her head toward him for a moment and smiled more warmly. "That's very sweet of you," she said, and turned back toward the road. "But I mean that I considered going into cooking. I thought about opening my own catering business. It's a silly idea, of course."

"Why?"

"It just is," she said, then thought about it for a moment. "I mean that it simply isn't practical. There isn't a lot of security in that kind of thing. Plus I think my father would have fainted if I told him I wasn't going to be a teacher. You should have heard him when Vince said he was quitting his job to be a painter."

"You didn't want to be a teacher?"

"I just never had the chance to consider anything else." She sighed. "Life was so much simpler back then. The choices seemed so easy because they were made for me. I just worked hard and achieved what I was working for. Now it seems I never know what's going to happen, no matter what I do or how well I plan."

"Maybe life is actually simpler now that you can do what you want to do."

They drove on for a few moments in silence.

"In any case," she said, "it all worked out. I love teaching—it's a part of who I am."

"I can tell."

She glanced at him briefly. "How about you?" she asked. "Did you ever think you'd do something different?"

He seemed to consider. "Not really."

"Do you like what you do?"

"Yeah." He paused again. "I like it. I don't know that it's what I really want to do, though."

"Oh? Why is that?"

"Painting is fine; there's nothing wrong with it, I guess."

A couple of moments went by.

"But?" she ventured, when he said nothing more.

He took a breath and shifted in his seat. "Nothing," he said, seeming to relax. "I was just thinking that I'd like to go back to carpentry, like my dad." He was silent a few beats. "Maybe I will, one day."

Meredith had an idea. She approached the topic with hesitation. "I don't suppose you would..."

He looked at her. "I would what?"

"That...that you'd consider helping build the set. For the play.

My principal mentioned they need someone." She waved her hand. "Don't worry about it, though. It's a really big ask."

"I'll do it."

She met his gaze. "You will?"

"Sure." His eyes were bright; they crinkled in the corners. "I'm happy to help. Besides, it'll be nice to jump back into carpentry."

"As long as you're sure."

"I'm sure."

She turned to him and smiled. "Thanks."

He met her smile with his own. "You're welcome."

She reached her hand out, and he took it. Meredith marveled once again at how good this intimacy felt, this physical contact with another person, the embracing of vulnerability and the exchange of each other's trust. Her heart pulsed in a quick, happy pattern. She watched the road before her with excitement, the sparkling lights twinkling in the darkness.

"Sandy seems pretty upset about Vince," Nick said after a time. "I feel bad for her."

"Me too," Meredith agreed heartily. She sighed. "When you two were away from the table, she grilled me about whether he mentions her. She's been through this so many times with him, but she never sees it coming." She paused. "I shouldn't be critical. Sandy's not a bad person."

"You didn't sound critical."

Meredith frowned. She had known Sandy for a long time, and while she'd never felt a strong connection with her, Sandy hadn't made her uncomfortable as she was doing this time around.

In any case, she shouldn't hold it against Sandy. It wasn't Sandy's fault. It was her stuff, not Sandy's. Sandy undoubtedly had her own stuff.

After driving for some time on deserted roads past farms and woods, they began approaching the lights and activity of a town. Bars and restaurants began popping up, and soon, as Meredith slowed her speed, they saw people hustling by, bundled up in the cold, walking to their cars after enjoying an evening of dinner, theater, and company.

"What's this?" Nick asked, gazing out the window.

"Framington," Meredith responded. She had been here many times. It was a posh, cozy town that boasted antique shops and bookstores but also a bustling nightlife.

"Let's stop," he said.

Meredith glanced at the clock; it was after eleven o'clock. She was beginning to grow tired, and she had no idea when Vince was returning home. She hesitated.

He looked at her. "Don't you want to?"

"It isn't that, Nick...It's just..."

"Just what?"

"Well, I'm a little overdressed."

"You're not overdressed. And anyway, does it matter?"

"I guess it doesn't." She paused thoughtfully. "Also, who knows when Vince is coming back home?"

"Vince won't be back until morning," Nick said with certainty. "Besides, he's got to find out sometime." He looked at her and smiled wryly. "He can't expect us to just sit around and wait for him."

"You're not too tired?"

"I just want to have some fun. Let's go to a bar."

The thought of going to a bar with him thrilled her. They hadn't been out in public together, just the two of them. It would be like a real date. She didn't generally go to bars, and she grew excited at the idea of doing something new. Without further hesitation, she pulled into a parking spot on the street and turned off the car.

He patted her hand and smiled. "Ready?"

"I'm ready," she said, returning his smile and leaning in for a swift kiss. "Let's go."

They climbed out of the car, and Meredith met him on the sidewalk. Despite the late hour, throngs of people milled about, going in and out of buildings and loitering on street corners. Nick took her hand and led her up the street, glancing into each open door and pausing in front of an English tavern with heavy beams for a ceiling and wide wooden planks for a floor. He drew her inside and up to the bar, where he helped her onto the only empty stool. He stood protectively behind her, his arm on her shoulder, while he ordered a beer and a glass of wine from the bartender.

She swiveled on her stool to face him. He was looking around the room, and she thought his angular features in profile appeared even more chiseled. His throat looked thick and sinewy with his head turned to the side, and her heart beat faster as she recalled what it felt like to kiss him there, the way he looked with his eyes closed and the way his chest heaved with hurried breaths.

The music was blaring, and the clamor of so many people carousing was making her head hurt. She knew they wouldn't be able to talk much here. Still, she was exhilarated. He sipped his beer and looked down at her. He stroked her shoulder, gently neatening her hair around her neck.

When he leaned in to kiss her, she let him, but flinched.

He stopped. "What's wrong?"

"Nothing." She was gazing about the room. "It's just, there are so many people here."

A sparkle of amusement touched his eyes. "And?"

She was drawn into his hungry stare, his eyes' blue clarity and the playful upturn of his lips. She breathed in; the self-consciousness was already seeping out of her.

"And nothing," she whispered. "Kiss me again."

They flirted like this for a quarter of an hour. Meredith slowly nursed her wine. She wasn't much of a drinker and had very little tolerance. A thought occurred to her.

She reached her hand toward him and placed it on his shoulder, drawing him in close. She said, "Do you mind driving home? After a couple of drinks I won't be able to see straight."

"No problem," he said, and then grinned. "And you won't need your eyes open later anyway."

Meredith lost her breath. Her heart fluttered a little, and she felt her eyes darken sensuously. "And why is that?" she teased. She was already starting to feel the dizzying effects of the wine.

She bristled pleasantly as he drew even closer, delighted by the mischief in his eyes.

"Because I'm going to kiss you here," he whispered, touching his lips to her shoulder, his voice soft like rose petals—"and here," he went on, gliding them up her neck—"and here." He playfully nipped the underside of her jaw, making her giggle. "So you see," he concluded, with a kiss on the lips for good measure, "all you need to do is lie still and let me do it. If you want to."

His finger grazed her cheek, and she inhaled shakily. *If you want to.* Yes...yes, that would do. The gentleness of his touch and the velvety desire in his voice had set her insides on fire. It was all she could do to sit still on her barstool; she was enlivened and energized, sensation sparkling beneath her skin.

"Hey," she said suddenly. "I feel like dancing." The words sounded odd to her even as they were coming out of her mouth. She didn't enjoy dancing and had never been good at it. She didn't know what had come over her.

He took the last swig of his beer and placed the glass on the bar, then removed her glass from her hand and placed it next to his. "Let's get out of here," he said.

He wrapped his arm around her waist and gripped her tightly. Her head had begun to spin, but she was enjoying it. He led her to another bar two doors down, this one darker and louder than the last. They walked inside, barely able to move in the crowd. He stopped at the bar and turned to her.

"What would you like?"

"Surprise me."

He said something to the bartender, who turned to fill the order, returning with a cool, gleaming cocktail. Nick passed it to

Meredith, who took a generous sip. She didn't know what it was, but it was red, sweet, and delicious.

"If I have much more than this, I'll fall asleep," she said woozily to Nick. "All I'll be good for is a cuddle."

"That would be okay, too."

She finished the drink more quickly than she had thought she could. Nick pulled the cherry from the glass and, with a sensual smile, slowly brought it to her lips. She opened her mouth and took in the cherry, closing her lips around it, and sucking.

"Mmm," he breathed, leaning in close and kissing her behind her ear. His lips were moist and warm. "Do you have any idea how beautiful you are?"

Her eyes closed as she rolled her neck to the side to give him easier access. Her hand reached for his face, which she stroked as he kissed her. His hair felt soft in her fingers. It smelled of him, and she inhaled deeply.

She felt herself melting. "Forget about sleep," she murmured, her eyes still closed. "I'll do whatever I have to do to stay awake for you tonight."

"I was hoping you'd say that."

Her vision was blurred; she wasn't sure if Nick or the alcohol was more intoxicating. She smiled dizzily. She opened her eyes and admired him, his eyebrows furrowed seductively and his lips pink and luscious. She drew him into a slow, delicious kiss. His hand gripped her neck, pulling her close to him.

He detached his lips from hers and brought them to her ear. "Let's dance," he whispered.

He drew her from her barstool and led her to the center of the room, where he pressed her close and moved rhythmically with her amidst the crowd. She moved with him, but warily; she couldn't focus, her eyes taking in the other dancers and her mind tormenting her with horrifying images of her own inept dancing.

"You look so beautiful," he whispered, his breath warming her ear, his voice tantalizingly intimate. "Just have fun. Don't worry about anybody else."

"I'm sorry, Nick. I..." Her eyelids drifted shut as his lips nibbled the lower curve of her neck, into her shoulder. She sighed aloud. "I guess I should relax."

"I guess you should." She could hear his smile, and she smiled in return. His hands slinked along her hips and over her back, where they splayed across her, hugging her tight. "Maybe I can help with that."

His hands traveled up and down the length of her body as he playfully seduced her with a licentious dance. She laughed and played along, pressing herself to him and letting him lead her. He stepped and swayed with her, holding her close and not taking his eyes off her. His rhythm was perfect, and his subtle movements brought attention to his slender strength, his lithe, muscular build. She thought he couldn't have looked sexier.

After some time, they made their way back to the street, where they walked hand in hand until it grew too cold. The streets were emptier now, and as they approached Meredith's car, they appeared to be alone. Meredith dug for her keys and, finding them, handed them to Nick.

He opened her door for her but held her arm before she could climb in. He kissed her lips, then looked at her.

"Did you have a nice time?"

She kissed him, then peered into his eyes. His arms were wrapped around her waist, hugging her possessively. Her hands were clasped behind his neck. "Nick," she said.

"What is it, beautiful?"

Her heart flipped at this term of endearment. She said hazily, "Every night I have with you is the best night I've ever had."

His face softened, and he inhaled sharply. Without a word, he leaned in and kissed her. He stroked her back and played with her hair, twirling it between his fingers. Finally his hand rose to her face, which he kissed once more before looking at her squarely.

"Let's go home now," he said. "I'll make sure this is the best night you've ever had."

~

MEREDITH HAD HAD the time of her life. As she sat in the passenger's seat, Nick driving, she felt wonderful, like every day was precious and exciting. She felt sexy, beautiful, and alive. It was so freeing to let go, to do what felt good, regardless of those around her. She loved that it came so easily to him and that he taught her to be that way, too. And after this night out, she knew they had reached a new level of intimacy. She was so full of joy she thought she might cry.

They rode home in relative silence, Meredith directing him where to turn and Nick wordlessly obeying. Meredith, most definitely feeling the effects of her drinks, fought to stay awake. Whenever she felt drowsy, she glanced over at Nick and was instantly alert.

They arrived home just before two o'clock in the morning. Vince's car was nowhere to be seen.

Nick pulled into the driveway, then met her at her door to help her out. They walked up to the house, holding each other in silence. Nick unlocked the door and shut it behind her.

The house was dark. They removed their coats and hung them on the coat rack, stumbling a bit in the darkness. They stood wordlessly for a few moments. Then Nick approached her and drew her by the waist so she was pressed against him. She lifted her chin, and they took each other in a long kiss, beginning gently but growing deeper as the moments passed. Nick reached for her backside and squeezed, pulling her hips to his and drawing a soft moan from her throat. Without a word, he took her hand and led her upstairs to her bedroom, where he shut the door behind them. He unbuttoned her sweater, letting it slip off her shoulders and onto the floor, and fumbled for a moment with the clasp of her bra before it snapped in his fingers. Meredith stood still, her eyes closed, feeling as if she might fall but incapable of moving. She sighed as he kissed her, his hands now at the zipper of her skirt; now she felt her skirt being slipped from her hips and down her legs, and she stood there, naked and trembling, as he lay her gently on the bed. He undressed in front of her, the broadness of his chest and the tight muscles of his arms looking glorious in silhouette as he lifted them over his head to remove his shirt; his hands went to the button of his trousers, which she soon heard rustle as they fell to the floor. Soon he was on top of her, and she embraced him willingly, her legs wrapped around him and her chin lifted as he nuzzled his face in her neck, his lips teasing her and tickling her skin. He sighed as her hands swept over his shoulders, back, and hips. He entered her swiftly and perfectly, and she gasped aloud. As he drew her further and further toward paradise, she gave herself to him completely, in mind, body, and heart.

CHAPTER EIGHT

SANDY

*M*onday morning, Meredith arrived at school early to meet with Ana, whose parents had given her the idea for the study club. Ana was the first student to join.

"This paragraph is good," she told her, as the two looked over the first draft of Ana's essay. She pointed with her red pen to a passage on Ana's screen. "But there's some overlap with the next one. Right here. See?"

Ana studied the paragraphs for some time. "I don't see it." She frowned. "I'm sorry."

"No need to apologize." Meredith patted the girl's hand. "That's why we're here. It's hard."

Ana smiled gratefully.

"Now, why don't you tell me again—what is the main idea of this paragraph?"

"How Frankenstein's actions go against nature."

"Right. And what is the main idea of this paragraph?"

"How nature restores Frankenstein's health."

"Good. But this final sentence here, in the first paragraph—"

"It's about nature restoring his health."

Meredith smiled widely. "That's right."

"I get it." Ana's eager fingers cut and pasted the sentence into the next paragraph.

"Good, but put it after the topic sentence. You still want to introduce the paragraph with something more general."

"Right. I totally get it. Thank you!"

"No problem." Meredith relaxed in her chair, delighted. "And please feel free to ask questions in class, too. We're all learning together."

Ana's face fell, and she shrank back a little. "It's hard for me to ask questions in class. I...I feel embarrassed."

Meredith's eyes softened. "You do? How come?"

Ana shrugged. Her voice grew quiet. "I don't like anyone else to know I need help."

Something inside Meredith stirred at Ana's words. She watched her for a moment, moved.

"I understand," she uttered, and cleared her throat. "And I think that's totally normal." She smiled. "That's the great thing about what we're doing right now. You'll get all the help you need, just you and me."

Later, Ana packed up her things, cheerfully telling her she'd see her in class. She was more confident now, and excited, and Meredith's heart flew high. As the girl left Meredith's classroom, Meredith's joy tapered a little: she was nervous about the next task at hand.

She followed Ana out of the classroom and walked down the hall, then took a deep breath and knocked tentatively on Kevin Williams's door.

"Meredith," he said brightly, waving her inside. "Please, come on in."

"Thanks. How was your weekend?"

"Oh, lovely, thank you. I saw a lot of my grandkids, which is always the best." Kevin glanced at her face and did a double take. "Everything okay?"

Meredith straightened, taken aback. "Of course! Why do you

ask?"

"As I said, Meredith, you'll be a great supervisor, but you're not a very good actress." His voice became quiet. "I can see it in your face. What's going on?"

Meredith sighed. She had been wearing what she thought was an easygoing, relaxed expression. She guessed Kevin was right about her acting skills.

"I need to be upfront with you, Kevin," she said. "I had mixed feelings about the play because drama was Adam's thing."

Kevin's face gentled. "Oh. I'm sorry."

"No, no, you have nothing to apologize for." She smiled kindly. "I actually thought it would be good for me. It would help me move forward even further, and it would be fulfilling one of his dreams. And I was really excited for another opportunity to work one-on-one with the kids. But I was worried that if I did it *only* for Adam, it wouldn't be about me, and that didn't seem healthy at all."

Kevin nodded. "I understand."

"I've been thinking hard about it, and I don't think that's why I'm doing it. I feel good, Kevin. I feel ready. I want to do the play, for me. I can do it, and I can do a good job." She swallowed. "But *Romeo and Juliet* is going to be tough for me."

"I see." Kevin didn't seem to need an explanation as to why; the reason, evidently, was clear. "Well, as for *Romeo*, we'll just do a different play. No problem."

Meredith's heart leapt. "Really? You mean that?"

"Of course, Meredith. You're more important than that play."

"Thank you so much." Meredith could feel the anxiety seeping out of her chest, gratitude taking its place. "That is so very kind of you."

"It's nothing. And if you don't mind my saying so," he went on, "I'm happy you decided to do this. I really think it'll be good for you. You just let me know if it's too much. Okay?"

"Okay." She smiled. "Thank you."

"Now, which play do you think we should do?"

Meredith wrinkled her brow and rubbed her lips together, thinking. "I'm not sure."

"Well, they were going to rewrite *Romeo*. Why don't you have them write the whole play, on a topic of your choosing?"

Meredith looked at him wide-eyed. "Now that's an interesting idea."

"I think it's a great idea, if I do say so myself." Indeed, he looked quite pleased; he bounced a little on the balls of his feet. "The only question is the topic. What's something that interests you, Meredith?"

Meredith stared at him blankly. "Food," she said, without thinking, and laughed. "Cooking, to be exact."

"That settles it, then. I guess the play is about food."

Meredith laughed again, more relaxed now. "I wasn't serious, Kevin. I'm not sure that would work."

"Why not? An ice cream sundae on a first date. The first Thanksgiving after Grandma died." A flash of sadness crossed his eyes, but was gone as quickly as it was there. "The point is that food is at the center of our lives; it isn't just something we eat to survive."

"I actually love that." *A home-cooked meal between formerly estranged siblings. Hot chocolate after ice skating, the sweet early stages of a new romance.* A spark of excitement flared in her gut; the gears in her mind were turning wildly. She imagined herself working with the students, talking with them individually, getting to know them, helping them put their experiences to paper. She could feel the possibility coursing through her blood. All at once, she knew this was the task for her, that somehow, it was key to her wellbeing. "It's a great idea. Let's do it."

∾

MIDTERMS WERE THE FOLLOWING WEEK, and Meredith prepared to sprint toward her holiday vacation.

She had half days every day. However, every night would find her grading the exams, in addition to the term papers she hadn't yet completed. Exam weeks were mixed blessings. On the one hand, she enjoyed being home for lunch and having quiet time by herself to complete her work. The prospect of vacation shone brightly, spurring her to complete her tasks as quickly as possible. However, the week would be particularly stressful for students, which meant frantic last minute questions, tears from those who were cracking under pressure, and possibly demanding phone calls from desperate parents. Meredith would have strict deadlines this week and would need to manage her time wisely if she was to finish on time. At the end of it, though, she would be free for a week.

Most important was the fact that she would have a happy Christmas this year.

Christmas fell on a Saturday, which meant she would work Monday through Thursday, administering her last exam Thursday morning. Friday night the three of them would go to Tara's house; Tara and her family had invited them for dinner before they left on Saturday for their Christmas in the Washington suburbs. Meredith's plans for Christmas were minimal, but she was looking forward to relishing a cozy holiday at home with people she cared about. She imagined Christmas music in the background, curling up in pajamas in front of the fire, and sitting around the table to enjoy a nice meal together. She only wished she and Nick could be open about their relationship; as long as they were keeping it a secret, she wouldn't truly be able to enjoy his company on Christmas.

"Then let's tell him," Nick said one night as they undressed for bed: Vince had gone out for the evening, giving them some unexpected freedom. "That way, you can enjoy Christmas."

"I can't." She surprised herself with how forcefully she said these words. She climbed beneath the blankets. "It's tied up in the fact that it's a secret. He thinks it means I don't trust him. If we tell him we've been together all this time, that's exactly how it will look."

"Isn't that all the more reason to tell him? Before it gets even worse?"

She understood this logically. But no. "The timing isn't right. It has to be done at the perfect time."

"Okay." He stepped out of his jeans. "It's just that I feel kind of guilty, to be honest."

"I know." She kissed him as he slid into bed beside her. "It's because you're such a nice person."

"I just think we'll both feel better when this is out in the open."

"I know," she said again, but she knew she wasn't going to do it. She frowned—she hated to make Nick an accomplice, but she could not bring herself to risk losing her brother again. If Vince needed her to trust him, she had to do it, or at least appear to. She wrapped her arms around him. "Let's talk about it tomorrow."

Meredith felt herself falling for Nick with more intensity as the days passed. She was mesmerized by him. He seemed to live in uncomplicated peace; he wasn't materialistic or temperamental, and he made her more easygoing, as well. He saw the world as a good place, the source of unlimited opportunities for self-expansion, self-fulfillment, and fun. She loved listening to his soft, steady voice as he talked dreamily about Maine, the formidable rocky coastlines and the way the cliffs turned purple in the light of the setting sun. He found sacredness in nature and saw it as a place in which he could discover something bigger than himself. Meredith liked his vision; it made her feel that life was full of possibilities. She appreciated that he understood what drew her toward the mountains and the woods and that he was so eager to hear stories of her own adventures. He was unlike any man she had ever met.

Nick was different from Adam in a lot of ways. Whereas Adam had been vibrant and gregarious, Nick was subdued and contemplative; people had been drawn to Adam's personable charm as if by a magnet, but one had to get to know Nick in order to see his depth and kindness. Adam had been professionally driven; he had raced through his graduate program and already had been head of the English department at the school where he had taught. Nick saw his own job as the means to an end, a tolerable but mundane task to which he had committed so that he could enjoy his true interests on his off time. Adam had researched neighborhoods and school districts where he thought he and Meredith would like to buy a house one day; Nick had moved around haphazardly, renting whatever space was available where he needed it. Adam had liked to examine problems and carefully work them out; Nick saw things more simply and relied largely on common sense.

With these thoughts tumbling around in her mind, she went through the motions each day, trying not to look at Nick as they ate breakfast together, settling in at work, administering her exams amidst grumbling and knuckle cracking, and returning home to chug through her stacks of scribbled penmanship and to calculate her grades. The days passed without incident, her students handling the stress of exams with impressive fortitude; Meredith had to comfort only one crying student this year, and she received no phone calls from any parents.

On Christmas Eve, they headed over to Tara's. Tara was on her best behavior, refraining from teasing and double entendres of any kind. Meredith relaxed with relief and with a nice cocktail, content to be with Tara and her happy family. She loved doting on Tara's sweet daughters, and she was pleased that Tom, Vince, and Nick got along so well.

After dinner, Meredith helped Tara clear the dishes while the girls played in front of the Christmas tree. The men stood to help, but Tara insisted they remain in the living room to chat.

Once she and Tara were in the kitchen, Meredith knew why. Tara pulled her into a corner and asked how things were going.

"Great," Meredith said, not even trying to keep the gushing emotion out of her voice. "It's amazing. He's amazing. I'm so happy." She was startled to feel the welling of tears.

"Oh Merry, that's fabulous."

"I love where we are right now. It's so easy and comfortable. He's helped me so much, in ways I can't even explain."

Tara clasped her hands together as she listened, her face contorting with happiness.

"He's opened up so much to me," Meredith went on. "He's still the same quiet, gentle person—but now I see the man behind it." She shrugged. "And I really like what I see."

"It's a credit to you too, honey. He's opened up to you because he knows that he can."

"And I love that he has. I love that he trusts me. There's some sort of understanding between us. When we're together, it's like we escape the stresses of everyday life."

"I'm so happy for you. If anyone deserves it, you do."

"The only problem is Vince," Meredith said, frowning.

"You still haven't figured out what to do about that?"

"No," Meredith answered, looking at Tara inquisitively.

"Don't ask me," Tara said. "You know your brother better than I do. At some point you're going to have to tell him, though. You know that, don't you?"

"Yes, of course. I just..." She sighed. "I just don't want this to end. I know once we tell Vince, things are going to change. It will be a lot more tense around the house."

"At least you'll have Nick to help you forget your troubles."

They finished cleaning and dried their hands. Tara held Meredith's arm back as she prepared to join the others.

"Are you okay?" she asked. "I know this is a hard time of year for you."

"I'm wonderful," Meredith assured her with a smile. "I have many welcome distractions." She kissed her friend's cheek. "Thank you for asking."

"I'm glad you met Nick when you did. You needed him now."

"Tara," Meredith said, her eyes wide and deep with sincerity. "He's brought me back to life."

"And I love him for that," Tara said, returning the kiss.

Vince, Nick, and Meredith stayed through dessert and then headed home, wishing everyone a merry Christmas and a safe trip to Virginia. Vince surprised Meredith and Nick by dropping them off and telling them he'd be home by Christmas, then wishing them a good night before speeding off alone.

"Well," Meredith said as she and Nick stood on the sidewalk. "I guess he and Sandy are going to have their own little celebration."

"Good for them. I think we should go celebrate, too."

They wrapped their arms around each other's waists and went into the house.

They enjoyed a delightful, enthusiastic night together, grateful that for once they had no need to keep their voices down. Meredith brazenly made a trip to the kitchen wearing nothing but Nick's shirt, returning with a bowl of grapes and some water, which the two of them shared happily in bed. They rolled around playfully, laughing as they teased and joked with each other. Finally, they fell into a deep, contented sleep.

They were awakened by the sound of someone pounding on the front door. They sat up in bed simultaneously, confused and alarmed. Meredith glanced at her nightstand; the clock told her it was just shy of three o'clock in the morning.

"Wait here," Nick whispered, patting her hand and kissing her forehead. He slid out of bed and into his pants, then glided out of the room and down the stairs.

Frightened, Meredith waited, straining her ears. She heard the front door open. Immediately she heard frantic shouting, but to her surprise it was the voice of a woman. Cocking her head, she realized the voice was Sandy's. She jumped out of bed and threw on her bathrobe, determined to find out what was going on.

Peering over the railing, she saw that Sandy was in the house, crying and shaking, while Nick was shutting the door behind her.

"Sandy?" Meredith said with concern as she hurried down the stairs. "What's wrong? What are you doing here?"

"He's with another woman," Sandy shouted through tears. Her face was red, and her makeup, usually perfect, was smudged and runny. "I know he is. I thought I'd catch them here."

Meredith had the feeling she had had too much to drink. She directed her eyes toward the window and saw that the car sitting out front had its headlights on and that two women inside were peering at the house to see what was happening.

"He's not here," Meredith told her as she approached the doorway. "We thought he was with you."

Sandy stared at her. "Is that what he said?"

"No, he just said he was going out."

Sandy pouted and began crying again. She dabbed at her eyes and nose with an already overextended tissue. "Well, he wasn't with me. I've been with my friends all night. He was supposed to join us, but I never heard from him. When I called him an hour ago, a woman picked up."

Meredith's face hardened. She guessed she should have prepared herself for this; she'd known it would be coming, but she'd been too preoccupied to think much about it. She had no doubt about what would happen next. She'd comfort Sandy, finding just the right words to express kindness while being careful not to criticize her brother; then she'd field weeks of questions, sent via desperate text messages or midnight phone calls, until Sandy, like Vince, moved on to the next thing. Though Meredith had been through it many times before, and while it had been vaguely frustrating, it had been mostly harmless, and she'd tolerated it. This time, though, it was different; this time, the harm was real. The anticipation of this drama nauseated her.

"I'm sorry, Sandy," she said, the exhaustion more evident in her voice than she'd expected.

"Yeah, I'm sorry too." She blew her nose. "Did he give you any indication of where he was going? He didn't mention our plans at all?"

Meredith shook her head but said nothing. She could not go through this again. She glanced at Nick. He was watching Sandy with a frown. She went to him, standing close enough to feel his breath on her face.

"I can't believe he did this to me again," Sandy was saying, scrolling through her phone and, evidently finding nothing from Vince, shaking her head with disgust. "I just can't believe he keeps doing it. Every time we get back together, it's the same thing. I don't know why I put up with it. It never changes. I mean for him to keep making the same old promises, convincing me this time will be different, and then to continue to cast me aside like this, it's just—it's just—" She paused, looking at Nick and Meredith with an odd expression on her face. Her forehead creased, and her eyes rounded with understanding.

Meredith stepped away from Nick. She looked down at herself. She was wearing nothing but her bathrobe, tied hastily at her waist, and her hair was mussed and knotted. Nick was wearing only his dress slacks and belt, and while he at least had zipped up and buttoned the pants, the belt stuck out in an unseemly fashion from his waist, not having been dealt with at all before he opened the door. His hair was in even worse condition than hers, sticking up awkwardly in places and falling almost comically straight in others.

"Oh, my God," Sandy uttered as she covered her mouth with her hand.

"Sandy," Meredith began, but she knew it was no use.

"Don't 'Sandy' me. What is with you people? Here's Vince running off with every woman in sight while the two of you sneak around behind his back. I've never seen such a mess. I'm out of here." Sandy promptly turned away, storming out and slamming the door.

Meredith let her go. There was nothing she could do. She knew that no amount of begging would convince Sandy to keep her relationship with Nick a secret; if Sandy was inclined to tell Vince, she was going to do it no matter what Meredith did or said. Begging probably would only make it worse. Now all she could do was sit back and wait, and hope.

She turned to Nick. He was standing very still. She glided gloomily to him and rested her head on his chest. He brought his hands to her shoulders and kissed her softly.

"Nick," she said.

He lifted her chin so she was looking at him, then brushed his knuckles across her cheek. A gentle smile crossed his lips. "We wanted to tell him anyway. Maybe it's for the best."

"But I'm not ready for that confrontation just yet." She and Vince had just gotten to know each other again; the gap he'd left during their estrangement was finally refilling, and she'd finally felt complete. She was overwhelmed by a sensation of sinking; her heart seemed to fold in on itself, consuming her from the inside out. "I can't stomach the thought of something coming between us now that he's back in my life after all this time. And he'll be furious if he thinks we were hiding it from him."

"I guess we'll find out in the morning."

Sighing, she nodded as he led her upstairs, pausing in front of her door.

He seemed to be waiting for an invitation, to be told it was okay. She smiled ruefully: it was quintessential Nick. Despite her worry, she was comforted. She sighed again, resigned. Whatever would happen, would happen; there was no point in secrecy now. And she was tired of being afraid to live her life.

"Come on," she told him, taking his hand, pulling him inside. She closed the door, shutting out the world, and her worries, for the night. Why not, she figured. Both would still be there tomorrow.

CHAPTER NINE

CONFRONTATION

*M*eredith finally fell back to sleep after staring into space for a long time. She knew that if Sandy told Vince about her relationship with Nick, the romance would change. Vince couldn't stop them from being together; however, Meredith dreaded the tension that would flood the house if he were to find out that she had not only ignored his advice but also hidden it from him. She would miss the carefree innocence of the last two weeks, the ease with which she and Nick were getting to know each other and the joy of renewing her relationship with her brother. Things were just getting back to normal; she was finally feeling right. She was terrified by the thought of normalcy being once again disrupted, of having to pick up any more pieces.

When she awoke on Christmas morning, Nick wasn't beside her, but she heard him puttering around downstairs. She guessed he'd risen early on the chance Vince was home, to put off the confrontation as long as possible. She took her time getting dressed, fearful of what was going to happen. Finally she couldn't put it off any longer. She sucked in her breath and walked with assumed confidence downstairs.

Nick was sitting at the dining room table mechanically sipping a cup of coffee with a newspaper in front of him, though he looked distracted; she doubted he had read a word of it.

"Hi," he said, sitting up straight and smiling at her as she walked into the room. "Vince isn't home yet," he added, and leaned his head back as she kissed him. "Merry Christmas."

"Merry Christmas to you too," she said pleasantly. A wry smile crept onto her face. "I gathered Vince wasn't home yet; I didn't hear any screaming."

"Maybe Sandy won't say anything."

"Only time will tell," she said, and headed to the kitchen for her coffee.

As she poured the coffee, she heard a car pull up in front of the house. Peeking out the window, she saw that it was Vince's. She braced herself.

"He's here," she said from the kitchen, unable to move. This was it, the moment of truth.

Meredith heard Vince march up the walkway. The door opened, then closed loudly behind him as he entered the house. He stalked right into the dining room, not bothering to take off his coat. Meredith stepped into the doorway of the kitchen, watching.

"Hey, Vince," Nick said casually. "How was the rest of your night?"

"Cut the crap."

Meredith's heart sank.

Nick rose slowly to face Vince. "Excuse me?"

Vince's voice was hoarse with repressed, barely controlled anger. "Just cut the crap and tell me how long you've been fucking my sister."

Everyone froze. Vince's words hung in the air like an echo, the sound of the one important word lingering long after it had been said.

"Two weeks," Nick said, his face devoid of expression.

"Two weeks," Vince repeated. His eyes blackened. "That's almost exactly how long we've been here."

"Yes."

"So you've been sneaking around together since the very beginning."

"That's right."

Meredith was horrified. Her mouth was dry. She realized that it had been hanging open, and she closed it with effort. Her eyes were wide with shock. She gripped her coffee in her hand, terrified she would drop it to the floor.

Vince turned to her. "Do you want to explain why you flat out lied to me?"

She stared at him, unsure of what to say and unable to find her voice anyway. Her heart was racing, but her mind stood frighteningly still. She tried to pull herself together. She squared her shoulders in an attempt to appear strong and unperturbed.

Vince was glaring at her, his eyes sharp with anger. She looked at Nick. He was remarkably composed. His long lips were straight, and his eyes focused on hers. His brows were slightly furrowed, giving his expression a more serious appearance; otherwise, he did not appear flustered by Vince's words. As she looked at him, his face melted almost imperceptibly into the soft expression she now found so comforting. His eyes creased at the corners with a smile; they encouraged and supported her, telling her everything would be okay. Fortified by this subtle communication, she turned her attention back to Vince.

"This is none of your business," she said quietly but firmly.

Vince's jaw elongated. She could see his chest heaving as he tried to control himself. "It's my business when I've made clear to you how I feel about it."

Meredith was silent for a moment as she attempted to gather her thoughts.

Vince was shaking his head with disgust. "You two must think I'm pretty stupid," he said, then lifted his burly arm and pointed his finger angrily at Meredith. "I knew something was going on between you two. I've seen the way you look at each other. I just didn't think it had gotten this far."

"What is the big deal, Vince?" Meredith asked, annoyed out of her shock by Vince's condescending tone. "I'm not a child. I'm capable of making my own decisions. I just don't see what this has to do with you."

"Well, for starters, he's supposed to be my friend, and he shouldn't be sneaking around with my sister behind my back," he shouted, his eyes now pointed at Nick.

"That's not his fault," Meredith said. "He wanted to tell you. I—"

"Then there's the fact that I've told you that he's not right for you. And don't tell me I don't know what I'm talking about," he said, cutting off Meredith, who had opened her mouth and put her hand in the air, ready to protest. "I know more about it than you think—just ask Mom and Dad. Do you really want to be with someone who drifts from place to place in a dead-end job, someone with no goals and no prospects? Someone who could have been something but instead is going nowhere? What kind of a life is that? Not a glamorous one, Merry, take it from me. Just trust me on this. I'm saving you from yourself."

"Then that's what this is about." Meredith was shaking; she wasn't used to fighting, and she was terrified that every word they said would make reconciliation less and less possible, but she was angry, and she was hurt—for herself and on Nick's behalf. "It has nothing to do with Nick, or even with me. You're unsatisfied with your own life, and you're projecting it onto me."

"You don't get it. I'm trying to protect you."

"No, you're not. You're trying to undo what you see as your own mistakes."

"You told me nothing was going on. You told me if you trusted me, you'd tell me."

"What was I supposed to do?" She was growing frantic; she

could sense they were about to say things they'd regret, but she didn't know how to stop it. "You put me on the spot. You made it impossible for me to answer."

"You agreed with me, Merry. You told me keeping it a secret would mean you don't trust me."

"Well, what did you expect?" She was breathing hard now, her face burning. She couldn't believe the words that were coming out of her mouth. "Why would I trust you after everything that happened? You think having my 'trust' means you can just move on from what happened. It'll make you feel better. But trust is earned."

"You insisted it was fine! You said it over and over. Every time I bring it up, you tell me not to worry."

"Maybe it bothered me more than I knew." Tears sprang to her eyes, and she blinked them back. "Maybe I didn't want to admit it to myself. It was one less thing for me to deal with."

This seemed to hit home. The darkness in his face changed, somehow, the anger in his eyes weakening into something more like pain. Meredith ached for him, but she was angry, now, herself.

"It's not about me, or Nick," she said, her voice shaking. "You're trying to alleviate your guilt."

"And what if I am?" Vince's voice grew louder, and Meredith jumped back. "Just because it's true, it doesn't mean it's wrong."

"Vince." Momentarily, Meredith's anger subsided; she was transported backward six years, to the day her brother told their father he was quitting his job, the day he told her he was lost. She'd seen how much pain he'd been in that day, the look on his face as he stood up to their father and how much of a risk his decision had been. "I can understand why this is important to you. But that's on you. I'm a different person. And besides, we're not even talking about huge life changes. We're talking about a relationship. Why does it matter to you so much?"

"Because relationships lead to changes. Come on, Merry, don't be so naive."

Meredith frowned. She knew his behavior was deeply rooted in insecurity, and she had almost been inclined to forgive him, until this condescending accusation.

"I'm not naive," she told him. "I'm just not so cynical. Don't worry about me. I can be relied on to make good decisions."

"Exactly. Which is why you should be with someone reliable. Not someone like Nick. Someone like Adam."

Meredith froze, astounded that Vince had hit her there.

Vince was silent for a moment, then said, his voice more even, "I'm sorry, Merry. But it's true."

"Well," Meredith said calmly, but her voice was shaky. She lifted her chin a little in defiance, attempting confidence. "I'd appreciate it if you wouldn't tell me how to run my life. I've made it this far without your help. I don't need you to come back after all these years and tell me what to do."

"What the hell does that mean?"

"You know what it means. You weren't there for me last year; you've said so yourself. It's the reason we're having this argument in the first place. So you have no right to waltz in here and tell me what is right for me and for my life."

"How wasn't Vince there for you?" interjected Nick.

Vince and Meredith stood motionless, as if time had stopped.

Their silence increased Nick's curiosity. "Meredith, how wasn't Vince there for you?" he asked again.

Meredith took a deep breath. "Vince wasn't there for me when Adam died," she said, her voice low and even. Though she was talking to Nick, her eyes were intent on Vince.

"What do you mean?"

Meredith's jaw was clenched, her entire body numb. Her eyes were dark and burning with the tears she could feel rising in her.

"He didn't come to the funeral. In fact, he didn't come to me at all." The pounding of her heart was making her lightheaded. "I needed my brother." She swallowed back her emotion. "I couldn't even reach him. We spoke about it once, and he vanished."

Meredith did not know how Nick received this news; her eyes were fixed on Vince, who was breathing heavily. She had hoped that the sharpness of the words would reach her brother, showing him how out of line he was, but she couldn't read him. Her eyes shifted to Nick. He was staring at Vince. For once he was unable to keep his composure; his expression was stunned.

Meredith turned back to Vince. "Don't talk to me about Adam. You have no idea what we went through."

"You should be ashamed of yourself. How do you think he'd feel if he could see you acting this way?"

Meredith felt the breath leaving her lungs, and her eyes opened wide with disbelief. She put her hands on her hips in a gesture of challenge.

"Oh? And how am I acting?"

"Like a slut."

Meredith stepped backward as if Vince had physically hit her with the word. She was overcome with fury; she had been rendered speechless and motionless.

Nick, however, had become animated by Vince's insult. He stepped forward, his eyebrows furrowed sharply and his mouth turned down with anger. "Hey," he admonished, his voice fully impassioned. "Don't you ever talk to her like that again. I won't stand for it. Just who the hell do you think she is?"

"Who the hell do *you* think she is?" Vince asked with a dark laugh. "You don't even know her! You just met her."

"Apparently he knows more about me than you do," Meredith said, having found her voice. "Where do you come off, marching in here and throwing accusations around? Why don't we ask Sandy how 'reliable' you are, Vince? I'd love to hear her answer." She shook her head. "You call me a slut, and yet you slink off with a different woman every night. It's a double standard, and it's disgusting."

"It's different with those women, Meredith! None of them

expect anything from me; none of them want me to be something I'm not."

"I'll tell you what, Vince. You call up Sandy and ask her what she expects from you. Her expectations couldn't be higher—it's why she keeps coming back, time and time again. You hypocrite," she spat. "You dare to come in here and tell me what to do, when the reality is you're the last one who should be offering advice."

"Sandy should know better," he said, his voice reflecting his irritation. "I never made her any promises.'"

"Please, Vince. With you it's line after line after line. You do everything in your power to convince women you care about them, just so you can get what you want. You move from one woman to the next without a backward glance."

"And you think he doesn't?" Vince exploded, extending his arm and pointing an angry finger at Nick. "You think he's so different? You don't think you're just another woman to him? You don't think you'll end up alone? Face it, Meredith—you're no better than Sandy."

Meredith shook her head with disbelief. She turned to Nick. His jaw was firm, and his eyes, fixed on Vince, were serious.

"You shouldn't talk about things you don't know about," he said, his tone more annoyed than angry. "It isn't anything like that."

"Come on," said Vince. "You act like we don't pick up women everywhere we go, like I haven't watched you do the same thing a hundred times. And you expect me to sit around and watch you use my sister too?"

"I've never 'used' anybody. It just didn't work out. I don't believe in leading someone on if it isn't going anywhere."

"That's bullshit, and you know it. You've never stuck with any woman any longer than I have."

"I can't help it if I'm meeting all the wrong women. They want all the wrong things. Maybe that's the problem, that I'm looking in all the wrong places."

"This being one of them."

Nick turned to Meredith. His voice grew earnest, and his eyes softened. "Please, Merry," he pleaded. "Don't listen to him. I've never felt this way about anyone." His chest rose and fell a couple of times. His expression then hardened, his jaw set and his mouth straight. "I can't make you believe me, but I hope you'll use your judgment. I'm not perfect. But I'm always honest."

Meredith believed him, her instinct telling her this wasn't a line, that everything they had experienced together had been real. She didn't care what his past looked like. She could go only by what she knew of him from her experiences with him, living with him and talking intimately with him, lying with him in the dark and getting to know him as they opened up their lives to each other. She had seen disappointment in her life, and she believed she knew sincerity when she saw it. She might be vulnerable and gentle-minded, but despite what Vince might have thought, she was not naive.

She returned his gaze confidently, smiling and cocking her head with fondness. His face lit up with relief, and he went to her, placing his hand on her shoulder and kissing the top of her head. Meredith was unused to openly sharing affection with him, and the freedom felt glorious.

Vince was shaking his head, disbelieving and defeated. "I just thought you were smarter than this, Meredith," he said, and turned to walk toward the front door.

She followed him, leaving Nick behind to wait for her. Vince walked out the front door and paused, turning to her.

"So this is how we're leaving it, then?"

"I guess it is," she replied, and brought her hand to the door. "You know where to find me when you're ready to apologize." She slammed the door in his face.

❦

MEREDITH STOOD FACING THE DOOR, dumbstruck, for several moments before finding the strength to turn back toward the house. As she did, Nick walked from the dining room to the entryway. He embraced her and held her close as they let the last few minutes sink in. He pulled away, his arms around her waist and his hands knotted at the small of her back. He looked at her, a gentle smile in his eyes.

"It'll be okay."

Meredith nodded. "I know."

"Just give him time to cool off. He'll come around."

She nodded again but said nothing.

He held her silently, stroking her between her shoulders and brushing his lips against the top of her head. Meredith closed her eyes and sighed.

"So now what?" she asked, beginning to feel a little calmer.

"Let's go to the movies."

Startled, she pulled away and stared at him.

"The movies? Of all things, why the movies?"

He shrugged. "Isn't that what normal couples do when they have no other plans?"

She smiled, considering seriously now what her confrontation with Vince meant for her and Nick. She thought about all the things they had missed out on because they had been required to keep their romance a secret, all the things normal couples take for granted. She realized that now they would be able to indulge in all those experiences. He wouldn't have to leave her room at night anymore; she could wake up in his arms every morning. Her sense of doom dissipated. She grew excited.

She kissed him, her hands pressing his face. "Thank you," she said.

"What for?"

"For being so reasonable. For bringing me back to reality. For putting everything in perspective." Her eyes grew warm with affection. "For making me happy."

His hands drifted to her face, which he cupped gently as he moved in and kissed her. Her eyes were closed, and she sighed again, feeling pleasantly lightheaded.

He spanked her playfully, breaking the spell. "Go get ready," he said. "We have a date."

CHAPTER TEN

THE PERFECT PEACE

*M*eredith had never been to the movies on Christmas, but the way her Christmases had been going she felt she'd might as well try something new.

Nick drove her car, obeying her directions on where to turn and squeezing her shoulder at the red lights. She flipped on the radio. Christmas music chirped happily in the background.

Meredith was grateful to be able to relax. She was resigned to making the most of the fact that her secret was now public knowledge by enjoying her time with Nick to the fullest. She'd worry about Vince later.

They pulled into the parking lot of the movie theater. Nick took her hand and led her inside where, bristling after the cold, they stood, hand in hand, gazing up at the screen, deciding what to see.

"I've never heard of most of these," she said, shaking her head.

"Me neither."

"What are you in the mood for?"

"Anything. How about that one—'Darkness of Night'?"

"Sounds as good as any other," she said, shrugging.

They bought a large tub of popcorn and found their theater,

which already was filling quickly. Choosing two seats on the side, they listened to the chattering crowd, the tub of popcorn between them and leaning toward each other as if sharing a secret. Their hands bumped each other as they reached for the popcorn, and their knees rubbed each other playfully.

When the movie started, his hand abandoned the popcorn and reached around her shoulder. Meredith felt giddy, like a teenager on her first date.

They had had no idea what the movie would be about and groaned when they realized it was a gory horror film whose target audience appeared to be high school-aged kids. They sat through the loud exclamations from the audience, casting each other amused glances at the superfluous blood and violence and the half-hearted special effects. As the movie went on, they began to enjoy themselves, getting caught up in the far-fetched plot and commenting with the rest of the audience. Meredith laughed when, during the climactic conclusion, Nick cried out with disgust as the movie's heroine suffered a brutal blow. As the lights rose and the credits rolled, he shook his head with disbelief, but his face wore a lighthearted grin.

"I'm getting too old for this kind of thing," he said.

They stood, stretched, and hurried out to the car, holding each other to fight the cold. They decided to go out for a late lunch, Meredith blithely abandoning her big plans for Christmas dinner. As they walked hand in hand into the restaurant, she again was surprised to find that they were far from alone, and they settled in to enjoy their meal alongside other carefree couples.

When they arrived home, Vince's car still wasn't there. Normally they would relish the fact that they had some time alone at the house; now it didn't seem to matter whether he was there or not. They strode up the walkway, arm in arm, and into the house, depositing their coats and shoes in the entryway. Nick promptly picked her up, sweeping her off her feet and eliciting from her a delighted squeal, and carried her upstairs to her bedroom, where he closed and locked the door behind them before falling on top of her on the bed. He slid his hands under her sweater, grabbing her flesh and squeezing her breasts, kissing her neck and warming her with his breath. She smiled and closed her eyes, running her fingers through his hair and over the taut muscles of his arms, chest, and back. He drew her sweater over her head and reached his arms high as he pulled off his own shirt. She undressed and slipped under the blanket while she waited for him to strip naked, his body a gray silhouette against the soft light peeking in from behind the curtains. He slid into bed with her and engulfed her in a heated, frantic embrace; his skin was smooth and warm, and she sighed as his arms and hands slinked around her back, enclosing her. He waited to enter her, teasing her by kissing her neck, shoulders, breasts, belly, and thighs, finally culminating with the tender, aching flesh between her legs. She gasped as his lips and tongue caressed her, digging and stroking and circling until she was delirious and desperate, her breathing fast and her hands grasping herself—at which point he stopped, swiftly brought his hips toward hers, and entered her, thrusting powerfully and needfully, groaning as her hands grabbed him from behind, pushing him deeper. They moved together perfectly, as two people who had been together enough times to have found their rhythm, and before long they reached sweet oblivion, falling together happily as they clutched each other, then slowing as they returned to the earth, their skin sweaty and vibrant and alive with delight. They almost immediately fell into a beautiful, deep sleep, during which they dreamed about each other and from which they awoke with joy, still in each other's arms.

"WHY DOES Vince think you're unreliable?" Meredith asked. He was lying on his back stroking her hair; her head was resting on his chest, her arm around his waist. She lifted her head to look at his face. "I'm sorry, Nick. I have to ask."

"It's all right. I understand," he said, smiling kindly, then looking away and closing his eyes. He took a deep breath. He opened his eyes. They were clear and calm.

"I think you had it right before. Vince has regrets about the direction of his own life," he said as his fingers toyed with her hair. "He thinks he's settling for less than what he could have had. He's not happy with the decisions he's made. He's just trying to make sure you make better ones."

Her heart thumping, she asked, "But what about women? Why did he say you're no different from him?"

"He's wrong about that. Yes, I've shifted around in the past. Maybe I haven't settled down as soon as I had hoped. I'm thirty-five years old, and I've never been really serious with anyone. But it isn't what he thinks it is. Mostly I'd just never met anyone I had enough in common with. I'd never met anyone who wanted the same things."

He paused for a moment, watching her carefully. She felt a little flutter in her chest.

"Have you ever been in love?" she asked.

"I guess not." His hand stroked the back of her head, drifting down to her shoulders and back, tickling her. She shivered. "The truth is, Merry—things start out okay and go downhill pretty quickly."

"Why is that?"

"Because these women I meet on the road, it always seems so empty with them. It's hard to have a real conversation about anything important."

Meredith thought about this and thought about him. "I think I know what you mean."

A smile touched his eyes. "I know you do."

They both sighed. Nick let his fingers drift up and down her arm.

"In any case," he said finally, "I've never deliberately hurt anyone, and I've never used anyone. Vince assumes everyone is like him, and he doesn't want his sister treated the way he treats women. He could never understand."

Meredith took a deep breath and looked away for a moment as visions of a younger Vince fluttered through her mind.

"Vince started dating really young," she said. A smirk lifted the corner of her mouth. "I shouldn't say 'dating.'"

"I know what you mean."

Her smirk melted; she turned serious once more. "I always felt he was using sex to feel alive. Relevant, even." She sighed. "Maybe partly as rebellion. But also as distraction."

"Distraction from what?"

"I know he's hidden a lot of pain," she said, wistfully. "He uses sarcasm to hide it, but my parents hurt him more than he'll ever admit. There was this one time...I'll never forget it. He was maybe twelve or thirteen, and he failed a math test. My father was livid when he found out, telling him he'd never make anything of his life if he didn't apply himself. To try to compensate, Vince showed him an art project his teacher had praised." She frowned at the memory. "My father pushed it away without so much as looking at it, asking if Vince expected him to be proud. He said he was wasting his time."

"Awful," said Nick, tucking her hair behind her ear. "I'm sorry."

"That's not the half of it. That night when I went to wish him goodnight, I couldn't find him for half an hour. I eventually discovered him sobbing in his closet, clutching scraps of paper. He had torn his art project to pieces."

Nick's face hardened. "Jesus."

"I picked up the pieces from the floor," she went on, tears gathering in her eyes. "He was too defeated to stop me. When I put them together, I saw the emotion on that page. I realized it then, even as young as I was. He was baring his soul in his art, in all the ways he couldn't at home." Her voice caught; Nick wiped a tear that was falling down her temple toward the pillow. "It must have killed him to be rejected like that."

"Poor kid." Nick watched his fingers thoughtfully as they smoothed her hair back. "I didn't know that about him. It makes sense. That's a lot for anyone to deal with, especially a teenager."

"Exactly." Meredith sighed as he tenderly rubbed the small of her back. "It's why I've always forgiven him for all his flaws and indiscretions. It's why I try to see people's motivations. I spent years trying to make up for it, filling the void left by my parents' lack of interest by telling him how talented he was and how proud I was of him. I didn't want him to feel like a failure. I wanted him to feel important."

"I understand." He laid a gentle kiss on her lips; he locked eyes with her, and smiled sadly. "I'd do the same thing."

She remained silent a moment as he kissed her forehead. "It makes me sad to think he feels he's not good enough," she said then, looking at him again. "But it makes me mad that he apparently feels the same way about you."

"It's okay. I know it's not really about me."

Meredith nodded, her face somber.

Her thoughts took a turn. She smiled.

"How about you?" she asked, kissing his nose. "Did you start dating early?"

"Hardly. I was a late bloomer."

She pulled back to look at him, surprised. "Were you?"

"I was shy."

Meredith was charmed. Her face crumpled with affection, and she stroked his face with her fingers. He nuzzled closer, and she kissed the top of his head, his hair tickling her lips.

Her smile faded as her thoughts turned once again to Vince. "I wish I had told him earlier," she said. "I hate that he found out this way. You were right that keeping it a secret only made it worse."

"Vince will be okay," he said, closing his eyes again. "It won't hurt him to have some time to himself to think. You'll talk it out, eventually. And in the meantime, I'm glad we had those two weeks."

"Me too." She felt satisfied.

He opened his eyes and looked at her, his face more serious. "He needs to apologize for what he said to you. It was wrong."

"I know." Meredith frowned. "On several levels. I mean, the accusation itself shouldn't even be an accusation."

"Right." He took a deep breath and brushed her cheek with his finger. "Whatever the level, you didn't deserve it. I hope you know that."

"Thanks," she said, smiling. "I know that." Her smile turned into a smirk as she slid her hand between his legs. "Well, maybe I did just a little bit."

"Tell me more about Adam," he said as they lay facing each other, their eyes drifting open and closed, their fingers lightly touching each other's faces.

Meredith said nothing for a moment or two. "What do you want to know?"

Nick shrugged. "I don't know. Anything."

Meredith didn't know what to say. "He was a very good teacher."

"What else?"

"He loved the theater. He knew a lot about art."

"Just like you."

She furrowed her brow. "Why do you want to know all this?"

Nick took a lock of her hair between his fingers and twirled it. He brushed the end of it across her lips, and they both smiled. "No particular reason. I guess I'm just curious to know what kind of man Vince thinks is 'reliable' enough for his sister."

Meredith chuckled. "You're worried about what Vince thinks makes a person reliable?"

"I didn't say I was worried."

Meredith's face turned more serious. "It's funny that Vince is always railing against our parents' criticism, yet he's the first to agree with them when it comes to telling me what to do with my life."

"If your parents have high standards, it's probably just because they want the best for you."

"I'm not so sure about that. I was a very convenient public relations tool for my father, being a teacher."

"He must feel strongly about education, though."

"Of course. But if he felt strongly about the space program, I'd be an astronaut."

"I'll bet he was thrilled that you were going to marry a teacher."

"Oh, he was, especially since Adam was about to become a Ph.D, had interviewed my father for his dissertation, and was writing articles for *The Philadelphia Times*. My father pulled some strings for Adam to have some guest spots."

"Adam sounds pretty great. I can see why everyone loved him so much."

"My father certainly did. I think he looked forward more to seeing Adam than to seeing me. My grandfather was a city councilman. My father had this grand fantasy that Adam would top that by serving as Commissioner of Education."

They said nothing for a few moments. Nick watched his fingers as they twirled her hair.

"How about your mother?"

"When Adam died, my mother was more interested in whether I still planned on entering the doctoral program than she was about whether I could sleep at night."

Nick's eyes met hers. "I'm sorry."

She softened. "It's okay," she said, and kissed him. "They are who they are, and I've accepted it. I learned long ago not to let them bother me. Thankfully I don't depend on them for comfort."

They each took a deep breath and lay in silence for some time. Savoring the safety of their embrace, Meredith let her eyes drift shut. When she looked at him again, she found that his eyes had been wide open. He appeared to be staring into nothingness.

"You seem lost in thought," she said with a smile, bringing her hand to the side of his face and letting her thumb delicately trace the outline of his jaw. "What are you thinking about?"

He met her gaze and returned her smile. He kissed her lips and tucked her hair behind her ear. "Nothing."

"Are you sure?"

He stroked the corner of her eye with his thumb, letting it then graze over her temple. She sighed contentedly. "It's nothing," he said again. "Just how accomplished your family is."

"Accomplishment is subjective." Meredith snuggled in closer. "Let's talk about your family," she said, and rubbed his back with her fingers. "Tell me about your mother."

"She was a very good cook."

"She was?" Meredith asked, delighted.

"Yes. She used to enter bake-offs all the time, and she always won. Strawberry pie was her specialty. She baked it with strawberries she grew in her own garden. She was very proud of it." Abruptly he laughed. "My father used to joke that he wanted to die first, just because he couldn't live without her pie."

A wave of affection rushed through her. "Your family sounds so different from mine."

He smiled. "We're small-town folk. Not like your sophisticated parents."

"I didn't mean it like that. I mean it sounds like your family was very close."

"My parents grew up in the same small town and went to the same high school. Their families knew each other well. My grandmothers volunteered in the same soup kitchen, and my grandfathers used to play poker together every Thursday night. In fact, it was a running joke between them that my mother was forced to marry my father because her own father lost her in a poker game."

Meredith laughed. "There were a lot of jokes in your family."

"Yes, there were," he said, joining in her laughter. "Not so many anymore, though, now that most of them are gone."

They passed some more time in silence.

Nick said, "Why didn't Vince to go the funeral?"

Meredith's face turned solemn, and she stroked his cheek. "He never told me. I think he just couldn't handle it."

"I would have gone if I had known."

She felt her eyes grow misty. "I know."

He drew her gently in and kissed her forehead. "I want to be there for you now, though."

She looked at him then. Tears welled in her eyes in spite of her attempt to hold them back. "You already have," she said, her voice trembling. "And more."

∽

THEY WERE SITTING in the living room, Meredith in red flannel pajamas, Nick in sweatpants and a t-shirt. They were snuggled together under a fluffy blanket in the middle of the couch, Nick's arm around her shoulder and her head resting on his chest. Meredith was reading a lighthearted paperback while Nick dozed, his head leaning against the back of the couch.

The doorbell rang, rousing them. Meredith turned her head toward the door while Nick stood and walked to the entryway. She heard the door open and a woman's voice greet him politely. It was Sandy.

Meredith rose to her feet but stood still where she was. Within seconds, Sandy entered the room, Nick behind her. Sandy was looking at Meredith, her eyes searching for a hint of how she was about to be received. There was a moment of awkward silence.

Nick said he was going to take a shower and walked out of the room. Sandy waited until his footsteps had faded before speaking.

"Meredith, I'm so sorry. Can you ever forgive me?"

Meredith sighed. "Of course I can forgive you, Sandy," she said, motioning for Sandy to sit down with her on the couch.

Sandy sat next to Meredith, but faced her, one foot on the floor and the other tucked beneath her. Tears gathered in her eyes as she spoke. "I was trying to hurt Vince by telling him about you and Nick," she said, wiping the tears with the back of her hand. "I never meant to hurt you." She sniffled. "I shouldn't have said to you what I said last night. I'm so embarrassed. I was upset, and I took it out on you. I've been in agony about it all day."

Meredith smiled sadly. "I appreciate that, Sandy. Thank you for coming here." She sighed again. "Don't beat yourself up over it. It's good that Vince found out. It had to happen at some point."

"Thank you," Sandy said meekly, with a frown. "I hope it wasn't too terrible. He was furious when he left this morning."

"It was pretty bad," Meredith said, bristling again as she recalled his insult. "But Vince is an emotional person. I'm sure he'll calm down and see reason soon enough." She didn't know who she was trying to convince, Sandy or herself.

"He came by my place early this morning," Sandy said, her voice more steady. "He gave me a song and dance, trying to explain what happened last night." She rolled her eyes. "He was pretty mad when I didn't buy it."

"Vince doesn't care if you buy it, Sandy," Meredith said gently. "He only cares if you give him a hard time about it."

"Well, I gave him a hard time about it. I said it was always the same, that he always made all these promises and they never came true, that it was like he was telling me whatever was convenient so he could have a good time before taking off in the end."

"What did he say?"

"He said it wasn't his fault that I had made assumptions, that it was stupid of me to have any expectations and that I needed to open my eyes." She shook her head and looked away. "That's when I told him if anyone should open their eyes, it was him, because..."

Meredith flinched, unable to keep a grimace from creeping onto her face.

"Well," she said, with effort, "it's over now. No need to fixate on it." She took a deep breath. "How did you leave it with Vince?"

"He said I could call him when I had calmed down. Then he left."

Meredith shook her head. "Typical."

Sandy looked at her frankly. "Tell me the truth, Meredith. Do you think he's been playing me all this time?"

Meredith returned her gaze. "Yes."

Sandy shook her head. "I can't believe I'm so stupid."

"No," Meredith gently scolded, leaning forward and placing her hand on Sandy's. "Don't do that to yourself. You can't judge yourself based on one situation. Besides, you're not the first woman to fall for Vince's act, and you won't be the last. He knows all the tricks." She leaned back and crossed her arms over her chest. "My brother is a good person. I love him dearly, but he has no respect for women."

"He has respect for you. You should have seen how worried he was when he found out what's been going on."

"He's only thinking about how it affects him."

"That's not it," Sandy insisted. "He adores you, Meredith. He was so excited when he was picking out those flowers for you. He kept talking about how much you've done for him and how much you've been through, and how he was finally going to be able to repay you. I can't tell you how many times he's described you as 'the perfect sister.'"

Meredith listened skeptically, but her eyes had begun to soften.

"That's why he was so upset this morning," Sandy went on. "He just wants to make sure you don't get hurt. Maybe he goes about it the wrong way, but he means well." She frowned, then sniffed. "When it comes to you, at least."

"Yeah, well." Meredith's nose curled a little with distaste. "I'm starting to realize that meaning well may not be enough." She took a breath. "But I do have trouble finding that balance, I guess."

A few moments of silence passed.

Sandy asked, "So I take it you don't think it'll change."

Meredith shook her head. "Honestly, I don't."

Sandy frowned. "I don't know where to go from here."

"I think that's up to you. I've just seen you go through this a dozen times; I can't see it working out any differently. You just have to decide if you want something casual or nothing at all."

Sandy thought about it. "I don't have anything against casual. I'd be okay with casual, except that I feel like it makes me look clueless."

"Who cares?" Meredith asked this question with more force than she had expected. She looked at Sandy thoughtfully. "Does it matter what other people think, really? If you want to do something, just do it because you want to, because it makes you happy. No one else knows what's right for you right now. Just do what makes you happy."

Meredith sat on her own words for a moment. They seemed even more important than she'd realized when she'd said them. The nagging thorn that had been twisting in her stomach seemed to fade a little, somehow.

"You're right." Sandy sat straighter, her expression brightening. "Thanks so much, Merry. I really appreciate it." She smiled. "I always liked you, you know. You always seem to have it all together."

Meredith laughed. "Well, I don't, at least not anymore."

"Why do you say that?"

Meredith shrugged but didn't say anything; she didn't want to get into it with Sandy. "Several reasons, I guess. I mean, look how I handled this situation with Vince."

"I thought you just told me I shouldn't judge myself based on one situation."

Meredith's lips upturned into a slow, wry smile. "You're right, Sandy. I did say that, didn't I?"

Sandy shifted further into the couch, assuming a more casual position. "You know what would really make everyone feel better," she said, grinning knowingly. "A party."

Meredith shook her head. "No, Sandy."

"Come on, it would be so much fun." Sandy tapped Meredith's knee. "I don't even mean for your parents. Just a party, with some friends."

"No." Meredith fidgeted nervously with the hem of her shirt. The nagging thorn was returning, and bile gathered in her gut. She was beginning to understand why she had been so resistant to Sandy this time around. It was because Sandy made her feel pressured, somehow—pressured to make small talk, pressured to be the person she was before, pressured to be someone she no longer was. It was ironic—but moving forward as the Meredith of five years ago was actually moving backward. And something about Sandy's repeated drama with Vince—drama Meredith herself always had to clean up after—seemed to pull her back to a chapter she had closed. She was trying to forge a new path, not continue on the old one; "normal" wasn't normal anymore.

Sandy was a person who never seemed to change. Watching Sandy make the same bad decision over and over made Meredith anxious. Repeating history was the opposite of what she needed.

The thorn inside her was twisting and gnawing; she wrapped her arms around her stomach, wishing it would stop. The situation just wasn't as complicated as her subconscious seemed to think it was; she was doing, clearly, just fine. Look at all the wonderful ways she was moving on!

Meredith took a breath against the wrenching of the thorn, and the moment passed. She turned her attention once again to Sandy. She tried to be sensitive; she knew Sandy really did mean well.

"Sandy, I don't want a party," she said, making her voice kind but firm. "It's just not something I can do right now. I really need you to understand that."

"Okay." Sandy's face had turned serious. "I understand. I won't ask you again."

"Thank you." Meredith offered a little smile.

They sat in silence for a moment or two, letting the conversation sink in.

"Well," said Sandy finally, "I should probably go." She looked at Meredith. "I guess I'll stick it out with Vince for now. I mean, as long as he's here. Might as well."

"Good. Just as long as you know what you're getting into."

"I do. Thanks." Sandy smiled. "And what about you?" She tapped Meredith's knee again. "You and Nick? How's that going?"

"Good." Meredith rubbed her lips together; she didn't really want to discuss it with Sandy and hoped Sandy wouldn't ask her any personal questions.

Thankfully, Sandy seemed content to keep her comments light.

"Well, I'm glad," she told her. She cocked her head. "Why were you keeping it a secret, anyway?"

"It's complicated." Meredith sighed. It seemed too much to explain, and she was growing tired of talking. "Vince and I had just reconnected, and I didn't want to jeopardize that. I just wanted everything to be perfect."

"It can still be perfect," said Sandy eagerly, and Meredith suspected she was trying to make up for having revealed the secret. "At least now you can be open about it."

"Yes." Meredith smiled politely. "Yes, I suppose that's true."

"I mean, you're practically perfect yourself," Sandy went on, with her usual ebullience. "I'm sure you'll end up with the perfect life."

"The perfect life," Meredith repeated, but she did not say any more. Somehow the word "perfect" now tasted different on her tongue. Life was messy, and beautiful, and heartbreaking, and unsure. If perfection did exist, it must be nuanced, as complicated as life itself.

Sandy stood and gathered her purse, then brought Meredith in for a hug. "Well, thanks again for your help, Merry. I really appreciate it. Hey, can I tell you a secret?"

"Sure."

Sandy pulled away and looked at her frankly. "I think I probably already knew what I was getting into. With Vince. I mean, there's definitely a pattern. I guess I just wanted things to be a certain way, and I let myself believe it."

"That's a courageous thing to say," said Meredith, a weight lifted; she knew the cycle was over. She smiled in earnest. "I'm glad you feel that way."

"It's tempting to delude yourself, you know? Like sometimes it's easier to lie to yourself than to work through the truth."

Meredith stared at her, sensing the importance of her words but not yet able to decipher what it was. She hadn't been denying the truth about anything—so why did Sandy's comment resonate so deeply inside her? She didn't have time to think about it, however; Sandy was waving goodnight. Meredith followed her through the entryway and closed the door behind her, sighing deeply, with relief, as she shut out the world beyond.

MEREDITH CREPT UPSTAIRS, having turned off all the lights and leaving the house in quiet, expectant darkness. Vince still wasn't home. Meredith had no idea when to expect him back, if at all. At the moment she really didn't care.

The shower in the hall bathroom was running; the light shone from under the door and into the dark hallway. Nick's bedroom door was closed, and no light shone from underneath. Meredith walked past this room until she reached the bathroom. Without hesitation, she turned the doorknob and let herself inside, locking it behind her.

She undressed quickly, letting her clothes fall to the floor in a heap. She tossed her hair out, then pulled the shower curtain from the wall and stepped inside.

She had been worried about startling Nick, but he seemed to have been expecting her. Instantly he began caressing her shoulders and back with his hands. Gazing up at him through the steam, she pressed herself to him as he leaned in and took her in a deep, blissful kiss.

NICK AND MEREDITH, wearing nothing but towels, hurried across the hall to her bedroom, unsure if Vince had returned during their shower. Meredith was determined not to hide from Vince, but she wasn't ready to let him see her and Nick emerging from the shower just yet.

The first thing Meredith noticed as she entered her room, Nick closing the door behind them as he followed, was a pair of blue cotton pajama bottoms folded neatly on the bed. Nick must have placed them in here before his shower, expecting to make her bedroom his last stop of the night. She smiled as she considered the prospect of spending all night with him, not feeling the lonely cold of his absence when he slid out of bed and left her each night.

The second thing Meredith noticed was a present sitting on

top of the pajamas. It was wrapped simply in red paper, and it was topped with a white bow.

He placed his hand on her back and gently nudged her forward. "Open it," he said softly.

She glided toward the bed and sat down. She took the present in her hands. It was about the size of a sheet of paper, and quite thin. She opened the sides and back of the paper, then placed it on the bed as she turned the gift over to look at it right side up.

It was a picture frame, bordered by a simple ribbon of silver. Inside the frame was a print. It was the Impressionist painting they had discussed at the art museum, the one in which the woman was holding a bouquet of roses.

Meredith's eyes widened, and her mouth dropped open. Her breathing quickened as she stared at the print, dumbfounded. She turned to Nick, who stood before her wearing his towel around his waist, his half-dried hair falling in blond clumps over his forehead and temples. His lips wore a wide grin.

"I love it," she said, looking back down at the frame. "Thank you." She stood and, placing the frame on the bed, wrapped her arms around his waist, nuzzling her face in his neck and stroking his back with her fingers. He smelled fresh and sweet after his shower, and she removed her face from his neck reluctantly. Her eyes met his. His face portrayed ill-concealed triumph; he was delighted by her reaction.

"Merry Christmas," he whispered.

"Merry Christmas," she repeated, tilting her head up for a kiss.

She pulled away from him, a sly smile on her face, and went to the top drawer of the dresser. She withdrew a white envelope, "Nick" written neatly in the center.

She handed it to him. He took it silently and slid his finger along the rim to open it. He pulled out a card, a simple winter scene with the words "Merry Christmas" in gold script.

He opened the card, pulling from it two tickets, which he momentarily ignored. He looked at the card. "To Nick, the best

Christmas present I could have asked for. Love, Merry," he read. He met her gaze for only a moment before turning his attention to the tickets. "The Villard Arboretum," he said quietly, reading the bold print. He looked at Meredith.

"It's one of my favorite spots for walking," she said. "I know you enjoy the outdoors, and you said you like winter activities." She shrugged. "I thought we could go together, you know, one day when—"

"It's perfect," he interrupted, his eyes round as he looked from the card to the tickets, and then finally to her. "Everything. Just perfect." He swallowed. "Thank you." His lips were turned into a little frown, but a smile touched his eyes.

She took the card and the tickets from his hand and placed them on top of the frame on the bed. She wrapped her arms around him again and was surprised when he did not reciprocate immediately. After a slight hesitation, he slowly embraced her, but he seemed distracted.

She looked up at his face. He was staring off to the side, his eyes still wide. He appeared to be deep in thought.

"Nick," she said, her brow furrowed curiously.

He met her gaze, but there was a faraway look in his eyes.

"Nick," she said again, more loudly this time, bringing her hand to his cheek. "What is it?"

His eyes bore into hers. "Nothing."

"Are you okay?"

Seeming to sense her worry, he snapped back to reality. "I sure am," he said, and embraced her in earnest. "I don't know that I've ever been better."

NICK AND MEREDITH climbed quietly into bed that night, switching off the light and lying contentedly next to each other, their legs intertwined and their arms around each other. Both of them were thoughtful, considering the repercussions of the day's events and trying to regroup so they could begin a new chapter in their relationship tomorrow. They had exchanged slow, intimate kisses and fallen into a comfortable sleep, happy that they could remain entwined in each other until morning.

After Nick fell asleep, his breath warm on her face and his chest heaving evenly against hers, Meredith thought about Adam, her eyes wide open as she allowed the memories to overcome her. She was thinking about the time she and Adam hosted a dinner party for Vince when he was visiting for the weekend. Meredith had invited some colleagues who had never met Adam before. One of these colleagues, Mark Bailey, had struck up a conversation with Adam and, glancing over, Meredith had noticed that Mark's face had been contorted into an expression of shock and alarm. Approaching, Meredith had heard Adam telling Mark about the trip to the Hamptons he and Meredith had taken, how wonderful it had been to wake up together to the sound of the ocean. Meredith had realized that Mark had incorrectly assumed that Adam was the brother for whom Meredith had thrown this party; laughing when she corrected him, he had told her she and Adam looked, sounded, and acted so much alike he hadn't even thought to ask.

She thought about how everything in their apartment had been set up in twos: two sets of black shoes under the table in the hallway, two stacks of student essays on the dining room table (topped with two red pens), two New York University coffee mugs hanging from hooks in the kitchen, two khaki-colored raincoats hanging in the closet, two copies of *The Great Gatsby* on the bookshelf, each marked with comments and conversation starters for their individual classrooms. She smiled as she recalled how friends used to jibe them affectionately when they went out to eat, for most of the time they ordered identically, from drinks to dessert.

Life with Adam had been perfect. Everything had been understood. There were never any miscommunications because they were so much alike and could anticipate each other's needs and desires. It had been a carefree, idyllic life. They enjoyed the same activities, and never argued about what to do in their free time. They both were neat and orderly, and never argued about housework. They had similar habits and philosophies regarding money and therefore never argued about finances. They could finish each other's sentences and therefore never suffered any misunderstandings.

Meredith had forgotten about his eyes. After he passed away she thought the image of them would never fade from her mind, the molten, warm look of them, how people could not help but instantly adore him, never failing to sense his gentle nature and his inherent goodness. They seemed to reach out, to invite people to confide in him and to assure them that he would have the answers they needed. Meredith knew his innate ability to relate to people was partly what had made him such a beloved teacher. He had exuded happiness, and people had been drawn to him, Meredith included.

The day they received his diagnosis, they had sat in shock in the car while they attempted to let the news sink in. She could vividly recall him staring straight ahead as they sat motionless in the parking lot of the hospital, his brown eyes wide and thoughtful. After many minutes of silence, she had placed her hand on his shoulder, bringing him back to the moment and making him turn in her direction. His eyes had bored into hers, and Meredith knew what he was thinking. He was thinking that he didn't know how many more times he would be able to look at her, and that it didn't seem possible that this could even be a question.

Meredith had lived in denial for several weeks, not knowing how she could go on without him and therefore refusing to consider it, convincing herself that if she didn't prepare for it, it wouldn't become a reality. As he had grown sicker, though, she had been forced to come to terms with what she knew instinctively was about to happen. They had attempted to go about their lives as normal, but Meredith couldn't look at him anymore without staring at him for minutes at a time. After five years in their blissful relationship, she had felt the need to cram a lifetime of happiness into the few months they had left.

Toward the end Meredith had steeled herself, making preparations and trying desperately to keep Adam as comfortable as possible. Adam, usually a life-loving, vibrant person, grew tired and troubled, and Meredith sensed when he had resigned himself to his fate. Struggling to keep his eyes open as he fought determinedly to look at her, he told her he loved her and ordered her to be happy. The day he passed away, Meredith had sat motionless in his hospital room, holding his hand and looking at him with concentration, talking to him through her mind and hoping and praying that in the inscrutable grandness of the universe he would find a way to hear her from wherever he was.

Vince had not gone to her. He had been gushing in his sympathy, but he had not rushed to her side as she had been hoping he would, in fact all but disappearing shortly after. Meredith's parents were genuinely bereaved; they had loved Adam, especially Harold, and they mourned with her at his funeral. When it was over, however, rather than comfort her or ask her what she needed, they had pressed her about her plans for the future and warned her not to take too much time from work; they'd spent what little time they had left with friends, then sped back off to who knows where, leaving Meredith alone. During this time, and the months after, in which she had been forced to adjust to life without Adam, her rock had been Tara, who gladly took late night phone calls and traveled frequently to New York to cook her dinners, accompany her to the grocery store, and even sleep with her in bed on nights when Meredith had been feeling particularly lonely. Tom had fully supported and encouraged Tara in her being there for her friend. Meredith had never been able to express to Tara and Tom how much their support had meant to her, how she felt she never would have made it through those months without them. She doubted she'd ever be able to do so.

Meredith had let herself grieve for a couple of months, finally packing away the pictures and other remnants of their life together, when it had become clear to her that she could grieve for a lifetime if she let herself. She bravely finished her school year, mechanically going through the motions of her day alone, merely trying to survive until she could start a new life where there were fewer memories. When her parents suggested they needed someone to watch the house as they took their next round of vacations, Meredith had figured the house where she had grown up would be just as good as any other house, for her to try to move on. At that point she was eager to be anywhere but where she was, and she had willingly taken on the responsibility. She started her school year fresh in a new job with new people and finally had begun to feel as if she was making a new life, albeit in a familiar place. Unfortunately she had found that she was a very different person than she had been the last time she had lived there, and she felt more out of place than ever.

Nick stirred in his sleep, moving his hand from her back to her waist and lifting his head slightly on the pillow. Meredith looked at him as he slept. Tender affection filled her heart. She realized as she gazed at him that she had not moved on with her life, that despite what she had told herself—despite her desperate attempts to appear as if she was okay, to others and to herself; despite her conviction that moving on meant she was strong—in fact she had been stuck in a half-life of grief that had stolen her enthusiasm and extinguished her optimism. She carefully brushed his hair back from where it was falling over his eyes. She sighed inwardly at how beautiful he was. Warmth filled her when she thought about his gentleness toward her, toward the world. She loved his kindness and his generosity. She loved his sharpness, his subtle wit and his refusal to be intimidated—by Vince, by unfamiliarity, by doubt, by the world. She loved the simplicity of his perspective, his respect for nature and for all that was beautiful. She loved how his calm composure deceptively hid a passionate enjoyment of life—of fun, of art, of food, of sex, of her. She had not shed a tear while reminiscing about her time with Adam, but as her eyes examined Nick as he slept, she found herself weeping silently, her pillow damp as if tears had been falling there for several minutes without her knowing. She knew instantly in her heart that she loved him, though the thought seemed absurd, seeing as she had met him such a short time ago. She didn't know where they were going, where life would take them or what the universe had in store for them—but she knew that whatever happened, she would never be the same. Nick had renewed her passion for life. He had reminded her that there was beauty to be found in every day, that one need not look so far to find it. He had shown her once again that she had a place in this world, that she was not meant to drone on mindlessly every day, that she was entitled to happiness. She loved him for giving her life back to her; she would always be grateful to him for that.

She listened to his peaceful, even breathing, feeling soothed and happy. Darkness still permeated the room, only a fragile sliver of moonlight shining from behind the curtains. Her eyelids had grown heavy; she decided to try to sleep. She took one last look at Nick. "I love you," she whispered as quietly as she could, to avoid waking him. She closed her eyes.

"I love you too," he whispered back, and drew her close before falling almost immediately back to sleep.

CHAPTER ELEVEN

THE SNOWY FIELD

The blue haze of dawn crept into Meredith's bedroom, its cozy glow sneaking along the wall. Meredith felt a gentle touch behind her ear and on her neck; she smiled as her body registered warm skin against hers. She opened her eyes and looked right into Nick's. He was tucking her hair behind her ear.

"Good morning," he whispered.

"Good morning."

He kissed her softly. "You look beautiful in the morning."

She laughed. "I doubt that."

"It's true," he said, and kissed her again.

In a flash she remembered what they had said the night before, and her heartbeat accelerated. She didn't know if she wanted to bring it up, unsure whether he had even been conscious when he had said it. He might not even remember. She decided to put it aside for now.

They lay in comfortable silence until the morning light turned golden, drawing them from their dreamy intimacy and making their senses more alert. Meredith encouraged him to collect his things from his room; he returned dragging his suitcase and carrying a pile of clothes over his arm. Together they organized his few clothes into her dresser and closet.

Meredith had no idea if Vince was home. As she stepped out into the hallway, she saw that his door was shut and that the light was off. She and Nick descended the stairs together, unsure of what to expect.

The house was quiet. They shrugged and went about their day.

They decided to visit the arboretum with the tickets Meredith had given Nick. After breakfast, they bundled up in their coats, gloves, scarves, hats, and boots, and climbed into Meredith's car, Meredith driving, Nick gazing out the window in the passenger's seat. It was a sunny, cold day, and they squinted against the sparkling snow that covered the lawns and rose in tall mounds on street corners.

They drove ten miles to the Villard Arboretum. Meredith was soothed by the peacefulness of the grounds as soon as she pulled into the entrance, and as she drove up the winding road, she remembered again how she adored the arboretum's many open fields and quiet corners. Seeing as it was a cold, snowy Sunday, very few cars were in the parking lot, and Meredith was glad they would have the park largely to themselves. She pulled into a spot and met Nick as he climbed out, standing tall so he could take in the meandering paths and rolling hills.

Hand in hand, they walked downward toward the entrance of the trail, taking their time and reading signs informing them of the species of trees, plants, and flowers along the way. The fact that it was winter meant that the scene was barer than at other times of the year, but Meredith, though she loved the dazzling colors and fullness of the park in spring and summer, thoroughly enjoyed the sparseness of winter. She felt there was something beautiful in its modesty, almost as if the life here were hibernating.

They paused in the rose garden, observing in silence its

uneven stumps and imagining its bloom and fragrance in spring. Nick wrapped his arm around her waist as they stood there, his hand resting on her hip as he pulled her close, his eyes taking in the stubbly scene. They turned and walked back up the steps to continue on the trail.

As they walked, Meredith pointed to the left, noting the holly and camellia that bloomed in winter. Nick and Meredith deviated off the path so they could take a closer look, huddling together as they marched clumsily through the snow.

They strolled by a great open field that sloped downward toward a creek. In the distance they could see a bridge that overlooked the scene. Nick paused, his eyes soaking in the seemingly endless ocean of white.

Meredith watched with him. "It's beautiful," she said. "Total purity."

"Perfection."

Meredith turned to him. He was gazing at the snowy field, untouched and stretching on until it dipped into the creek below. Meredith took his arm and let him stand there in silence for some time. Finally, he turned to her and smiled.

He took her hand. "Come on. Let's keep going."

They continued on, the crackling of the snow beneath their feet the only sound. As they turned toward a small wooden bridge that would take them over the creek, Meredith noticed Nick's eyes on a large shrub with yellow blooms.

"Witch hazel," she said.

They came to a fork in the path. Meredith knew that the lower branch, to the right, would lead to a swan pond and log cabin. The path on the left would draw them up to an overlook, which would give them a view of much of the grounds. Nick paused, silently waiting for her to lead him. She decided they'd look at the swan pond first, then double back to the overlook.

It was shady down by the swan pond, and colder. The pond itself was half frozen, and no swans were in sight. She drew him by the hand onto a smaller path that led to the log cabin. Nick looked like a giant in the miniature house, his head nearly brushing the ceiling. He walked to the tiny window, his footsteps reverberating as they pressed against the wooden floor. He bent at the waist and looked outside.

Meredith followed him, her arm taking his as she peered out with him. She leaned up and kissed his cheek, which felt warm against the cold.

He glanced at her, his expression inscrutable, before taking her hand and leading her out of the cabin.

They made their way back around to the other path, the one that would take them to the overlook. They breathed more heavily as they climbed the steep hill, and Nick placed his hand on her back to prevent her from slipping on the icy ground. When they reached the overlook, they inhaled with satisfaction and leaned over the side, taking in the scene.

She turned, sensing Nick's eyes on her. Startled, he smiled awkwardly and turned back to look at the field beneath them. His elbows were leaning on the stone wall of the overlook, his hands clasped in front.

Meredith turned toward the field and gazed at it with him. With its undulating softness, the snow white and pristine, and its vast endlessness, it seemed to represent unlimited possibilities. Meredith couldn't help but think about the new possibilities for her own life.

Nick faced her.

"I love you, Merry," he said. "Is it too soon to say it?"

Meredith was overcome by a warm rush that made her feel a little dizzy. "No," she said, a bit breathlessly.

"I've never done this before. But I feel at home with you." His blue eyes were wide and radiant. They sparkled against the brightness of the snow. "I love that you brought me here today. And I love that I can talk to you."

She wanted to respond but couldn't. She swallowed, holding back tears.

He neatened her hair where it had escaped from under her hat. His eyes met hers, and his expression became serious. "What Vince said," he began. "I've been thinking. I wonder if there's any truth to it. I guess I have been a little directionless."

"Nick," she said finally, sensing darkness in his voice. She took his hands in hers. "Don't let Vince's accusations haunt you. It's as you said—he couldn't understand."

"I don't have a lot, and I'm the furthest thing from a Ph.D. But I want to give you everything you deserve. I just hope I can."

Meredith embraced him tightly, nuzzling her face against his chest. He lay his cheek against her head. Soon she looked upward and smiled, and she felt him relax.

"I love you too," she said. "There's more to life than Ph.Ds. And you've already given me everything. I was lost before I met you. And I didn't even know it until you brought me back."

THEY WALKED hand in hand down the steep hill, then marched quickly as they approached another sharp incline that brought them past the greenhouses and the back side of the rose garden. They paused here and took a breath, gazing around.

"This was really nice, Merry," Nick said, and kissed her forehead. "Thank you for bringing me here."

"I'm glad you liked it. I love coming here in winter. It's so peaceful."

"Maybe one day you'll come to Maine, and I can take you to my favorite places."

She looked up at him. She longed to tell him how much he already meant to her, that he made life simple and full of joy, that she so appreciated that when she was with him she could look forward and not back, and that the world seemed straightforward and the future bright.

Overcome, she said nothing, but his eyes told her he understood. His arms circled her waist; he grabbed her from behind and pulled her in close. He leaned in and kissed her. "Let's go home," he said. "I want us to appreciate the rest of this day."

THEY TREKKED up toward the car and climbed in, shivering against the cold. Meredith drove off feeling calm and happy, Nick sitting beside her with his head leaning against the back of his seat. Vince's car was not there when they reached the house. Meredith wondered what he had been doing all weekend.

They fixed a quick lunch and ate it standing up in the kitchen. Then they walked upstairs to Meredith's bedroom, where they lay together on the bed, huddled closely for warmth and comfort. Soon they had dozed off into a cozy midday nap, lulled to sleep by soft kisses.

When they awoke, they continued to lie there, talking quietly. Toward evening, Meredith sneaked downstairs and made a couple of sandwiches, sliding a bottle of wine under her arm and then returning to the bedroom. They remained there for the rest of the night, covering themselves beneath the blankets when the sun went down, their enthusiasm renewed under the sleek velvet of darkness. During the day they had found comfort and peace, but the night invigorated them. Dizzy with wine and with each other, they delighted in losing themselves, gleefully forgetting the world around them. As they lay exhausted and glowing, waiting for their heartbeats to slow and their breathing to calm, the silver moonlight illuminating their skin through the open curtains, Meredith let her happiness engulf her. Nick, his face turned upward and his breaths still coming quickly, his eyes closed and his chest heaving, reached for her hand; he brought it to his lips and kissed her fingers, sensuously wetting the tip of each with his soft lips. Meredith closed her eyes, letting him take over her consciousness, which he always did.

MEREDITH SLIPPED into her bathrobe and walked carefully downstairs in the dark. She was carrying the lunch dishes and empty wine bottle, which she was planning to exchange for two glasses of water. She lamented the fact that Nick had to go to work the next day. She was off from school all week, and the house would seem lonely without him.

She stepped into the kitchen, which was dark except for the little light above the stove. She placed the bottle in the sink and then jumped with shock when she saw Vince leaning against the counter, staring at her.

"Damn it, Vince!" she cried, her heart racing. "Why didn't you say anything?"

"I figured you'd see me eventually," he said, taking a long sip from the glass he held in his hand.

"How long have you been home?"

"Long enough," he said, averting his gaze.

Meredith felt lightheaded as the color drained from her face.

"Vince—" she began weakly.

"Don't say anything," Vince interrupted, putting his hand in the air to stop her. "I don't want to talk about it."

Meredith was silent. Don't say anything? But there was so much to say. They'd fought more viciously than they ever had in their lives, and she hadn't seen him since. He'd said things to her, horrible things, things she couldn't just forget. She wondered what he'd been doing since that morning. She wondered whether he was okay. She wondered if they would ever recover their closeness, or if they were simply too different. With a tightening in her chest she remembered the fight he'd had with their parents. Part of her worried he'd take off this time, too, that they'd become estranged again.

And there was something else, something she couldn't quite explain. She put her hands to her stomach, the thorn twisting like a knife, pulling her apart.

"I think we need to talk about it," she said, flatly, deliberately keeping the emotion out of her voice. "I don't think we can pretend that nothing happened."

"Look," Vince said; Meredith thought he sounded tired. "I don't want to fight with you." He placed his glass on the counter and crossed his arms, finally looking at her. "We'll talk about it. Just not tonight. Okay?"

It wasn't, and part of her resented having to do this entirely on his terms. But he wasn't shying away this time; he wanted to work it out. The tightening in her chest unraveled somewhat. "Okay."

"Tell Nick to meet me downstairs tomorrow and we'll go to work."

"I will."

Meredith waited, but Vince appeared to be finished speaking. She awkwardly filled two glasses with water, conscious that he was watching her, and was about to leave the kitchen when he stopped her.

"Merry."

She turned. "Yes?"

She straightened with surprise as Vince approached her and kissed her forehead. Without another word, he strode with heavy steps up to his bedroom and closed the door.

Meredith indulged in a couple of deep breaths before returning upstairs. She glanced at the mess of lunch dishes in the sink. Everything was so messy—life, love, relationships. Her relationship with her brother was no exception. As she quickly cleaned up the dishes she found herself thinking that the thing about a mess was that it meant you had done something. It seemed anything worth doing involved a mess of some sort. She

was beginning to see how aptly this described the human experience, how light and darkness were intertwined, how one couldn't
exist without the other, how easily the two became each other.

Barred clouds bloom the soft-dying day, she thought, recalling the
poem she'd taught her students only weeks before, *and touch the
stubble-plains with rosy hue*. It was beautiful, she had told them,
despite the imperfections. In fact, the imperfections were what
made it so beautiful in the first place.

She retrieved the water from the counter and hurried upstairs,
back to Nick.

CHAPTER TWELVE

GOOD

The following morning, Meredith had the pleasure of waking up next to Nick once again. He lay sleeping beside her, the thick darkness of the early winter morning still heavy in the room.

She rose, stretched, and stopped at the window on the way to the bathroom. She touched her fingers to the curtain and pulled it aside.

Vince's car was in the driveway. He was home.

Meredith swallowed, bracing herself. She took a breath and headed to the bathroom for her shower.

Later, Meredith and Nick walked downstairs together, Meredith with her heart in her throat.

Vince was sitting at the dining room table eating a bowl of cereal and scrolling on his phone.

"Hey," he muttered under his breath as they walked past him to the kitchen.

"Good morning," she returned, and followed Nick out of the room. They grabbed their breakfasts and joined him at the table in silence.

It was ridiculous to her that they should sit here and not

address the elephant in the room, that he would rather endure this tension than work through it. Also, he owed her an apology; she could not move forward, not completely, until he addressed what he had said to her. So they endured breakfast wordlessly, the strain almost unbearable. She and Nick braved glances at each other, but their synchronization was off; they never managed to look at each other at the same time.

The silence was broken when at one point, in her absentmindedness, she reached for her phone and accidentally swiped her coffee cup with her hand. The cup tipped over, and coffee spread over the table.

"Damn it," she muttered, rising, and looking about for a napkin.

Nick took his own napkin and reached forward to wipe up the spill. Vince rose and went to the kitchen; he returned a moment later with a roll of paper towels.

He passed some to Meredith, then took a few in his own hand and caught the coffee as it threatened to spill over the side of the table. Eventually, the table was dry. Vince and Meredith looked at each other from opposite sides.

"Thanks," Meredith whispered, offering a short, mild smile.

Vince was staring at her, eyes wide, like he was going to say something. Meredith waited, holding her breath.

But whatever it was that was on his mind, he thought better of saying it. Instead, he gathered the wet paper towels, nodding in acknowledgment of her thanks.

"You're welcome," he uttered blandly, then turned toward the kitchen to dispose of the trash.

When they were ready to leave, Vince walked into the entryway, and Meredith heard him putting on his boots and coat. She and Nick followed. Vince was ready to go and stood waiting by the door, his gaze cast downward. Nick put on his coat and boots and stood before Meredith.

"Okay then," he said, and leaned in to kiss her cheek. "I'll see you later."

Vince rolled his eyes and opened the door, stepping out without a word. Meredith wished Nick goodbye and waved dreamily as he followed Vince, closing the door on his way out.

She cleaned up from breakfast and settled in to a peaceful, easy day at the house, reading and tidying up. That evening, as she sautéed the mushrooms and onions she would place atop roasted chicken—the savory aromas of sage and rosemary filling the air—she peeked outside frequently, hoping to see Vince's car pull up to the house. She was eager to see Nick and also curious to hear about their day, whether Vince had talked to him at all about what had happened.

Finally they arrived. Meredith straightened her hair and looked over the dinner table, then stood between the dining room and entryway to wait for them.

The door opened, and they stepped inside. Vince nodded hello and proceeded to remove his coat and boots before heading to his bedroom; Nick stayed behind and kissed her, pressing his hands to her waist and chilling her with his cold hands.

"How did it go?" she asked.

Nick shrugged. "Fine, I guess. He didn't say anything."

"About us?"

"No, I mean at all."

Meredith's eyes opened wide. "The two of you didn't talk all day?"

"No. When he wants to apologize for what he said to you, I'll talk to him. Until then, he can have his silence."

Meredith was crestfallen. "I was sure you would have gotten things straightened out." She frowned and shook her head, then sighed. "I was going to wait for him to come to me, but maybe I'm being petty. I hate that we're quarreling. Maybe I'll just say something."

"No," said Nick, with more vehemence than usual. "You aren't being petty. He's wrong. He needs to come to you first."

"Is that really how you feel?" Meredith looked up at him curiously. "For some reason, I thought you'd be in favor of working it out as soon as possible."

"Usually I am. And you should do what feels right. I just think in this case you should stand firm."

Meredith wrapped her arms around his waist and smiled coyly. "You're so calm and peaceful, but you also don't back down." Her eyes sparkled mischievously. "It's sexy."

"Glad you think so." His words were muffled as she leaned upward for a kiss.

He squeezed her hand as Vince came downstairs and headed into the dining room, awkwardly inquiring how he could help with dinner. Meredith mumbled thanks but served dinner herself, no longer interested in their reactions, her only goal to get through the meal as quickly as possible so the discomfort would be over.

After dinner, the three of them sat reading in the living room. Occasionally Meredith or Nick would ask a mundane question about the other's day. Other than that, they passed the time in silence.

Finally they all retired to bed, Meredith wishing Vince goodnight and receiving an uncomfortable "Goodnight" in return as he tried not to notice Nick joining her in her bedroom. Nick and Meredith climbed into bed with relief, happy to put the day behind them, and eager for the night.

THE SITUATION with Vince was weighing on Meredith, and not only because of their fight. There was a weird, inexplicable impasse, something she couldn't explain but knew wasn't really about Nick. Neither Vince nor she addressed it—indeed, they did not speak to each other. They nodded curtly in acknowledgement of each other's presence, but quickly left the room, each solid and steadfast, refusing to fold first. And so, the tension mounted. The thorn that had been plaguing her was sharper than ever, twisting and turning deep inside her. A feeling that had lingered in the background, biding its time, seemed now to demand her attention. She knew it wouldn't rest until her quarrel with Vince was made right.

Thus the week passed, the three living as non-speaking room-mates during the day, Nick and Meredith opening up to each other at night and cherishing the little time they had together each morning. Meredith spent her days relaxing and taking care of odds and ends around the house, occasionally meeting Tara and her daughters at Tara's house, where the little girls played while the two friends chatted over coffee. Meredith enjoyed her time with Tara, who listened with interest to Meredith's stories and squealed with delight in all the right places.

She and Nick texted each other throughout the day, exchanging little pleasantries and notes of affection. Each night as they undressed, they told each other about their day. It was mundane, it was what couples did; it was so charmingly, refreshingly normal. Meredith was surprised by the delight their new routine brought her. She loved getting to know him in all the little personal ways people can only get to know each other by waking up together, by living their daily lives together; she loved learning about his little idiosyncrasies, and letting him learn about hers, witnessing all the little ways in which he showed gentleness and joy. It brought her new life; it made her feel more than ever that she was on the path forward. By the end of the week, she was feeling thoroughly refreshed.

New Year's Eve was Friday. Vince left without a word just before dinner, leaving Nick and Meredith to celebrate quietly by themselves. They toasted the new year as they sat bundled up under a blanket on the living room couch, watching the ball drop in Times Square. Meredith contemplated the new year, grateful that it was looking like a happy one. That weekend, they avoided the house as much as possible during the day, instead choosing to take a winter hike, go out to dinner, and stroll around hand in hand, just happy to be together. They eagerly fell into bed together at night, having anticipated this time all day and not wanting to waste even a second.

MEREDITH WAS sad that her quiet week at home was over, but part of her was looking forward to going back to work and being occupied productively during the day. Monday morning they ate breakfast downstairs in their usual silence, Vince's aloofness almost a tangible presence in the room. Nick kissed her goodbye, whispering "I love you" in her ear and sending a warm shiver through her veins.

Meredith drove to school filled with hope and optimism. She greeted her first class cheerfully, ignoring the sneers of students who were not as accepting as she of the fact that their vacation was over. She dove into her lessons, feeling revitalized and full of energy. It was a day that reminded her why she enjoyed teaching.

She had just sat down for lunch in the faculty room, relieved to be off her feet and to have a few minutes to dive into a new novel, when she was interrupted by a tap on her shoulder.

"Pardon me, Meredith," said Kevin Williams, "but your brother is here to see you."

Meredith was shocked speechless. In a daze, she closed her book and stood, then followed Kevin toward the faculty room door. As he pushed it open, Meredith caught sight of Vince, whose lips were turned up into a friendly smile. Meredith didn't know what surprised her more—the fact that Vince was visiting her at school or the fact that he was smiling at her.

Hope bubbling in her chest, Meredith composed herself and

thanked Kevin, who quickly scuttled away. She turned to Vince. He stood before her, his eyes intently on her face, his expression warm but serious.

"You're on your lunch break, right?" he asked her. "I tried to plan it so I wasn't interrupting."

"Yes, I'm on lunch. What are you doing here?" Meredith asked. "Is everything okay?"

"No, it's not."

Meredith's heart sank. "What is it?" she asked, her thoughts frantically turning to Nick.

Vince sensed her concern and gently touched her shoulder. "No, no, it's nothing like that. It's just..." He hesitated, but his eyes remained on hers. Finally, he sighed. "I couldn't wait one more minute to tell you I'm sorry. I've been so embarrassed I haven't even wanted to face you all week." His entire face drooped into a frown, and for a moment Meredith feared he might weep. "I said some terrible things to you, Merry. I had no right to say them. You've been through so much and have handled it all so well. I'm really proud of you." He took a deep breath. "I hope you can forgive me, but I wouldn't blame you if you couldn't."

Meredith's eyes were blurred with tears; she wiped them with her hand. It was finally over—they really were going to be okay. Nearly breathless with relief, she took the tissue he held for her, and sniffled. "Thank you, Vince. I really appreciate that."

"Shit, Merry. Please don't cry. This is all my fault. I don't know why I said what I said. You're an angel." He put his hands on her shoulders. "You've been nothing but generous to me, not just in the last few weeks but always. You were right—I am a hypocrite. I'm the last person who should lecture someone about relationships—about anything, for that matter. And you were right about the double standard." He grimaced here, and swallowed, the distaste clear on his face. "That thing I said you were. You aren't. But if you were, you'd be allowed. Wait. I mean, that's not what I mean." His eyes widened, and he shifted where he stood. "What I mean is, what I said, it isn't—I mean, it shouldn't be something that we—it isn't something anyone should—"

"I understand." She had to cut him off; it was too painful listening to him stumble. "Thank you."

"Okay. My point is, I get it. And I'm ashamed of myself." He shook his head. "I want to say thank you, for taking care of me and for putting up with me, even when I haven't deserved it."

"I love you, Vince," she said, and patted his arm. She smiled up at him through glassy eyes, elated with the lifting of this burden. "You're my brother. You're not perfect, but neither am I."

"Actually, while we're on the subject of not being perfect, I want to clear the air about Adam." His jaw tightened, and he sighed. "I was weak, Merry. Your pain was so deep…I didn't know what to do for you, so I ran away. I couldn't handle it, but I should have stepped up and handled it. For you." His frown grew more severe. "I guess I was also afraid. Somehow his dying made me feel like even more of a failure. It hit too close to home, and I couldn't deal with it. Plus I knew if I returned I'd get hell from Mom and Dad. I'm just so sorry. I—"

"Stop," Meredith said, placing her hand on his arm. "I understand, and it's okay. It's in the past. You're here now, right? Let's just move on."

"Yeah, but I know it bothered you. On Christmas, you said—"

"On Christmas, I was mad," she interrupted again, "just like you were mad. Maybe it bothered me, but not enough to matter now. Truly, Vince. I'm fine."

"It was terrible. I failed you. But I won't fail you again."

"You could never fail me." She hesitated. "I'm sorry I wasn't honest with you about Nick and me."

"No, I don't blame you. It's like you said. I was trying to make myself feel better, but that isn't your problem."

She took a breath. "So I guess we're all good."

He pulled her close and hugged her. "Thanks. You know I love you, right?"

"Of course."

He squeezed her tighter. Meredith closed her eyes and basked in the comfort of her big brother's embrace. The air around them felt lighter; the path forward looked clearer and less complex. She hadn't realized how she had been holding on to his absence after Adam's death; she had pushed it away, for his sake and for her own. His apology meant she could really move on.

Vince held her for a few more moments before separating from her.

"Listen, Merry. I understand what you're doing," he said, his voice rather grave. "You've been lonely for a long time. But I'm scared for you. Just put aside for a second what I said the other day about Nick. Even if everything is perfect between you two, you're still going to have to deal with the problem of his moving away from you soon."

Meredith with effort kept her face expressionless; she had been toying with the idea of broaching the topic of moving to Maine to be with Nick, but she had held off, wanting more time to pass first. She knew it was absurd to even consider it at this point.

"It's a risk I have to take," she said. She tried to keep the emotion out of her voice, but failed. "The fact is that Nick makes me happy. Really happy." She stopped talking before the tears rose again.

"I know," Vince said. "You think I don't see that?" He sighed and rubbed his face in his hands. Finally he looked at her again. "I'm glad you've found happiness, Merry. I really am. And I'll be the first to admit that my own insecurities probably made me judge Nick too harshly. He means well, and he's been good to you. How can I tell you not to be with someone who makes you happy when I myself couldn't step up and be there for you?"

"So you approve?"

"Let's not go overboard," Vince said, and smiled. "I'm your big brother. I don't think I'll ever approve of anyone you bring home.

I still wonder if you'd be better off with someone who can relate to your life a little more." He chuckled. "You know, someone more in your lane."

"He's a painter and I'm a teacher, Vince. There are no 'lanes.'"

"Yeah, but you know. Mom and Dad." He didn't have to say any more than that; their father's prestige and ambition, of course, often were a presence in the room, even when the man himself was not. "Anyway," he said, "it's your call. I'll support you no matter what."

Meredith's face brightened. "Thank you. That means a lot to me. Truthfully, Vince, I've been trying to tell myself it didn't matter what anyone else thought, but I feel better having your blessing." She paused and rubbed her lips together. They were being honest with each other, and there was the specter of a worry lingering in her mind's darkest corner. "Can I ask you something, though?"

"Anything."

"It's just that..." Her heart was thumping; she pushed through. "You asked what Adam would think about all this. I just—"

"Stop," he interrupted her, surprising her by placing his hands gently on the sides of her face. "Of all the shitty things I said, that was the shittiest. Don't listen to me. Adam would want you to do this."

"Okay." Relief washed over her. She let a few tears fall, though like raindrops in a sun shower, they fell over a smile. "I know that. I guess I just needed to hear it from you."

"I was never worried about that. You have every right to move forward. That's the last reason not to do it."

Meredith inhaled deeply, closed her eyes, and nodded. "Thanks."

When she opened her eyes, he was smiling. "Adam would give his permission. And I give my permission, too, not that you need it."

Meredith pulled him in for a final embrace. "I admire you, Vince."

"Well, that's your first problem."

"No." She stood back and slapped his arm. "I'm serious. I think you should stop your self-deprecatory jokes. You seem to think you've failed, but you haven't. You weren't afraid to do something different. You stood up to Dad. You're living your life." She nudged him again, but gently this time. "Don't you think that counts for anything?"

Vince looked skeptical, but his face had softened. "I appreciate it, Merry. I just wish I'd done what I set out to do."

"But you took a big chance, and even though things didn't go as planned, you make the most of it. You should stop beating yourself up. Well," she added, a crooked grin sliding across her face, "over this, at least."

"If you say so."

She swallowed. "It took strength. And I respect it."

He smiled. "Thanks, Merry. I respect your strength, too."

As she looked at her brother's sympathetic face she felt she finally understood. Strength wasn't standing firm. It was knowing when and how to bend. It was refusing to let anyone define your path. A weight seemed lifted from Meredith's chest. She felt the thorn that had been nagging her dissipate into dust.

She punched his arm, and he punched hers back. They both laughed.

"Hey," she said, her voice lighter, "now we can go on proper double dates with you and Sandy."

Vince snorted. "Sandy's been kind of cold with me. I don't know if we'll be seeing much of her anymore."

"You mean you haven't been with Sandy all week?"

"No," he said, his face turning sheepish.

"Then what—"

"Don't ask."

Meredith let the topic drop; Vince probably didn't know they had spoken. She guessed Sandy had decided it wasn't worth it after all.

"Well," he said, stepping aside to make way for a couple of teachers exiting the faculty room, "I'll let you get back to your lunch. I'm on my lunch break, too. I need to get back anyway."

"Okay. Thanks for coming by. You made my day."

Vince smiled. "You really are the best, Merry. I don't deserve you."

"No, you don't," she said, and punched his arm again. "Now get out of here."

Meredith watched Vince for a moment as he walked away, his hands in his pockets, his easy swagger seeming to own the narrow hallway. He disappeared around the corner, and she took a deep, calming breath, relishing the lightness in her heart. As she returned to her seat to resume her day, the room looked different —brighter, somehow, with the knowledge that sometimes things really did work out.

MEREDITH WAS eager to see Vince and Nick that night, curious whether Vince had extended his hand in peace to Nick the way he had to her. She finished dinner early—lemon dill salmon and vegetables spanning all colors of the rainbow—and left it in the oven to stay warm as she changed into jeans and a sweater and sat on the couch to prepare the week's lessons.

When she heard the front door open, she placed her work on the coffee table and crept toward the entryway. Vince and Nick were removing their coats and boots, but they were also engaging in polite, quiet banter about their workday. Meredith was overjoyed. She allowed her pleasure to show on her face, and as Vince approached her, she looked up at him, her eyes hopeful and questioning.

He patted her shoulders. "We're good, Merry," he said, and went to wash up for dinner.

When he had gone upstairs, Meredith turned to Nick, who was watching Vince as he strode up the stairs. When Vince's door closed, he turned to Meredith and tenderly kissed her lips.

"So?" she asked. "Did you talk?"

"Yes. As Vince said, we're good."

"What happened?"

"Vince told me he was sorry and that he was okay with our being together as long as you're happy, because his only concern is that you don't get hurt."

"And what did you say?"

"I said it was good that we were on the same page and that I was glad to hear he wouldn't hurt you again."

He kissed her again and went to wash for dinner, nodding amicably to Vince as they passed each other on the stairs.

CHAPTER THIRTEEN

POSSIBILITIES

*D*uring the weeks that followed, Meredith was kept busy not only with school but with her study club. She was meeting Ana twice a week. She so enjoyed this quiet, contemplative time, when her student could be honest about her questions and concerns. She loved witnessing the look on Ana's face when she accomplished something difficult. And it was only made better when she gained a second student: Ana had learned so much and gained so much confidence that her friend Kim joined her. Before long, Meredith had a handful of students eagerly enlisting her help.

Meredith also spent many hours after school with the students who were writing the play, reading over rough drafts and correcting grammar. The script was coming together, already containing six scenes in which students recreated memories surrounding dinner tables, first dates, school lunches ruined by bullies, and wedding banquets. Meredith was having fun and was glad they were having fun, too. She was particularly grateful for the relationships she was forming with the students. Her shift to one-on-one instruction felt like an exciting new path.

In the last days of January, when the script was complete,

Meredith asked Nick to meet her after school so they could discuss with Kevin his role in helping with the set. That morning, she was especially giddy as she kissed him goodbye, knowing she'd see him earlier than usual that afternoon. She was jittery all day, and as the last minutes of her final class ticked by, she couldn't help but glance at the door frequently, hoping to catch a glimpse of him. Finally the bell rang, and she dismissed her students. As they trickled out, their attention seemed to be attracted to something to the left of the door. Watching, Meredith saw Nick's face as he peered around the doorway, patiently waiting for the students to exit. Several students glanced back at Meredith as they left, and grinned.

When the last student had made it through, Nick casually strolled into her classroom, a friendly smile on his face, his eyes bright. He looked around the room, taking in the posters displaying common grammar mistakes and paintings of famous poets, the bookshelf lined with extra copies of the works they were studying, and her desk, on top of which lay neat piles of assorted student essays, quizzes, and evaluations. As he approached her, he turned toward the door; seeing that he wasn't being watched, he leaned in and kissed her, then pulled away and looked at her expectantly.

"I love that you're here," she said, looking up at him fondly.

"I love you," he replied, and kissed her again.

She led him to Kevin's office and knocked on the door. Kevin called to them to enter, and they stepped inside. Kevin looked up and smiled.

"Hello, you two," he said. "Nick, I want to thank you again for helping us out. I can't tell you how much we appreciate it."

"Please don't mention it," said Nick, returning Kevin's smile. "It's my pleasure."

"Has Meredith told you what we need?"

"Three attached walls, each with a door in the middle," Nick said. "All I need are the details."

Meredith sat and listened while Kevin and Nick discussed the practical aspects of the set, delighted to hear Nick talk about his work. Finally they all stood. Kevin and Nick shook hands, agreeing that the set should be built by the end of February.

"You're really helping us, Nick," Kevin said. "We're very grateful."

"As I said, it's my pleasure," Nick responded. "I like to help in whatever way I can."

Kevin walked them to the door of his office. Meredith thanked him, then escorted Nick out to the parking lot.

"I'm so happy you're doing this," she told him as they made their way toward the doors. "The play is something new and interesting for me, something important. It's so nice to have you involved."

"It's new and interesting for me too." As he spoke, Meredith smiled and looked at him; though serious, as always, his voice held latent enthusiasm. "It feels like something I'm supposed to do."

"You mean because of your father?"

"Yes. It's just the kind of thing he would do. It's almost like I'm doing it for him."

He walked her to her car and glanced over his shoulder at Vince's, which he had borrowed for the purpose of the meeting. "I need to go back and pick up Vince," he said. "I'll meet you back home."

"Back home," Meredith repeated thoughtfully. She gazed up at him. She thought about how she had learned to read his expressions, how subtle were the changes in his face.

"What is it?" he asked. His hand rose to her face, and he gently tucked back her hair. His fingers tickled her, and she smiled.

She was on the verge of saying something she had been thinking but was afraid to talk about. Her chest began rising and falling more hurriedly as she prepared herself to risk it all. She decided to be blunt.

"When you go back to Maine," she said, her breath almost choking her. She swallowed, but her throat was dry, and when she spoke again her voice was almost a whisper. "I want to go with you."

Nick's expression remained unchanged as he absorbed her statement. His forehead then creased with emotion, which crept down to his eyes and made them bright and alert. "I would love that," he said, his voice quiet but the words coming out quickly and with excitement.

"You would?" she asked, barely able to believe she could be endowed with this much happiness.

"Yes," he said, his voice firm and certain. He lifted his hands to her shoulders and caressed them affectionately. "There's nothing I want more than to stay with you."

"I'm so glad," she said, not bothering to hide her elation. "I thought maybe it was too soon."

"I don't care how long it's been," he replied. "I just know I have to be with you. End of story."

She felt as if her knees would buckle; she placed her hands behind his neck and pulled him down into a long kiss. His arms encircled her as he buried his face in her neck, his breath deep and warm against her skin.

MEREDITH BEGAN IMAGINING the possibilities for her move the moment she and Nick discussed it. She was eager to slow down, to stop chasing something she no longer wanted. Truth be told, though she intended to make every effort to find a teaching position, she felt she would not be devastated if she made a career change. She adored teaching; however, she knew Nick would have to travel again soon, and she wanted to be able to follow him when he did. Predicting that she would be gone for weeks at a time, she began considering possibilities for jobs that would allow her to be flexible with her schedule, such as catering for events. She also felt that not having a classroom would enable her to spend more time tutoring, to have that one-on-one time she had come to cherish so much this year. She saw her move as the perfect opportunity for her to explore her interests, to focus on what was most important to her—to be free.

Somehow with Nick the superficial details of her life seemed unimportant; as long as she was with him, as long as she had the peace he brought her, she would be happy.

The following Friday, the first week of February, after her final class of the day, Meredith mustered up the courage to submit her letter of resignation to Kevin. She wanted to do it soon, to give him a greater chance to find a replacement before the start of the next school year. But she had been putting it off, as her heart broke at the thought of saying goodbye to him; he was such a genuine person and kind leader, and his support had meant so much to her as she'd precariously built her new life.

"Your encouragement has been invaluable," she told him as he brought her in for a hug. "I really appreciate it, more than I can say."

"It's been my pleasure," he said, pulling back and smiling. "We'll miss you, but I'm happy you're going to be happy."

Meredith had suggested to Nick that they also break the news to Vince that night; she felt that she should strike when her momentum was up. Back at the house, her anxiety growing every minute, she awaited their arrival as she distractedly prepared dinner, burning her sauce and forgetting to turn on the oven altogether.

When Vince and Nick walked in the door that evening, they found cartons of Chinese food displayed on the dining room table, resting on trivets and surrounded by candles. Meredith had tried her best to make up for the fact that her home-cooked meal was a bust.

"To what do we owe this elaborate feast?" Vince asked as she unceremoniously stuck a spoon into each carton.

"I'm a little absentminded today. My dinner didn't turn out."

Vince glanced up as he scooped cashew chicken onto his plate, his eyebrows raised with interest. "Really? That doesn't sound like you. Everything okay?"

"Sure," she said, her voice stifled by a large bite of egg roll.

Nick was looking at her. Her eyes wide with terror, she returned his gaze, seeking reassurance there. He nodded, encouraging her.

"Vince," she said, her voice breaking, and she cleared her throat. "Vince, Nick and I have something to tell you."

Vince's hand, which grasped a fork full of food, stopped midway to his mouth; a shrimp fell with a plop down to his plate. "Oh, my God—you're pregnant."

"No!" she exclaimed, her hand flying to her face. "No, no," she said again, and laughed. "It's not that. It's just that," she began, and swallowed, "I'm going to Maine with Nick." She paused. "I'm moving."

Vince was silent, his face stony. Meredith was still, but her eyes darted to Nick, who was turning his head toward Vince.

"Well," Vince said finally, rubbing his hands together and avoiding eye contact.

"Is that all you have to say?"

"No," he replied. "I'm just not saying it."

Meredith sighed. "Vince, I thought you were okay with us."

"Whatever, Meredith. It's your life."

"I thought maybe you'd be excited. It means I'll live near you, too."

"How nice," he muttered, standing.

"Vince," Meredith said, also rising. "I'm going to be with Nick. You must have known this was coming."

"Yeah, well, I was going be with Heather, too."

"It's not the same, and you know it. This is a good thing for me. I can stay with Nick, and I can start fresh somewhere in a life I truly want."

"So you're going to quit your job and move to Maine to follow your dreams. Because you've seen how well that's worked for me."

Meredith's hands rested on her hips. "What's wrong with following my dreams? It's the perfect opportunity. Maybe it's time I did something different for once. Maybe as long as I'm making a change, I'll pursue my cooking like I've always wanted."

Vince laughed. "Same old Merry, naive and idealistic as ever."

"What's that supposed to mean?"

"You know what it means. It means that I thought I was going to pursue my dreams, too, and where the hell am I now? Nowhere."

"Vince," she said, "I know you're concerned for me. But I can't spend the rest of my life at a standstill. I'm not the same person I was all those years ago. Maybe my happiness is down a different path, just like you thought yours was. You told Dad it was time for you to take control of your own life. Now I'm taking control of mine."

"But I never did, Merry. That's what I've been trying to tell you. I quit a sure thing so I could end up as a failure. You sound just like I did six years ago."

"And you sound just like Dad."

Vince's eyes turned black, and he crossed his arms. He paused a moment before speaking again. "I'm only trying to help you."

"Then please just be happy for me. For us."

Vince's eyes met hers, and he looked at her for several moments. Finally, his expression softened. "I want to be, Merry. I really do. But I hate to see you throwing away the stability you've worked so hard for." He clenched his jaw, then threw his hands in the air in resignation. "If you think that's the right thing to do, then go for it. I just hope you know what you're doing." He picked up his plate, deposited it in the kitchen, and stalked upstairs.

Meredith sat back down with a huff. "I need a drink," she said.

"Come on," said Nick, rising from his chair and holding out his hand to her. "Let's go get one."

MEREDITH EXCUSED HERSELF, hurrying to her bedroom and exchanging her more formal work clothes for a pair of jeans and high boots, topped with a black sweater. She went into the bathroom and shut the door, then washed her face and touched up her makeup. When she emerged, she was pleasantly surprised to find Nick in a state of half undress, zipping up a pair of dark slacks; he had already exchanged his old work shirt for a sleek charcoal-colored sweater that hugged his frame alluringly.

"I've never seen that," she said with a smile as she admired the sweater.

"It's new," he replied as he buttoned the pants.

"You bought new clothes?"

"Yes."

"When did you do that?"

"When I realized I had someone to impress."

She was both flattered and amused. She watched him as he scrutinized himself in the mirror; he smoothed down his clothes and straightened his hair, then turned to her.

"Very nice," she said silkily, her eyes taking him in. She placed her hand on his shoulder and rotated him, playfully checking him out from behind.

"I approve," she added, spanking him lightly.

"So do I," he said, taking her waist in his hands as he looked her over. "I may not let you out of this room after all."

"There's plenty of time for that," she said. "Let's walk over to Tony's. I'm looking forward to that drink. You can have me to yourself later tonight, and every other night. Does that sound good?"

"That sounds perfect."

They walked downstairs together, not bothering to tell Vince they were going out. They bundled up in their coats and gloves and walked outside, then headed off in the direction of Tony's, a local bar within a fifteen-minute walk. They shuffled cozily together along the sidewalk, which was lined with several inches of snow on either side.

Meredith had never been to Tony's before, though she passed it on her way home from work every day. On nights when she had to work late, she saw people loitering around the entrance and walking hand in hand from the parking lot. Tonight it was bustling with many other couples and hopeful singles seeking warmth on a cold Friday night. Nick and Meredith squeezed through the door into the well-lit bar, which was furnished with dark wood tables and stools and TVs displaying sports in the background. Lively music blared from unseen speakers.

Nick helped her onto a tall stool at a small round table next to the bar, then left her to order their drinks. Meredith told him to surprise her again, as he had at the bar in Framington. He returned carrying a beer and a fuzzy-looking peach concoction with an umbrella and a pineapple spear.

"Thanks," she said as he handed her the elaborate drink and sat down next to her. She sipped it; it was sweet and strong.

He took a swig from his own glass, then smiled warmly at her, finally leaning in and kissing her cheek. He withdrew his face but remained close to her, leaning toward her with his elbows on the table and his arms folded in front. Meredith rested her hand on the one closest to her.

"You look beautiful," he said, gazing intently at her. He kissed her lips softly, making her tingle a little.

They sat for a while, taking in the scene and chatting. Nick excused himself and headed for the restroom, and Meredith leaned against the back of her stool, looking around until he returned.

After a couple of minutes a man sauntered toward her, wearing suit slacks and a dress shirt, his tie loosened and the sleeves of his shirt rolled halfway up his arms. He was attractive and clean-cut, with a friendly smile. His smile widened as he approached her table.

Meredith's heart began thumping, and her anxiety grew as he took Nick's seat beside her.

"Hi," he said, holding out his hand for her to shake. "I'm Alex."

"Hi," she responded, indulging him in the shake but quickly withdrawing her hand.

"I'm here on business for the weekend, from New York."

"Oh," Meredith said, her face strained into a polite smile. "Welcome to town."

"Thank you," Alex replied, his voice kind. "Are you from around here?"

"Yes," she said, searching around for Nick.

"I'm in importing. I'm down here to meet a business partner. How about you? What do you do?"

"I'm a teacher," she said, rubbing her lips together nervously.

Meredith was just getting ready to tell him that she was waiting for someone when she spotted Nick striding across the room, his eyes on Alex, who was turned intimately toward her, asking more questions. He stepped toward the table and stood beside Alex, indicating with his closeness that Alex was in his chair. Alex looked upward and started when he saw Nick so close behind him.

"How's it going," said Nick.

Alex instantly made the connection and took the hint. "Ah," he said, throwing his hands up and smiling. He glanced at her only for a second before standing. "Sorry. All yours," he told Nick as he scuttled away, disappearing quickly into the crowd.

Nick reclaimed his seat. He wrapped his arm around her back

and held her shoulder, and kissed her passionately before she could say a word.

"I'm sorry, Nick," she stammered afterward. "I—"

"Don't apologize," he said, a smile crinkling his eyes. He kissed her once more. "It's not your fault you're so irresistible."

She smiled shyly as her eyes met his. They were clear and blue, and soft with affection.

"I love you," she said, feeling lightheaded.

"I love you too." He patted her thigh. "Come on. Let's have some fun."

They stood and abandoned their table. Nick drew her by the hand to the bar and ordered two more drinks. Standing snugly close among the crowd, they talked happily and observed the scene.

At one point, they were standing next to another couple when Meredith noticed that the woman was staring at her. Meredith smiled politely.

The woman said, "I'm sorry—I just feel as if I know you."

Meredith studied the woman's face, and the light of recognition hit her. "Yes, we went to school together. Marcy, right? It's me, Meredith."

Marcy's eyes widened, and she smiled. "Meredith, hi! Of course. We had algebra together the year Mr. Jamison retired and went to clown school."

Meredith laughed. "Oh yes! How could I forget?"

"So how have you been?"

Meredith nodded, knowing she couldn't possibly go into all she had been through since high school. "Good," she answered. "I'm great, actually." She turned to Nick and placed her hand on his arm. "Marcy, this is Nick."

Nick extended his hand and smiled. "Nice to meet you."

Marcy shook his hand. "Nice to meet you too." She turned to the man standing behind her. "This is my husband Trent. Trent, Meredith and Nick."

Trent wasn't paying attention; his eyes were fixed on the TV screen above their heads. He reluctantly drew his gaze downward at Marcy's insistence, finally extending his hand to them both.

"Trent and I just got married two weeks ago," Marcy said. She held out her hand for them to admire her ring.

"It's beautiful," Meredith told her, and smiled.

"Thanks. We just returned from our honeymoon in Paris. Have you two ever been there?"

"I went as a teenager, with my parents," Meredith said. "My father had a work engagement there. How about you, Nick?"

"No."

"Marcy wanted to go to Niagara Falls," Trent inserted on a commercial break, "but I told her I wasn't taking her to Canada when I could take her to France."

"It's just as well," Marcy said. "Niagara Falls would have reminded me of my ex-boyfriend. He had wanted to take me there, but it never panned out."

"Yeah, I stole Marcy away from some poor schmuck," Trent said absentmindedly as his eyes scanned the room.

"Oh, stop, Trent," Marcy laughed, and playfully hit him. "He was not."

"He was an okay guy, don't get me wrong," said Trent. "But he was a freaking painter, for chrissake. What kind of life could he ever give Marcy?"

Meredith blanched, and a dark frown crossed her face.

"He doesn't mean that," Marcy assured Meredith, noticing her grimace.

"I sure as hell do," Trent said testily. "There comes a point when you just have to get serious. If you want to bring home the big bucks, you can't spend all day painting goddamn walls. Not if you're going to have the finer things in life, anyway. A real man supports his family. That's why I got my MBA. I knew I would be the breadwinner someday."

Meredith was livid. She wanted to see Nick's reaction but was afraid to look. She said, "I think it's a perfectly respectable profession. I admire a man who can work with his hands and create new things from nothing. In fact, I think it's sexy," she added, a touch of challenge in her voice.

Trent smirked. "The way you talk, you'd think Nick here were a painter."

Meredith pursed her lips, too irritated to speak.

"Oh," Trent stammered, his eyebrows rising as he turned his attention to Nick. "Hey, I'm sorry. I didn't mean that," he said emptily, clapping Nick on the back. "I'm just busting on you. Haha!"

Meredith braved a glance at Nick. He was staring at Trent, his expression inscrutable. His lips wore an amused grin, but his eyes were dark.

Marcy slapped Trent's arm again. "Honey, how awful!" she scolded. She turned to Nick. "Don't listen to him, Nick. There's nothing wrong with being a painter. He's just showing off."

"Don't sweat it," Nick told her with a polite smile.

Meredith brought her hand to his back and rubbed affectionately.

"Hey, we'd better go," Trent said, looking at his watch. "I have to be up at five for golf tomorrow."

"All right," Marcy said. She hugged Meredith. "It was so good to see you. I'm sorry about Trent."

"Don't worry about it," Meredith said, forcing herself to smile in return.

Trent and Marcy walked off. Meredith watched them go for a moment before turning to Nick.

"What a jerk," she said. "Don't pay him any mind. He doesn't know what he's talking about. I'll take a kind-hearted painter any day over an arrogant MBA."

He placed his hand on her shoulder and drew her into a warm kiss. Pulling away, he smiled. "Trent doesn't bother me," he assured her. "Let's forget him. I'd rather focus on you." His hands dropped to her hips. "Dance with me."

They put Trent and Marcy out of their minds and enjoyed each other's company. Finally they had had enough, and they walked hand in hand outside into the cold. There were some stragglers hanging about, waiting for rides or mingling flirtatiously. Nick and Meredith walked on, huddled together against the cold, occasionally laughing as one or the other stumbled over a patch of ice or an uncleared stretch of sidewalk.

They arrived back home, their faces red and cold and their boots wet with snow. Meredith began to skip up the steps into the warmth of the house, but Nick held her back, gently tugging her arm.

"Merry."

She turned to him with curiosity. "What is it?"

"Thank you."

"What for?"

"For making me happier than I've ever been in my entire life."

Meredith's face melted into a smile, and she took his hand.

"I want to make you happy, Merry," he continued. "If I can't do that, then I can't do anything."

"Oh, Nick," she said, reaching her arms up and cupping his face in her hands. "If I could only tell you..." She stopped, unable to find the right words. There was too much. She feared anything she said would devalue her feelings; no words could do them any justice. "You've given me my life," she said.

"I love you, Merry."

"I love you too."

She kissed him. He kept his lips on hers for several moments before pulling away, resting his forehead on hers and closing his eyes.

Finally she patted his shoulder. "Come on. Let's go inside," she said. "It's time for you to have me to yourself, remember?"

THE NEXT DAY, Saturday, Tara called Meredith in a panic, telling her that her babysitter had just canceled and that now they had no one to watch the girls while she and Tom went out to dinner with Tom's boss. Meredith assured her that she would be happy to babysit the girls for however long Tara needed her. Tara thanked her profusely and told her she was welcome to bring Nick along, just as long as there was no "funny business."

They arrived at Tara's house at six o'clock and were warmly welcomed by Tara, looking stunning in a simple black dress and high black boots, her auburn hair pulled up and wrapped around elegant hair pins. Tom had dressed up for the occasion, as well, and was wearing a formal black suit and white shirt. His perpetually knotted hair had been combed through and tamed into a wavy coif. He had done a good job cleaning up and concealing his proclivity for a more bohemian look. The giveaway was his tie: it was speckled with purple peace signs.

Tara gave Meredith instructions and told her where to find important phone numbers; then she and Tom thanked them and rushed out the door. Meredith turned to Nick. He was being led by the hand out of the living room by Evelyn.

Meredith followed them into the dining room, where macaroni and cheese awaited Evelyn and Ginger. Nick and Meredith sat down at the table with them.

"Hi, girls," Meredith said cheerfully. "How is your dinner? Is it yummy?"

"No," Evelyn said. "I like the white kind."

Meredith looked down at Evelyn's bowl. The cheese was orange, not white.

She picked a noodle from Evelyn's bowl and popped it in her mouth. "Mmm!" she exclaimed. "I think this tastes even better than the white kind."

"No," said Evelyn. "It's worse."

"Do you know why that cheese is orange?" Nick asked suddenly.

Meredith turned toward him with surprise.

"No," Evelyn said shyly, but with interest. "Why?"

Nick leaned forward. When he spoke, his voice was quiet. "Because a leprechaun touched it. Everything a leprechaun touches turns to gold. Did you know that?"

"No," Evelyn whispered, her eyes wide with fascination.

"It's true," he said, and leaned back in his seat.

Meredith was staring at him, dumbstruck. His eyes met hers, and he winked.

After dinner, Nick and Meredith played board games with Evelyn, Meredith occasionally jumping up to prevent Ginger from climbing on the furniture or putting something unsanitary into her mouth. Meredith admired the way Nick indulged Evelyn but did not talk down to her. He spoke to her patiently as he would to a peer, and he seemed to relate to her with little effort. Meredith felt as if her heart would burst.

She left him downstairs as she took the girls to their bedrooms to change them into their pajamas and read them a story before bed. She kissed Evelyn goodnight and then stayed with Ginger for a few minutes, stroking her hair and caressing her face until the little girl drifted off into a happy sleep. Then Meredith tiptoed downstairs.

Nick was sitting on the couch with the remote in his hand, flipping through the channels mindlessly, his head leaning against the back of the couch.

He smiled as she descended the staircase into the family room. "Hi," he said, and straightened. He reached his arm across the back of the couch as she took her seat next to him, and pulled her close, his hand on her shoulder.

"Hi," she said, and snuggled into him. She reached up and took his face in her hand, and kissed him. "You were so sweet with the girls," she said.

"They're cute. It's easy to be nice to them."

Meredith wanted to ask the inevitable question, but she couldn't muster up the courage.

"Maybe I'll have some kids one day," he said, anticipating her question.

Meredith drifted off into a pleasant reverie revolving around Nick and a pretty blond child, walking happily through the woods or finger painting together. She put the thought aside, trying not to get ahead of herself.

She then found herself imagining Nick as a small blond child, sitting quietly reading a picture book or examining plants in his backyard.

"Do you mind if I ask you a difficult question?"

He lifted his head, which had been resting on hers, and looked at her. "Sure."

"Why did your father leave you and your mother?"

Nick took a slow, deep breath, and rested his head on hers once more. "He quit his job to go out on his own, but he never could get enough business. My mother didn't blame him, but he blamed himself. He became pretty depressed. Eventually he just couldn't face it, and he left."

"How old were you?"

"I was in high school."

"Did it affect your relationship?"

"At first. I couldn't understand why he did it, and I hated what it did to my mother. But he always made time for me no matter what, and he asked about her all the time. It was almost like he thought she was better off without him. He seemed so broken. After a while I just felt sorry for him."

Meredith was watching him with a sober expression. "When did he go back?"

"I told him she had cancer, and he realized it was now or never. They spent her final years together, but he never forgave himself for missing all that time."

Nick and Meredith spent a peaceful night, watching a little television here and there but mostly talking, reminiscing, and laughing. Tom and Tara returned just before midnight and found them sitting on the couch together, Meredith's head leaning on Nick's shoulder and Nick lovingly stroking her arm. They rose and stretched, assured Tara that the girls had had a good night, and waved goodbye. They drove home in serene silence, and once they arrived, they went straight up to Meredith's bedroom, where they climbed into bed, whispered "I love you," and, holding each other, quickly fell asleep.

CHAPTER FOURTEEN

SACRIFICES

The next week was Valentine's Day. Nick and Meredith went out to dinner with Vince and Sandy, who had been won over by Vince's charm and ability to talk his way out of anything.

They chose a trendy French restaurant. At Nick's quiet request, Meredith explained the various French terms and ingredients, careful to keep her voice tactfully low to avoid broadcasting his confusion.

After their main courses, they sat leisurely in their booth with wine and dessert, Vince and Sandy feeding each other macarons and ice cream. Nick's arm was around Meredith's shoulder; Meredith was settled comfortably by his side.

"This is much better than last Valentine's Day," Sandy was saying in between bites of ice cream.

"What happened?" Meredith asked, grinning.

"I was stood up. It was a first date, and the guy never showed."

"Lucky for me," said Vince, his voice syrupy sweet. In response, Sandy gushed and cooed, scooting in closer and kissing his face all over.

"It's okay, Sandy," Meredith assured her, trying to ignore this excessive display. "I was alone last Valentine's Day, too."

"Yeah, and that was even worse when you consider what you had been doing the previous Valentine's Day," Vince said, draining the last of his wine.

"Oh?" Sandy asked as she refilled his glass. "What did you do that year, Meredith?"

"I went to see a production of *Romeo and Juliet* on Broadway," Meredith told her.

"Oh!" Sandy exclaimed, clapping her hands together gleefully, her eyes wide. "How romantic! What happened to the guy?"

Meredith stiffened but managed to put on a polite smile. "He passed away."

"Oh, my," Sandy replied, suddenly solemn. "I'm so sorry. I had no idea."

"It's okay," Meredith said. She patted Nick's thigh and felt his finger rubbing her shoulder.

Sandy's eyes rounded. "That must be why you didn't want to see the show. You know, the one in the city that time."

Meredith took a sip of her water, offering a nod in response. She had come a long way since that night. It was the last thing she wanted to talk about.

But Sandy was relentless.

"How long were you together?"

"We were together for five years."

"How did you know him?"

Meredith was becoming uncomfortable, and she was growing irritated with Sandy for not understanding the delicacy of the situation. She forced herself to answer, but her voice was flat and cool. "I met him in graduate school."

"Romantic and smart, too? He sounds like the perfect guy! He certainly knew how to sweep a girl off her feet. Only the best for our Merry, right?" Sandy gushed. "How nice that he took you all the way up to New York."

"We were living there at the time."

"You lived in New York? That must have been fun!"

Meredith was finding it more and more difficult to suppress her exasperation. She attempted to relay her feelings to Sandy through her eyes, but Sandy was on a roll.

"Nick, it looks like you've got some big shoes to fill! A professional woman who has lived in New York City with a smart, exciting man isn't going to be content to just sit around and watch the snow fall in Maine. Don't you think Merry's a little out of your league?" She winked at him, then laughed.

Meredith was now genuinely annoyed, and when she spoke again she couldn't help the flush from creeping into her face. She tried to keep her voice calm and cordial. "Not at all, Sandy. That was a long time ago, and I was a very different person back then. I'm completely happy with my life now. I wouldn't change anything, not a thing. Please, let's not talk about it anymore."

Sandy was taken aback and looked hurt. "I'm sorry," she said, glancing from Meredith to Nick. "I didn't mean anything by it. I guess that was kind of stupid of me to say." She appeared to be on the verge of tears. "Please don't be mad. I shouldn't have said that."

Meredith ordinarily would have put aside her displeasure and forgiven Sandy, but she had been pushed beyond her limits. She didn't like to talk about Adam, especially not over dinner and in front of Nick. Most importantly, she didn't want Nick to fear that she longed for the more fast-paced life she had lived in New York; on the contrary, she was eager to join him in Maine and to put that life behind her.

"Let's just change the subject," Vince said, attempting a light-hearted tone. "Sandy, honey—why don't you tell Nick and Meredith that story you were telling me earlier? You know, about what happened to you at work yesterday."

Sandy eagerly obliged, but Meredith didn't hear any of what she was saying. She glanced up at Nick, nervous about what she would see in his face, but as usual, his expression was unreadable as he watched Sandy tell her story.

NICK WAS quiet for the rest of the evening, more quiet than usual. He seemed deep in thought. Meredith worried that he was growing self-conscious, between their encounter with the obnoxious Trent at the bar and Sandy's tactless comments at dinner. As they undressed for bed that night, she went to him, running her hands up his waist and chest and kissing him on his shoulders and throat.

He stood still, only his hands moving to rest on her waist as he let her kiss and caress him. Meredith glanced up at his face. His eyes were open, and his mouth was turned outward into a serious line.

Meredith pulled away. "What are you thinking about?"

He shrugged. "Nothing in particular."

She frowned. "You're not thinking about Sandy, are you?"

He grinned. "She's not my type."

Meredith playfully slapped his arm and smiled. "I'm serious. Please don't give a second thought to what she said. I don't know what got into her tonight." She kissed his lips and rubbed his chest with her hands. "I'm so happy with you, Nick. Just the way things are. You do know that, don't you?"

"Of course I do," he said. He returned her kiss, then patted her hip. "Come on, beautiful. Let's go to bed."

She joined him, taking the lead and kissing and stroking him as he lay on his back, doing her best to take his mind off whatever he had been thinking about. Eventually he turned her on her back and crept on top of her, burying himself in her and responding to her kisses—but his rhythm was slow, and his embraces passionless, and Meredith felt that his heart wasn't in it.

NICK HAD BEEN WORKING on the set for the school play. He had procured the materials and cleared a space in Meredith's garage, which was full of her old furniture and household items, for which she had no use in her parents' fully furnished house. Meredith kept him company as he worked. She enjoyed the chatter, and she liked to watch him as he carefully measured and cut the wood that would build the final structure. He was full of life during these times, animated and enthusiastic, and he threw himself into the work with excitement that thrilled her.

He finished his work the last week of February, and on Friday he borrowed a coworker's truck to deliver it to the school. He met Meredith there during rehearsal. The students cheered as Nick and another teacher carried in the pieces, and they watched as Nick assembled it before their eyes.

Kevin clapped when it was completed, then shook Nick's hand vigorously with gratitude.

"Once again, we thank you," he said.

"I'm honored to have been a part of it," replied Nick, with a warm smile.

"It's just a small way for you to repay us for stealing Meredith from us," Kevin joked, shaking his head as he watched her. "We sure are going to miss her around here."

"I'll miss you too, Kevin," she said, "you and everyone else. I'm so fortunate to have had such a wonderful year here. "

"I don't know how we're going to find anyone quite so special," Kevin continued. He sighed, then turned to Nick. "Meredith certainly is one of a kind, as you know."

"I know," Nick said. He rubbed her back and smiled.

"Have you found a job in Maine yet?"

"No," she replied. "I've been looking, but the population is a lot smaller than it is here, and they don't need as many teachers. It's okay," she said, smiling. "I'll find something. If I don't find a classroom right away, I'll tutor. I've really enjoyed that this year."

"I sure hope so. You were made to teach, Meredith. It would be a shame for you not to be in front of a classroom."

"Thank you, Kevin, but I know it's going to work out."

They chatted for a few more minutes. Nick and Meredith then left, Meredith to go straight home, Nick to return the truck and drive back home with Vince.

That night the three of them went to Tara's house for dinner. Meredith had broken the news of her move to Tara, who had teared up with both joy and sadness, for while she knew Meredith would be with Nick, she was sorry to see her best friend leave her.

"I don't know what I'm going to do without you," she said at dinner, squeezing Meredith's shoulders as she walked by to grab more wine from the kitchen. "I need to be able to see you at least once a week. I'll go through withdrawals."

"You'll be fine," Meredith laughed. "I'm the one who's going to be a mess. How will I survive without you to help me make all my decisions for me?"

"You'll have Nick to do that," Tara said on her way back to the table, a sly look in her eye. "And I have a feeling he'll always tell you to sleep on it."

Everyone laughed.

"I am going to miss you, Merry," Tara said solemnly now, placing her hand on Meredith's as she took her seat across the table. "I really am."

Meredith squeezed her friend's hand. "I'll miss you too," she said. "Painfully so."

~

"MAYBE I SHOULD JUST MOVE to Pennsylvania," Nick said that night as they climbed into bed. "Everyone is going to miss you so much."

"No," Meredith replied decisively. "I want to get out of here. I need a change of scenery. There's nothing for me here." She propped her elbow on the pillow and leaned her head on her hand. "I'm looking forward to going to Maine. I'm excited about it." She smiled as he climbed into bed next to her and wrapped his arm around her waist, pulling her close.

"My life is not that exciting. I hope you aren't disappointed."

"I don't want exciting. I'm ready for peace and quiet."

"But what about your teaching?"

"Honestly, I don't care anymore. As long as I'm with you, it doesn't matter what kind of job I have."

"I just want to do what's best for you."

"Let me be the judge of that," she said, and leaned in for a kiss.

IT WAS the middle of March. Vince and Nick were leaving to return to Maine in April. Meredith's parents were returning in August, when Meredith would move permanently to Maine to be with Nick. In the meantime, she would continue her preparations to move, consolidating her belongings and looking for a job, for though she had made many phone calls and sent out dozens of resumes, she had been unable to secure one. Though at one time this unknown would have frightened her, her inability to find a job made her upcoming move that much more exciting. She couldn't wait to focus more on her cooking. Also, she was growing more and more delighted by the idea of private tutoring. She felt for the first time that she was making her own choices, that her future was completely hers.

After their conversation the night they returned home from Tara's, Nick seemed especially thoughtful for a couple of days, and more than once Meredith found him staring at her with intensity, his face contemplative. Something about his expression frightened her. Meredith tried to extract from him what he had been thinking about, but he remained close-lipped about it.

Time comforted him, evidently, and before long they went back to their normal happy life, both growing more and more eager every day for the prospect of the big move. Meredith was exhilarated and looked forward to closing this chapter of her life and beginning anew in a new place, with the man she loved.

One afternoon, less than two weeks away from Vince and Nick's departure, Meredith was packing up after her last class when she heard a knock at the door. Lifting her head, she was delighted to see Nick, smiling and stepping unhurriedly into the room. Her face brightened, and she met him halfway across the room, embracing him and kissing him.

"This is a nice surprise!" she exclaimed. "What are you doing here?"

"Taking you out for an early dinner," he said, his arms around her and his hands folded together at her lower back. "Vince and I knocked off work early today. He's waiting in the car."

"How wonderful! Let me just grab my things."

She returned to her desk and picked up her messenger bag, and immediately her eyes fell upon a quiz she had forgotten to drop off for photocopying. She took it in her hands, intending to run to the office, when her door opened again. In stepped Ned, work bag and keys in hand.

"Hi, Ned," she said quickly. She turned to Nick. "Honey, I'll be right back, okay? I just need to run this down the hall."

"Okay," Nick said, a smile creasing his eyes. "I'll be waiting."

Meredith smiled and hurried from the room.

She was held up on her way back by a straggling student with a question about his grade. Meredith tried her best to comfort him, explaining what he could do to improve his writing and showing him a couple of examples from his most recent essay. Satisfied, the boy thanked her and walked away. Meredith returned to her classroom.

Ned pushed the door open to leave just as she was approaching. "See you, Meredith," he said, and walked briskly off.

Something about his expression made her uncomfortable, and when she entered the room, she was overcome by an ominous feeling. The atmosphere felt tense. Nick was standing where she had left him, in the middle of the room, but his usually composed face was white and unsettled. He didn't meet her gaze right away; she had to take a few steps toward him before he looked up. When he did, his eyes were wide and had the subtle sharpness of panic.

"What's wrong?" she asked, hurrying to him and taking his hand in hers.

He said nothing, but glared briefly at the door once more before turning his attention to her.

"Let's get out of here," he said, and, placing his hand on her back, he guided her from the room.

Meredith was rattled. She and Nick said nothing as they walked out to Vince's car. Once there, Nick gave her a quick kiss, then went right for the back seat and slid inside, closing the door with a thud.

Meredith wanted to greet her brother and ask to what occasion she owed this surprise, but she was too upset. Vince evidently sensed the tension.

"What happened?" he asked.

Meredith opened her mouth to tell him she wasn't sure, but Nick's voice sounded from the back before she could say anything.

"I'm not feeling too well," he said. "Why don't you two drop me off and then just go to dinner by yourselves."

Meredith turned to face him. She reached behind her seat to place her hand on his knee. "Please tell me what's wrong," she said, trying to keep the desperation out of her voice. "Did Ned say something to upset you?"

"I'll be fine. I'd just like to go home."

"I'm worried about you."

"Don't be," he said, forcing himself to look at her. His breathing was short and quick, as if his heart were pounding, and Meredith could see his chest moving up and down. He attempted a weak smile. "It's nothing."

She frowned, her own heart racing. She turned to face forward once again. Vince put the car in gear and drove off.

When they arrived at the house, Nick placed his hand on Meredith's shoulder and kissed her cheek, then swung the door open and stepped outside as quickly as he could.

"Give me a minute," she said to Vince, and climbed out of the car.

She stopped Nick as he was bounding up the walkway toward the house.

"Nick, please," she begged. "Something's wrong. Please tell me what it is."

He looked down at her with eyes full of emotion. "I just need some time to myself."

"What's going on with us? You've seemed so worried lately, and now—"

Nick pulled her in close, taking her face in his hands and kissing her firmly several times.

"It's nothing you should be concerned about," he told her. His eyes met hers. "I love you, Merry. Please don't ever doubt that."

"Why would I doubt that?"

He released his grip and looked at her as she stood before him.

"You shouldn't. I'll see you later, beautiful," he said, tucking her hair behind her ear. "I'm sure I'll be feeling better by then. Have fun with your brother." He kissed her, then turned and walked toward the house.

Meredith let him go, not knowing what else she could do. She trudged back toward the car. Her eyes fell on Vince in the driver's seat. He was watching her, his face dark with worry.

She opened the door and fell dejectedly into the car.

"What's going on?" Vince asked gently.

She bit her lower lip, holding back tears. "Nothing," she said. "Just drive."

Vince drove off. Meredith couldn't understand what had happened. They were so happy. They both were eager to begin their life together. They had been planning this for weeks and had talked with excitement about it every night. Now she had the uneasy feeling that it was about to fall apart. She was terrified.

As Vince pulled onto the main road, Meredith's thoughts drifted to Ned. She knew deep down that Nick had begun to worry about his ability to make her happy. Ned must have said something that further encouraged this absurd fear. She vowed to confront him about it tomorrow.

They pulled into the parking lot of one of Meredith's favorite Italian restaurants. It was early, and Meredith was the furthest thing from hungry. Even if she hadn't had a meal in days she knew she wouldn't be able to eat a bite.

She put her hand on the door to open it, but Vince's hand on hers stopped her.

"Are you okay?" he asked.

Meredith sat back in her seat and stared straight ahead. "I wish I knew what was going on," she said. She turned to him. "Has Nick said anything to you?"

"No. I wish I had an answer for you."

She studied his face. His expression was kind.

"Thanks, Vince," she said, her eyes softening. She closed her eyes and leaned back against the seat again. "Please," she said to no one in particular. "Please let it be okay."

They sat in silence for some time, Meredith falling deep into thought. She knew something was wrong. It wasn't like Nick to be so upset, much less to show it. The frantic look in his eyes had scared her. She hoped desperately that a couple of hours to himself would calm him down and make him more inclined to share his worries with her.

Her door opened. Vince was standing there, prepared to help her out of the car. She hadn't even noticed him climbing out of his own seat.

Numbly, she unbuckled her seatbelt and stepped out of the car, taking the arm he offered and following him into the restaurant. She endured dinner in a daze, merely picking at her food and gazing absently around her, unable to focus. Vince attempted light conversation but soon gave up and motioned to the waiter for the check.

They drove back to school in silence. Sick with worry, Meredith climbed into her own car and drove home. She pulled into the driveway a couple of minutes after Vince and met him in the entryway as he was pulling off his boots.

Nick, having heard them enter the house, was descending the staircase as she walked in. His eyes remained on her as she removed her jacket and stood there waiting for him to say something. Vince awkwardly excused himself and went upstairs to his bedroom.

"We have to talk," Nick said.

She stood still, afraid that if she moved she would faint. Her breathing was hurried, and her heart was thumping painfully in her chest. Making every effort to keep the fear out of her face, she watched him as he approached her and stood before her, his eyes dark.

The suspense was unbearable.

"Just tell me," she said. "Please."

He inhaled, steadying himself. He said, "I'm not going to lie to you, Merry. I'm worried. I don't know that I can do this."

Her composure left her, and her expression turned frantic. "I know Ned said something to upset you. Please tell me what it is so we can work it out together. I love you." She took his hands in hers. "Whatever is wrong, we can make it right."

"This isn't about Ned. I've been feeling this way for a while."

"But won't you tell me what he said?"

"He didn't say anything. Just forget it."

"This must be coming from somewhere. Yesterday things were fine."

"But they weren't fine. It's a hundred little things all adding up. It's just too much."

Meredith looked up at him, her mind spinning out of control. He was watching her, contemplation making his blue eyes deep and his long lips straight and stern. His hair looked swept backward, as if he had been running his fingers through it.

He rubbed her shoulders. "You know how I feel about you. I can't even imagine one day without you, much less a lifetime." His forehead creased with thought. "But I would only hold you back. I can't possibly give you everything you deserve."

"You mean a lifetime of love and happiness? I'll take that any day over money."

"It's not about money, Merry. If you come to Maine with me, you'll be leaving a stable job and the chance to live a stable life. I couldn't live with myself knowing I was the reason you weren't in front of a classroom, where you belong, especially if I'm not even home half the time. Who knows where I'll have to travel to a month from now? And even if I left my job for one that didn't require me to travel, even if I moved down here to Pennsylvania," he said, and instantly Meredith knew he had considered it, "I'd never live up to what you're used to or what your family wants for you. I'll never be the intellectual who writes editorials for the paper. I can't possibly compete with all that."

"Don't you see?" Meredith pleaded, placing her hands on his chest. "I don't care about any of that. I've spent a lifetime worrying about it. I want to go with you because those things don't matter when I'm with you."

He was watching her carefully now, his expression burdened

by conflict. "We have some time to think about it," he said. "I haven't made any decisions yet."

Meredith bristled and stepped back a couple of inches. "Please don't make decisions about my life without consulting me. Why do all the men in my life seem to think I can't make decisions for myself?"

"I'm only trying to help you."

"Then don't help me," she said, her voice choking with tears. "I love you, Nick. You said you love me. That should be enough."

"I do love you, Merry. I've never loved anyone else. There's nothing more I want than to be with you. But you deserve someone who can give you so much more. Maybe Vince was right after all. Maybe I'm not reliable enough. Maybe you would be better off with someone more like Adam."

Meredith's eyes widened. "That's what this is about? You're worrying over what Vince said? You said yourself that it wasn't about you. And I wish you wouldn't compare yourself to Adam. I'm with you now, and I'm happy. Who cares about the past?"

"How can I not care about the past when the differences are so obvious?"

"Honey, I love those differences. That's the whole point."

"But one day you might not. And they'll always be there in the back of my mind."

They stood in silence.

Finally, Nick kissed her forehead. "Let's not talk about it anymore right now. We still have a couple of weeks."

Meredith nodded and let him pull her close. She had never known anyone who could make life so simple; she wondered how he could make everything so complicated, at the time when it mattered the most. She returned his embrace in a haze, hardly believing this could be happening.

"I love you," he whispered.

"Please don't leave me," she replied, and pressed her face to his.

❧

THE NEXT DAY, Meredith kissed Nick goodbye and went to work early so she could visit Ned in his classroom before their first class.

She deposited her bag and jacket in her own classroom and reentered the hallway, headed down the hall. Ignoring her nervousness, willing her heartbeat to slow, she entered the room without knocking and spied him sitting at his desk, preparing the day's lessons. He looked up upon hearing the door open. When he saw who it was, he dropped his pen on the desk and sat back in his chair, staring at her.

"Hello, Meredith. You're here bright and early this morning. To what do I owe the pleasure of a visit from you?"

It took every ounce of self-restraint for Meredith to suppress the urge to tell him what she really thought of him, instead tightening her jaw and forcing into her voice a calm she did not feel.

"What did you say to Nick yesterday?" she asked.

"I don't know what you mean."

"I see. You're going to be a coward and deny it."

Ned seemed to be trying to decide what his approach should be. Finally he appeared to have come to a decision. He rose from his chair and faced her.

"It wasn't a big deal. We were just discussing *King Lear*."

Meredith was taken aback. She shook her head with confusion. "I don't understand."

"I asked Nick if he had read it recently, and he said he hadn't. I told him he should pick it up because he might get a kick out of it, seeing as it's full of guys who do dastardly deeds even though they appear to be good on paper."

"Ned, what's your point?"

"You've read *Lear*. You know all about it. I only mentioned it to Nick because you said you usually go for men who are good on paper."

Her eyes grew wide. She had begun to feel queasy, and her heart was pounding. "What are you talking about?"

"Don't you remember? You told Beth that being with Nick is different for you because he isn't good on paper."

"Oh, my God," she gasped, the heaviness of dread seeping into her chest. "You didn't tell him that, did you?"

"Of course."

"Oh, Ned." Her voice had begun to shake. "Ned, how could you?"

"Don't worry about it. I made clear that you meant it as a compliment. I said you had been telling your friend all about how you had only ever been with that type of man and never saw yourself going in any other direction. I told him he shouldn't be offended that you called him simple, either. You were just explaining that you were due for a change."

Meredith was furious. There was so much to say that she didn't know where to begin or how to calm herself. She thought about Nick, recalling all the times he had expressed insecurity, and though she resolved to explain what her meaning had been and that Ned had taken her words totally out of context, she knew the damage had been done.

"I can't believe you could be so cruel," she uttered through her pain. "You completely twisted my words. And now, because of you, Nick is seriously considering ending our relationship."

"You can thank me later. You'd eventually grow bored with a guy like that. I tried to talk to him. Not much of a conversationalist. There doesn't seem to be too much behind the eyes, if you ask me."

"I *didn't* ask you." She was keeping her voice constrained with effort; the rage was piling in her heart, her head, her throat. "You don't even know him, Ned. In the ways that matter, he's wiser than anyone I've ever met, and he's made me happier than I ever thought I could be after my life fell apart a year and a half ago."

"I could have done that, too, without requiring you to lower your standards."

His malice took her breath away. Tears stung in her eyes, but she ignored them. "I told you time and time again that I wasn't interested. You did this for spite, knowing it wouldn't do anything but hurt people."

Ned was unmoved. "Don't blame me. Frankly, I think you're very ungrateful, Meredith, for all the help I've given you since you've been here. The least you could have done was give me a chance."

Meredith realized that Ned had been exploiting her grief and her kindness the entire time, that he didn't mean well after all, that his ego was more fragile than his interest in her was strong, that the sick feeling she had in his presence had been justified, that she should have trusted her instincts instead of constantly giving him the benefit of the doubt and subverting her own feelings, that in this case, her optimism had been not only misguided, but dangerous—in short, that Beth had been right all along. She stood there, stunned, furious with him and furious with herself, vowing never to question her instincts again.

What was done was done. She was left to try to pick up the pieces. All she could do now was learn from this, and move forward.

"It wasn't really help," she said through her teeth, nauseated by his utter lack of remorse or apology, "not in the way you should have meant it. It was all for yourself, to get what you wanted. I don't owe you anything."

"Maybe you should calm down first, and then we can talk about it rationally."

It was the final straw. His contempt and misogyny were so obvious now, her having missed it seemed incredible. To think, she had been so worried about sparing his feelings, when he'd been using her all this time. And now that she was finally calling him on it, he was playing the victim. Everything was fine until she refused to be passive; once she stood up for herself, she was the dreaded hysterical woman. It was manipulation—it was gaslighting—and it had gone completely over her head. If she hadn't been so upset, she might have laughed.

"There's nothing to talk about. You hurt a nice person, on purpose, out of spite. I will never talk to you again."

She turned toward the door without waiting for his response. "I know you may find this hard to believe, but you don't know everything about everybody. What you don't know about Nick is that he is the kindest, most gentle-hearted man I know—and that's a lot more than I can say for you."

From the doorway, she faced him once more. "Congratulations, Ned," she said bitterly. "You succeeded. You've made me just as unhappy as you are." She placed her hand on the doorknob. "I hope you feel good about yourself."

With that, she stormed out of the room.

MEREDITH TAUGHT her classes with effort, hoping her lessons would serve as distractions from the terror that was oppressing her every second. Nothing she did that day was free of it; it was a presence in her mind and in her heart, and she went through the motions of the day in agony, counting the seconds until she could return home and try to straighten out the spiraling storm her life had suddenly become.

When she guessed that Vince and Nick would be on their way home, she threw herself into dinner, letting her mind drift, feeling tormented by a pang of fear whenever her thoughts returned to reality. She placed everything carefully on three plates and looked them over, not even knowing how they had gotten there.

Two minutes later, the front door opened, and Meredith heard Vince and Nick step inside. For the first time, she was afraid to meet them. She willed her legs to move toward the entryway, where she was surprised to see Nick standing alone.

"Where's Vince?" she asked, already feeling the tears.

Nick's face was grave, and he said nothing. Meredith waited for him to speak, too nervous to speak herself. Still he was silent. Meredith noticed that his jaw was working, his eyebrows were furrowed sharply and his chest was heaving. In an instant she knew that he was stifling tears of his own.

Overcome, she turned and flew up the stairs as quickly as she could. She heard him calling her name, but she was incapable of responding. She went into her bedroom and shut and locked the door, then locked herself in the bathroom. She left the light off and sat on the floor in total darkness, a darkness which mimicked the darkness inside her. It was the only thing she could think of to do.

MEREDITH DIDN'T KNOW how long she had sat in the bathroom; she felt as if she had left her body and floated away to a place where she couldn't feel the pain she knew was going to obliterate her as soon as she came back down. She put it off, floating above herself in numb oblivion for as long as she could. Finally she stood, arching her back painfully and realizing she must have been sitting on the floor much longer than she had thought.

She opened the bathroom door and emerged into the darkness of her bedroom. The clock on her nightstand told her it was after eight o'clock. She had been sitting in the dark bathroom for over two hours.

She desperately wanted to see Nick, to try to talk him out of his decision, to see his eyes crinkle kindly, letting her know everything would be okay. But she couldn't bring herself to open the door. She knew once she did she would collapse. She wasn't ready to hear the words just yet. She needed a night to revel in her memories before they were tainted with heartache.

She stripped off her school clothes and left them lying on the floor, then climbed into bed in the darkness and lay there with her eyes wide open, missing his presence next to her and realizing that this was what her nights would feel like from now on. Her hand dropped to his side of the bed, and the emptiness there was too much. The tears overwhelmed her, and she sobbed, her breaths choking her as she once again began understanding what it would be like to sleep without the man she loved beside her, to fall asleep cold and alone and yearning for a touch she would never feel again. In her mind she deliberately and painstakingly recalled every memory she and Nick had made together, from the night he had comforted her in her room to just the night before, when they had fallen asleep knowing that in the morning everything would change forever. The joy of those nights stood before her like a ghost, and she remembered every touch, every laugh, every sigh, every word.

She didn't know how long it had taken her to fall asleep, but her face was wet with tears when she awoke to her alarm. They continued to fall as she forced herself to shower and dress for school, not knowing how she was going to make it through the day.

When she had dressed and pulled herself together as best she could, she opened the door to her bedroom and stopped short. Nick was sitting outside her bedroom, still in his clothes from the day before, his feet planted on the floor and his arms wrapped around his bent knees, his back and head resting against the wall. He was fast asleep.

∼

MEREDITH TALKED ONLY when she had to that day. She scratched her lesson plans and assigned in-class essays in all four classes, ignoring the groans of her students. She pulled out a stack of papers to be graded, but she had no intention of grading them; she needed a pretext to sit and stare into nothingness, and to think.

When she pulled up to the house that afternoon, she was surprised to find Vince's car parked out front. She listlessly grabbed her work bag from the back seat and walked into the house.

Vince and Nick were sitting in the dining room, their elbows on the table as they leaned in toward each other, engaged in quiet conversation. At the sound of her approach, they stood. Vince kissed her forehead, lingering a second or two longer than necessary, and then headed up to his bedroom.

Meredith turned to Nick.

"I'm sorry I locked you out last night."

"I understand."

"It isn't that I didn't want to see you," she continued, trying to keep her voice flat. "I just—"

"It's okay. I understand."

They stood in silence.

He approached her, then placed his hands on her shoulders and stroked her arms.

"Can we go for a walk?" he said.

Meredith stared at him, then shrugged. Nothing seemed to matter anymore.

They walked out of the house and headed to the left. Her mind drifted to their first walk together, after their visit to the museum, when he had shown her his playful side by throwing a snowball in her face and tackling her into the snow. She decided they would walk back to the park.

He took her hand and walked with her in silence all the way to the park. She tried to absorb him, imprinting into her mind every detail of how his hand felt as it held hers. The first time they had visited the park together, the day had been cold, snowy and gray, but today was comfortably warm, and sunny. With sadness she remembered that they had first held hands while walking to this park, how they had talked about the beauty of Maine and then kissed in the snow.

They arrived at the park and stopped.

"I can't do this," she cried, and turned from him to head back home.

She felt his hands around her waist, pulling her back.

He brusquely turned her around so she was facing him; she was surprised by the force of his grip.

"Merry, this is killing me," he cried through a clenched jaw. "Absolutely killing me. Do you understand that?" His eyes were wild with pain, and his lips formed a long frown. He was practically shaking her, his hands clenching her waist. "Do you have any idea how hard it is for me to say goodbye to you?" He let go of her and spun around so his back was to her. He stood before her, his hands now at his hips and his face lifted toward the air as he gathered his strength.

"I never thought I'd have with anyone what I have with you, Merry," he said, more calmly now, though his voice sounded shaky and unfamiliar. With a frightened start she realized he was in tears; though his back was to her, she could see it in the way he was breathing, and she could hear it in his voice. "I thought we could put it all behind us and just be together. I kept thinking, 'Finally, someone I can see myself with. Someone who understands.' Only this time, I was the one who didn't understand. It isn't that simple. All the things I never thought were important— they are important. I just didn't know it. God, I've been so ignorant. I can't believe all the years I've wasted caring about all the wrong things."

"You had it right before," she said through her own tears. "Don't let everyone else make you feel like you didn't understand. You understand more than you think you do."

He said nothing, but looked at the ground and shook his head.

She took a step toward him. "Ned told me about your conversation yesterday. Don't take anything he says seriously. He has been after me since day one and is doing anything he can to pull us apart. I promise, I didn't mean it like he said. I was telling Beth about how refreshing it was to be with you. I also told her that you're good at heart and a nice person, but of course Ned twisted my words and left that part out. Nick, I love you. I would never say what he told you I said."

He turned to look at her. "I know you didn't mean it like that, Merry. I know you love me and that Ned twisted your words. You didn't do anything wrong. It still doesn't change anything."

"But why not? If you know that's how I feel, why does anything else matter?"

"Because it's been made clear to me in a hundred other ways. I know you meant it to be kind. You're a kind person. But however you meant what you said, the fact remains that you were right. I am a change of direction for you. And I feel like I'd never live up."

Meredith shook her head and wiped her eyes.

"Take the play," he went on. "Working on that set just reminded me how much I love doing things like that. Carpentry, creating something. Enjoying something. Following in my father's footsteps." He sighed and stared forward. "And I've never done anything with it."

"But you were," she told him, taking a few steps toward him. "Just like I was. It was a start. It was a possibility. It should make you feel good about yourself."

"It made me feel worse, because I've strayed so far from that path."

"There's nothing wrong with the path you're on. You have a good job, and you're good at it."

"There's nothing wrong with that path. But it's not *my* path. Even my father struck out on his own; even he took risks. I haven't taken any risks. I've done nothing. I've made nothing of myself, in all this time."

"You have your whole life in front of you, Nick. You have plenty of time to do whatever you want."

"I've done nothing," he repeated. "I need to figure out why."

Meredith's heart was breaking. She sighed and rubbed his shoulder.

"You just deserve more," he said. "I just can't be the person you always imagined for yourself. And if I can't do that, you'll grow unhappy. You think you won't, but I don't want to be the one you resent one day because I couldn't be everything you needed."

She shook her head sadly. "Nick, what you don't understand is that I don't need anything else. I'd live in a box on the street if it meant I'd be with you."

"It's not about that!" he cried, taking her shoulders in his hands. "It's not just about my job or where we live. It's about everything I'm not. Adam interviewed your famous father for his dissertation. I never even went to college, Merry." He frowned. "I want to think it won't mean anything. I really do. It's just that—"

"Oh, Nick," Meredith whispered. Every word sharpened the ache in her heart as she listened, and her view of him was clouded by tears. "What you are is gentle and kind. That's why I love you. I want you to take me away, to show me something new."

"You say that now, but one day you'll regret making these sacrifices. And I just can't be the one to let you make them."

"I don't want anyone else, and I don't want the life you want for me. The only sacrifice here is the one you're making."

He stroked her cheek and smiled ruefully as he tucked her hair behind her ear. "I'll bet you thought you would never find love again after Adam."

Meredith was silent.

"But you did. And you will again."

Sadness and frustration twisted deep inside her. She had to reach him.

She tried again.

"You're the one who keeps telling me not to worry about anybody else. And now here you are, worrying about everybody else, comparing yourself to ghosts."

"It's not the same thing."

"It is. It's like you think you don't deserve to be happy. It's self-flagellation. It's exactly what I was doing, but in reverse."

"I just can't do it, Merry. Not now."

Meredith wanted to continue to argue, to make him see. All this time, his uncomplicated wisdom had helped push her over the threshold toward the new normal she had needed. And yet he seemed totally unable to take his own advice, to do what made him happy, to take something broken and make something better with the pieces. She wanted to say all this, but her mind was growing numb. She wondered how it so quickly had become so hard.

She was exhausted. She gave up.

"Come on," she said. "Let's go home."

They held each other as they returned to the house. Wordlessly, they climbed the stairs together and walked hand in hand into Meredith's bedroom, but unlike other nights tonight the deep sleep they fell into held no comfort. Meredith awoke in the morning in his arms, like all other mornings, but instead of wondering blissfully what the day would bring, she found herself gloomily contemplating the rest of her life.

THEY SPENT one sad week like this, trying to enjoy the time they had left but living a shadow of their former life, doing everything they normally did but with the knowledge that it would be over in a matter of days. Meredith was numb. She was miserable at work; it was all she could do to smile for her students and not hide from her colleagues. She had barely spoken to Vince at all, unsure if he was more apt to be sympathetic or angry and feeling unable to deal with either.

On the final morning, Meredith and Nick awoke together for the last time. She dressed in a daze and could barely muster the strength to join them at the breakfast table. She ate not a bite and did not try to control her tears. She poured herself a cup of coffee but didn't drink it. Vince and Nick commented occasionally about their trip home, but otherwise everyone was silent.

Finally they returned upstairs to retrieve their suitcases. When she heard them descending, she placed her coffee cup on the counter and met them in the entryway. She closed her eyes against the vision of them preparing to leave her, but she couldn't escape the heaviness in her chest.

They put on their jackets and stood looking at her, each waiting for the other to begin.

Vince stepped toward her and embraced her. When he pulled away, Meredith saw that his eyes were full of tears.

"Merry, I...I just..."

"Please, Vince," she said. "Don't try to say it. I know. I just know."

He smiled sorrowfully as his eyes bore into hers. "I love you so much, Merry. I'm so glad I got to see you. I'm so glad we..." He stopped, his jaw working as he fought back emotion. He swallowed and rubbed her shoulder. "Thank you for everything."

"You're welcome. I love you too, Vince. Please call me."

"I will." He kissed her and walked out the door with his suitcase. Her heart seemed to go with him; she was empty and dark inside, made breathless by the force of her sorrow. She had spent so much time missing him, her friend and protector; she'd convinced herself her aloneness was preferred, but he had reminded her of how she needed her loved ones. His reappearance in her life, his boisterous presence, had soothed her more than she had known. Now that he was gone again, she was bereaved.

Eyes prickling with tears, she looked at Nick. He stood several feet from her, his hands in his pockets, and they looked at each other across this space. After some time Nick approached her with slow, even steps until he was standing just before her. He rubbed his finger against her chin, brushing her lips and then cupping her face in his hand. A sad smile creased the corners of his eyes as he attempted to relay in one look everything they had shared in the last four months.

He took her face in his hands and kissed her lips softly. "I love you, Merry," he whispered. "I'm sorry."

He tucked a stray lock of hair behind her ear. Meredith took his hand in hers as he stroked her neck, and lovingly kissed his fingers.

"I love you, Nick. Please come back to me one day."

She had so much more to say but couldn't bring herself to try. She held her face in her hands as he walked out the door, shutting it gently on his way out.

Meredith stood motionless for a few moments, staring at the closed door and wondering what she was going to do with herself, alone in this empty house all day and all night. She picked her phone from off the table and called her school, telling them she wouldn't be able to make it in that day. Then she called Tara.

"Tara," she said before breaking down. "I need you."

CHAPTER FIFTEEN

BE HAPPY

"I just don't get it," Tara was saying, shaking her head. "It just seemed to happen so suddenly."

Meredith nodded mechanically, her hands wrapped around a cup of coffee that had long ago turned cold.

"Maybe you still have a chance, honey. It's obvious he still loves you. Maybe he just needs to leave for a while to see that he can't go on without you."

"And what if he can?" Meredith said, looking up at Tara, her eyes red from crying. "What if he discovers that it isn't so hard? Then what?"

"Then it wasn't meant to be," Tara said kindly, holding her friend's hand.

Meredith turned her head toward the window. Her elbow propped up on the table, she held her chin in her hands. "I don't know, Tara. I just don't know how he can walk away from it all. When I think back to the times..." She stopped, unable to go on. Tara handed her a tissue. Meredith took it and wiped her eyes.

Tara was watching her, her brow creased with sympathy.

"It's just so wrong."

Meredith nodded again, and sighed.

Tara shook her head. "I guess he just needs to work some things out. You know what they say: if you can't love yourself, you can't love someone else."

Meredith frowned, more dejected than ever. "Maybe he'll work them out and feel better. Maybe he'll come back." She closed her eyes; she knew he wasn't coming back. "I just can't believe it's over."

They sat in silence for several moments.

Finally Meredith spoke. "I have to get out of here."

"Okay," Tara said, grabbing her purse. "I have the sitter for two more hours."

"No," Meredith said. "I mean, I can't stay here, not in this house. I have to move."

Tara sat back down. "Do you mean that? Or is that just the sadness talking?"

Meredith looked at her. "I've lived here almost my entire life. With the exception of college and my time with Adam, this town has been my home for as long as I can remember. It's time for me to go. I need to make my own life now. I can't stay here where there are so many memories."

Tara's eyes softened. "I understand." She once again held out her hand. "I'll be sad, but I understand."

"I wish I didn't have to leave you," Meredith said. "But I'll shrivel up if I stay here—especially once my parents come back."

"Yes, I agree."

"Now I just have to figure out where to go."

They thought about it for a minute or two.

"You can go anywhere you'd like," Tara said, trying to sound cheerful. "The world is your oyster now. You can choose for yourself what you want to do."

"There's the problem of money, of course. I don't have a lot, and I'd hate to sink what little of it I have into a house when I'm so constantly in transit. I'd be nervous about buying before I know where I'm going to be."

"You could rent."

"I'm so sick of renting," Meredith said, rubbing her face in her hands. "I want to be done with the temporary nonsense. I feel like I'm constantly uprooting. Just put me somewhere and let me be."

"Maybe this thing with Nick is for the best, then. He travels a lot."

"But the one consistent thing would be him. That's all that matters."

MEREDITH COUNTED the minutes until her spring break, which was ten days in the middle of April. She had about two weeks to go. The weather had grown warm and pleasant, and she was somewhat soothed by the longer days and the yellow glow of the spring sun.

She decided to take each day, each class, each moment at a time, and she managed to make it through those first two weeks, holding it together in school and grieving at home. She knew it would be a long time before she could wake up and not expect to feel Nick beside her, before she wouldn't peek expectantly out the window for Vince's car every night. She thought of Nick constantly. Not a moment passed when he wasn't with her. She wondered what he was doing, whether he was missing her, whether he was home or at work, what he was eating for dinner, whether he imagined her lying next to him at night as she imagined him.

She missed him terribly. She missed the way he greeted her with a lingering kiss, the way even the brush of his fingers on her back sent delightful shivers up her spine, the way they chatted quietly at night before climbing into bed, the way he joked with her and kept her company and loved her, and so appreciated her loving him. She thought of how he had forever changed her perspective and wondered how she would ever feel right again.

Finally she said goodbye to the school for spring break. The vacation's arrival was bittersweet, for while she was happy to have some time to regroup, she could not help but remember her last vacation and the happy times she had spent with Nick.

When she had been on vacation for a couple of days, she couldn't get a certain thought out of her mind. She picked up her phone.

"Hey, Merry," Vince's voice burst from the other end. "I've been meaning to call you. How are things?"

"Could be better," Meredith told him listlessly.

"Look, I'm really sorry about what happened. I didn't want you to get hurt. I wish I could take it away for you."

"I know. I appreciate it."

They let a few moments of silence pass.

"So," she began nervously. "Is there anything you want to tell me?"

"If you're asking me about Nick, you'll be happy to hear that he's been moping around like a sad puppy ever since we got back. He doesn't talk to anyone, and he never smiles."

Meredith's heart skipped a beat. "Has he said anything about what happened?"

"No. But he wouldn't."

Meredith paused, gathering strength. "Vince," she said. "I want to go up and see him. And you, of course. But I want to surprise him."

Vince was silent for a moment. "Merry, I don't know if that's a good idea."

"Why not?" she pleaded. "It's obvious he's just as sad as I am. Maybe if he sees me, he'll realize that he was wrong."

"What about school?"

"I'm on vacation for another week."

Vince said nothing, but after a few more moments, Meredith

heard him sigh. "All right, Merry—if you want to give it one last try, go for it. But do it soon, because he's leaving in three days."

Meredith's heart dropped. "Leaving? To go where?"

"To California. He'll be there for three months."

Meredith was shocked. "What about you? You're not going?"

"No. Nick specifically requested to go out on this job."

Meredith swallowed hard. "Give me his address. I'm leaving right now."

MEREDITH QUICKLY PACKED A SUITCASE, glanced around to make sure she hadn't forgotten anything, and hurried out her front door. She pulled out of her driveway at one o'clock in the afternoon. According to her GPS, she should arrive at Nick's door at midnight.

She was determined to drive straight through, stopping only for gas. She knew her way as far as Boston; after that she would be on her own in a strange place at night, guided only by the GPS. She was nervous but excited, full of anxiety but also of hope. At the very least she was thrilled that she would see Nick again in a matter of hours. Whenever she doubted the intelligence of this endeavor, she imagined him embracing her as they reunited, how he'd tuck her hair gently behind her ear—and she was spurred on.

By four o'clock she had made it as far north as Connecticut, beating New York City traffic by about an hour. Her heart lurched as she saw the familiar road signs of Connecticut for the first time since Adam passed away; they had come here frequently to visit his parents. Those had been happy times. As she passed the exit she would take if she were to visit them, she wondered how his parents and siblings were, how they were handling life without him. Meredith and Adam's family had kept in touch for a while after Adam's passing; they always had had a good relationship, and they genuinely cared about each other. After a while, however, it had grown too painful for everyone, and his siblings had scattered—and they had lost touch.

Meredith hit rush hour traffic near Hartford, and she sat almost still on I-95 as everyone inched painfully along. She sighed with frustration and leaned her head on her hand, her elbow propped against the door. At this rate she wouldn't be with Nick until after one o'clock in the morning.

After an hour of traffic, she resigned herself to pulling over for gas and dinner. By the time she returned to her car, the traffic had lightened, but she also had lost another half hour. Her blood was racing; she frowned at the thought that she would be oppressed by this stress for at least six more hours.

She crossed through Massachusetts, the memories of pleasant family vacations temporarily alleviating the burden of her anxiety. Meredith's parents had made time to take her and Vince to the Berkshire Mountains every year, spending a week in a cabin surrounded by nothing but trees, lakes, and open sky. It was there that Meredith had learned to love the outdoors. Frequently they had spent time in Boston and Cape Cod; her mother had family in Nauset Beach, and her visits here stood out as the happiest times of her childhood.

Her heart raced as she passed a sign welcoming her to New Hampshire. Now she was farther north than she had ever been. She stopped again for gas at the first convenient exit, not sure when she'd have another chance and wanting to do so before it grew too late. Before long she had left New Hampshire, and her heart flipped as she followed the signs toward Augusta. As she sped closer to him, her sadness melted, her memories of him feeling once again more and more real. She was certain she could change his mind, that once they were together he would not be able to resist the love they had, that seeing her again would revitalize him. She grew excited at the prospect of seeing where he lived, of strolling through streets he knew by heart and of learning even more about the peaceful life she had hoped to live with him.

Finally crossing into Maine, she veered off I-95 for the last time, now taking smaller highways that wound through wooded hills and quaint towns. She still had about two hours to go, and she felt she could barely sit still as she sped too quickly around poorly lit curves. She forced herself to slow down, not wanting to strand herself or worse before she even saw him. She was forced to slow down further when the streets became more local. The winding, steep roads frightened her in the dark, and realizing how exhausted she was, she strained to anticipate the curves and to see through the fog that had begun creeping through the trees. As the time on her GPS grew closer and closer, her speed slowed and slowed until she could safely take in the scene around her. It was mostly open space, a few small houses scattered here and there. She passed long driveways that led down to larger houses by the water. She was now about twenty minutes away; she should arrive at his door just before two o'clock.

She approached a narrow causeway that led across a small body of water—Yardley Reach, according to a wooden sign bearing its name in gold script. Meredith knew that just over the other side of this causeway was Blue Aster Isle. There she would find the small town of Dearham, and Nick.

As she crept over the causeway, the water still and black beneath her, Meredith felt her first pang of worry. She had no idea if Nick was even home, and if he was, if he was alone. The thought of finding him with another woman was so painful as to almost make her want to turn right around and drive back home. She edged on, though, knowing the reward was worth the risk.

She made it to the end of the causeway and stopped her car, unbuckling her seatbelt and climbing out to survey the scene. What she saw was breathtakingly beautiful. On either side of Yardley Reach, rocky shores were still and mighty as the water lapped and retreated. A few homes sat at the edge of the water, docks and boats dotting the blackness. She knew in daylight the beauty would be even more striking; however, she appreciated the calm and placidity of this vision in darkness. She returned to her car, took a breath, and continued on her way.

She drove through a tiny downtown, the buildings old and in need of updating and repairs. A post office, a small ice cream shop, and a dusty hardware store faded into the distance as she drove steadily through, looking for the final turn of her journey. She found it just beyond the downtown and made a righthand turn onto Hawes Drive with her heart in her throat.

Bare open fields straddled the road on either side, a budding cornfield visible in the distance. She grew nervous, having not passed a single structure in some time. Her GPS was telling her the house would be half a mile away; her eyes searched eagerly as the distance grew shorter and shorter. At last the house became visible. It sat about a hundred feet off the road, by itself in the open field, an older home covered with white siding badly in need of a cleaning, though Meredith noticed that the yard was tidy and quaint, a well-kept flower bed and vegetable garden sitting cozily between the house and the road, and the lawn carefully mowed. The small original house had been expanded by an addition that looked out of place, jutting from the side of the house and giving it an uneven appearance. A wide gravel driveway sat just beyond the house. Meredith pulled in behind a pick-up truck, its white paint dull with age but clean and in good condition. She retrieved her bag from the passenger's seat and stepped out of her car, shutting the door quietly to avoid making too much noise. She was surrounded by silence, her pounding heartbeat like a drumbeat in her ears. She felt as if she would faint from the suspense.

She strode up the cracked walkway to the door. There were two doorbells, next to each a name handwritten neatly in pencil. The plate by the doorbell leading into the house listed the names Mr. and Mrs. Clive Lipton. The other plate, leading into the smaller addition, read the name Mr. Nick Kelly.

At the sight of his name, Meredith's heart lurched with longing so intense it was almost painful. She was terrified to ring the bell, but the knowledge that he was just inside moved her arm involuntarily until her finger was on the button. Not pausing for even a second, not allowing herself the time to hesitate and change her mind, she rang the bell and waited in the darkness, the scent of salt water reaching her from a distance.

Meredith thought she saw movement from inside, but she couldn't be sure. She stood motionless, feeling on the verge of a breakdown. She had imagined that, if the door was to open, it would take several minutes, given the lateness of the hour. She was surprised when, mere seconds after she rang the bell, she heard a lock unlatching on the other side of the door. Her eyes opened wide with panic as she realized she had fewer seconds to prepare than she had thought; she had no idea what she intended to say to him.

The door swung open. Nick stood in the doorway, straight and tall, staring at her with his eyes wide and alert, his lips straight with shock. Meredith's face melted into a smile in spite of her nervousness; seeing him again made the force of her affection flood her in an ecstatic rush. He was wearing a white t-shirt and well-worn jeans, and Meredith thought she had never seen him look more handsome. His hair wasn't mussed as it would have been if he had been sleeping; she guessed hopefully that he had not been able to sleep from thinking of her.

His face brightened as he absorbed the fact that she was truly there, standing on his doorstep, having driven twelve hours in the middle of the night to see him. He closed his eyes and pulled her possessively toward him, his face flooded with relief.

She fell into him, dropping her bag on the ground and returning his embrace, her arms holding him as tightly as they could. They stood wordlessly for some time, pressed to each other, their rushed breathing the only sound. Then his hand slid to her waist and drew her inside; his other hand slammed the door shut behind them.

He took her face in his hands and kissed her. His soft sighs echoed in her ear, and she clung to him, the wild fluttering of her heart making her feel breathless.

Finally he pulled away. "What are you doing here?" he whispered.

"I had to see you," she said, misty-eyed, as she stroked the side of his face.

"I hate that you drove all the way up here by yourself," he said, the words made ragged by his deep breaths, "but I'm thrilled that you did."

She couldn't help but feel safe again as she looked up at him, all at once struck by the kindness in his smile and the crisp blueness of his eyes.

"I missed you," she breathed.

"I'd tell you I missed you too," he said softly, "but that doesn't even begin to describe it."

He took her hand and led her into the living room. It was dismally outdated and in need of a soft touch, but it was clean and tidy and obviously well taken care of. The carpet was gray and appeared to be older than they were; it was dull, having lost much of its color at least a decade ago. What little furniture there was appeared to have been collected from yard sales and college dorm rooms, mismatched and years from being in its best shape. A small television rested on a narrow bookshelf with three short shelves, three or four books on each. The room was dark, the only light glaring offensively from a tall brass lamp in the corner, with no shade; Meredith guessed the shade had been removed so the lamp would offer more light. A few house plants sat on window sills. In the corner Meredith saw a small round table with two chairs. Beyond that, out of view, appeared to be the sterile-looking white linoleum of the kitchen floor. Glancing to her left, Meredith caught view of an open door and the corner of a bed, dressed simply in a white sheet and topped with a dark blanket. It could have been gloomy, but its neatness and simplicity made it charming, and Meredith felt comfortable.

Meredith looked around, taking everything in, then smiled and wrapped her arms around him, resting her head on his chest.

"It's not much," his quiet voice sounded from above her.

"It's wonderful," she said, lifting her gaze to meet his. "I'm so happy to be here."

He continued to stare at her. "I can't believe you're here. I can't believe you did this."

"Can't you?" she asked, raising her eyebrows. "Why wouldn't I?"

His face turned more serious. "Merry, I'm leaving on Thursday, for three months. I'm going to California."

Meredith nodded. "I know. Vince told me when he gave me your address."

"Vince gave you my address."

"Yes."

Nick grinned. "Well, that explains it."

"Explains what?"

"We were supposed to see each other tonight, but he canceled at the last minute."

Meredith smiled. It appeared that Vince had warmed to the idea of the two of them being together.

Her eyes again met his. "Nick, you don't have to go. I'll just stay here with you, and not go back. Or I'll go with you to California. Whatever you'd like."

Nick frowned. "You know I'd love that," he said, a gentle lilt in his voice. "But I meant what I said. I just can't do it."

It was Meredith's turn to frown. She pulled away, feeling hopelessness sneak back into her heart. "But what about just now, in the doorway?" she asked, trying to conceal her panic and hurt. She pressed herself to him again, and rubbed his shoulders. "I thought if I came here, you'd rethink what you said."

"Merry," he said. She placed her hands on his waist and slid them under his shirt, then wrapped her arms around him, stroking the bare skin of his back with the tips of her fingers.

"Please," he groaned softly. "Please, stop."

She stepped away, knowing in an instant that he was unyielding, that she had made this trip for nothing and that she was going to have to face life without him. She felt tears gathering but held them back.

"Nick, there's no sense in this. Neither of us wants this."

He was watching her, his eyes wide and jaw tight. "Damn it, Merry," he said, and ran his fingers through his hair. "I can't. I just can't."

"Why not?"

"Because I don't want to hurt you. It just isn't right, not if we're not going to be together."

"Then let's be together." She took a deep breath, attempting to calm herself. "We should be planning our life together. Instead you're going all the way to California to escape me."

"I'm not trying to escape you, Merry. I don't want to go. Having you here, in my house, it's better than I had even imagined. But that's exactly why I need to go. I can't be here right now, where I wouldn't think of anything else."

"Anything else but what?"

"What it would be like if you stayed."

She took a deep breath. "Just stay with me now," she said over the breaking of her voice. "You don't have to think about it."

She sniffled. They said nothing for a few moments.

Finally he shook his head.

"God, Merry, you make it so hard for me to do this."

They were silent once more. Meredith dabbed at her eyes.

She steadied herself and looked up at him. "Stay with me now," she said again, her heart thumping. "Will you?"

His expression softened, and he hugged her close. Then, with a little sigh, his hand slid to her waist, and he guided her into the dark bedroom. When he slowly leaned in toward her, she closed her eyes and lifted her chin in expectation—but he only reached for the bed and removed a pillow, then straightened and kissed her forehead. His breath lingered on her skin, and his hand remained on her waist; she brought her hands to his chest, but he pulled away. "I love you," he whispered, and squeezed her hip. Then he walked from the room, closing the door on his way out.

MEREDITH SLEPT FITFULLY THAT NIGHT, knowing Nick was in the next room and resisting the almost impossible urge to go to him and try to force some reason into him. Sleeping in his bed— knowing he slept here every night, thinking of her—was unbearable. She was in torment. She knew she had one day and one night to reach him, and she was beginning to doubt she could do it. The part that upset her the most was that she knew he was resisting her on purpose, that he wanted to give in but wouldn't, for a misguided belief that by leaving her he was doing her some good.

She awoke in the morning to the tantalizing smell of a hot breakfast. She tried to arrange her hair as best she could, then grabbed her toothbrush and walked cautiously out of the room.

She sneaked into the small but clean bathroom to freshen up, then met Nick in the kitchen, where he was flipping pancakes on the stove. A plate of eggs sat on the counter.

"Morning, beautiful," he said with a sunny smile, glancing over his shoulder as she entered the room. They settled down at the table, Nick serving her for a change. She smiled.

"This is a switch," she said. "Everything looks great. I'm impressed."

"You're not the only one who can cook."

They dug into their breakfasts. Meredith looked around the small apartment. By the light of day, it looked much less gloomy. Cheerful yellow light poured in through the windows. Meredith could tell more clearly now how clean it was, how effort had been made to keep up with repairs so that time had not appeared to have taken so great a toll. The paint job appeared to be fresh; the white was clean and vibrant.

Nick noticed her examining his home. "I rent this space from Mr. and Mrs. Lipton," he said between bites. "They live in the main house. I pay only half because I do all the repair work for this apartment and the main house."

"That's nice," she said with a smile. "Have you lived here long?"

"About three years."

They ate in silence for a few minutes.

"I thought I could show you around Dearham during the day. Then at night we can meet up with Vince."

"Okay," she said. "How far does he live from here?"

"About a half hour, in Bar Harbor."

She swallowed, then looked at him. "When do you leave for California?"

"My flight leaves Bangor at nine o'clock tomorrow morning. I'll have to leave here around six o'clock."

If you leave at all, she thought, her heart thumping.

They stood and cleaned the dishes together, standing side by side at the sink and playfully splashing water in each other's faces, their elbows nudging each other. Meredith moved her hand to his waist and pulled him close, resting her head on his chest.

"I really want to have a nice day with you," he said, tenderly rubbing her shoulders. He brought his hand to her face, where his finger brushed her cheek. "I'm so glad you're here."

"I am too," she said, taking his hand from her face and moving it to her lips, and kissing it.

His expression turned serious. He turned from her and walked away with heavy steps, his face in his hands.

~

NICK WANTED to take her for a walk. The weather was chilly but clear, and as they walked hand in hand toward the road, Meredith couldn't help but feel her spirits lift. A light breeze guided them as they strolled along the road. There were no sidewalks, but there were also no cars, and they felt comfortable venturing out to the middle of the street, holding hands and pulling away from each other, laughing as they determined how far they could stretch before breaking their connection.

Meredith felt very happy here. There was something about being so far north, so far away from everything she knew, at the country's highest point on the East Coast, that appealed to her. The isle was small, and water could be reached by driving a short distance in any direction. Meredith felt isolated and safe, as if the walls of water around her served as protection against the harshness of the outside world. She relished the quiet. The open fields around her soothed her troubles, and as she listened to Nick tell her about the town, she felt sorry she wouldn't have more time here.

They walked for about a mile along the road, away from the town she had driven through the previous night. Where Nick lived, it was straight and open, but it soon began narrowing and winding, becoming darker and cooler under the shade of the trees. Here they walked closer to the side of the road, often taking a short detour around a tree or behind a boulder. Meredith grew cold, and she shivered; Nick wrapped his arm around her and held her close.

They arrived at an alcove in the trees. Meredith saw the clear space before they reached it. As they drew closer, she realized it was a small cemetery. The discovery surprised her; there was nothing else around, not a church or even a house.

"Oh," she uttered. "What an amazing little spot."

Nick led her into the alcove. The gravestones were old, many of them unreadable, the forces of nature having softened the engravings and forever obliterating the identities of the people buried beneath. Some of them boasted Civil War and even Revolutionary War service; others simply indicated dates of birth and death. Meredith frowned at the small tombstones of children.

They wandered around for some time, hand in hand, as they had at the art museum months before, commenting occasionally but mostly in comfortable silence.

As they exited on the other side, they faced each other.

"Should we head back?" Nick asked.

"Sure," Meredith answered. "I'd like to see more of the town."

Nick did not respond. He was staring at her, his face expressionless.

"What is it?"

He hesitated. After a moment he sighed, his chest heaving once and his shoulders rising and falling until they slumped downward with dejection. "Nothing," he said, and attempted a weak smile.

Meredith approached him and lay her hands on his chest. "Why this noble self-restraint?" she asked with a little frown, and he placed his hands on her hips as she stood there, his expression turning more tender. "Why work so hard for something neither of us wants?"

His eyes were fixed on hers. He swallowed, then shrugged. "I just can't let myself, Merry," he replied with a quiet, hoarse voice. "It's too tempting."

"Not tempting enough."

"Please don't think that." He looked troubled.

Her eyes grew soft, and she sighed. "Come on," she said, and forced herself to smile. "Show me the rest of your beautiful town."

THEY CLIMBED into Nick's truck. Meredith smiled as she indulged in a deep breath. The truck smelled of him.

"Ready?" he asked pleasantly, and patted her thigh as he backed onto the road.

Meredith watched him, his thighs pressed to the seat and his hand draped over the steering wheel. He opened the window, and his blond hair blew haphazardly over his face. Meredith leaned over and kissed his cheek. He moaned and smiled.

Nick parked his truck at a lookout off the main road, then met her on the curb and held her hand as she hopped down out of her seat. He led her down a steep hill, past cedar-sided houses built into the downward slope, until they reached the water. Here the water was lapping against the rocks with a soothing rhythm. Meredith looked down at her feet and cried out with surprise and delight.

She bent her knees and squatted to get a closer look. She had not been mistaken: the ground was covered with what appeared to be millions of seashells, none larger than her fingernail. They curled and curved and wrapped around themselves, in all colors, making the ground light up brilliantly like a rainbow. She dug her hand into the shells and picked up a handful. She let them trickle out of her hand back to the ground.

She looked up at him, her face bright with joy; she had never seen anything like this. Her expression changed at the sight of his face: it was stricken with grief. His eyes sagged in the corners and looked glossy with the beginnings of tears. She stood and took his arm.

"What is it, Nick? Are you okay?"

He pursed his lips. His jaw was tight, but his eyes were gentle. He said nothing, but took her hand and led her back to his truck. He pulled out of his parking spot and drove off to Bar Harbor to meet Vince.

THEY STOPPED at Acadia National Park to take advantage of the walking trails and majestic views. Nick drove them around Park Loop Road, with Frenchman Bay and the Atlantic Ocean on their left. Meredith leaned toward him from the passenger's side, straining to look out his window at the crystal blue water crashing against the rocky cliffs. Keeping his left hand on the wheel, he stretched his right hand around her shoulder and held her close.

He pulled over at an overlook under a canopy of trees. Meredith jumped out of the truck eagerly, her eyes opening wide with amazement at the breathtaking view. In front of her was the vast Atlantic Ocean, sparkling with a calm purity it lacked at the beaches where Meredith had seen it before. She couldn't believe the same ocean could look so different in two places. Before her was the rocky coast, proud stone cliffs rising from the water. The great expanse of it took her breath away.

Nick held out his hand in invitation. She took it and followed him to the cliffs, where they stood with nothing before them but the ocean and a green carpet of trees surrounding them. They paused for a few moments to admire the view.

"Incredible," Meredith breathed, the wind whipping her hair in long strands around her face. She felt as if she were flying. Her eyes scanned the horizon, which always moved her no matter where she was; she imagined how far she'd have to go to reach land and what she'd find when she arrived. She dared herself to look down. The cliffs were jagged and uncompromising far below them, but at their feet the ground stretched flat and smooth.

When she turned toward him, she realized he had been watching her and not the scene before him. In the bright open sky, his hair was the color of the sun, and as it whisked around his face in the breeze Meredith noticed the complexity of its color, the yellows and browns that, all together, gave his hair the appearance of spun gold. He was squinting against the sun; his lips were straight but turned up just slightly in the corners.

She felt the fondness in his eyes, and she couldn't help but smile. "What is it?"

He returned her smile. "You're beautiful."

Her heart seemed to turn over in her chest, and she took the arm he offered.

He patted her hand as it rested on his arm. "Come on," he said. "Let's go for a walk."

They walked along the platform of the cliff. Meredith looked downward and spotted a couple of fishermen on the rocky shore far below.

"Is this where you used to fish with your father?"

"No, I've never fished here," he said as he walked a few steps ahead of her, leading her by the hand. "He used to take me to more remote places, nothing as exciting as this. Mostly they were little coves along the road that nobody else had ever heard of." He cast his eyes at her and smiled. "That probably sounds pretty boring."

"Not at all," she replied, and returned his smile. "I think it sounds wonderful."

They were silent as Nick grasped her by the waist and hoisted her over a large crevice in the ground.

"How long has he been ill?" she asked as they continued walking.

"His most recent stroke occurred a few years back. But the first one was about ten years ago."

"That's when your mother passed away."

Nick paused for a moment to gaze out at the water. "He never really recovered after that. I think he just gave up." He looked at her. "He wasn't the same after he lost her."

His expression was heavy with meaning, and Meredith felt her face flush.

Still holding her hand, he began walking again. "I love my father. It's not easy for me to see him the way he is now. But I do my best."

Meredith stopped walking, and her hand held him back, stopping him in his tracks. He looked at her expectantly. He was standing with one foot on an incline, and he looked exquisite against the backdrop of the ocean and the rocks, his hair swept backward by the wind.

She stepped toward him and lifted her face to his, and kissed him slowly, bringing her hands to his shoulders and then wrapping them around to the back of his neck. He glided his hands around her back and pressed her in close.

She pulled away and looked into his eyes. They were clear and blue like the water.

"I love you," she said.

"I love you."

They kissed once more and then turned around to head back to the truck.

MEREDITH CLASPED her hands together with excitement as they drove into Bar Harbor. She immediately fell in love with it. It was a picturesque downtown, much larger than Dearham. Here there were exotic specialty shops, cozy restaurants, and taverns, scattered among which were antique dealers and coffee shops. The main street sloped steeply downhill, and at the bottom was the great blue expanse of the ocean. Nick again helped her out of the truck, then led her to a bustling pub that sat on the top of the incline.

Vince was waiting for them outside the door, standing among the throngs of people on the busy street. When he saw them, a wide grin crossed his face, and he opened his arms wide in invitation to Meredith. Meredith flew to him.

"Hey, Merry," he said, his arm around her shoulder. "I told you it wouldn't be long before we saw each other again."

"You were right. You're always right."

"Not always, but I'll take it. Come on, let's go inside."

The pub was dark and inviting, with neon signs on the paneled walls. The tables were close together and small, creating a cozy, intimate feel.

"So how have you been?" Meredith asked her brother once they had placed their orders. "No woman in your life? I thought for sure you'd have date here waiting with you."

"No," Vince said, sipping his water. "I'm laying off women for now." His eyes rose. "No pun intended."

"I was wondering whatever happened with Sandy," Meredith said. "We didn't see her around all that much toward the end."

"Sandy? She just wanted more than what I could give her, and things sort of fizzled out. You know, same old story."

Meredith didn't ask to what story he was referring. She had grown sad thinking about how much she had enjoyed her brother's visit.

The food arrived, and their chatter was replaced with the sound of the cracking of lobster tails and crab legs.

"So," Vince said, gnawing on a crab leg. "How is your visit going?"

"It's great," Meredith responded, unable to keep a smile off her face. "We've been having a nice time."

"What have you been doing?"

"We took a walk up to a little cemetery earlier today."

"A cemetery? How romantic."

"Then we went to a little lookout by the house. Just now we were at Acadia National Park."

"What did you think?"

"It's amazing," she said, remembering the grandness of the cliffs and the quiet force of the ocean. "It's no wonder you love it here. I've never seen any place so beautiful."

"It makes you want to stay forever, doesn't it?"

Meredith wasn't sure of Vince's meaning, and said nothing.

"So, Nick," Vince continued as he grabbed a roll out of a

basket in the middle of the table. "What time do you leave tomorrow?"

"Six in the morning."

"That doesn't give the two of you much time. Merry, it's a good thing we happened to talk yesterday; otherwise you never would have even known Nick was leaving town."

Meredith frowned, annoyed. She leaned in toward Vince. "Are you really going to do this right here, right now?"

"I'm sorry, Merry," he said, placing his hands on the table and looking squarely at her. "I'm not going to pretend it doesn't bother me."

"It's not your concern," she said, smoothing her napkin on her lap to distract herself from her irritation.

"It is my concern, because you're my sister and I love you. As I've said, I don't want you getting hurt. I know how it goes, believe me."

"Same old story?"

Vince and Meredith looked up, surprised. Nick's face was expressionless as he studied Vince, but his eyes were sharp. When Vince looked up, Nick lowered his gaze.

Vince frowned and returned his attention to his crab legs, but Meredith couldn't suppress a grin. She looked at Nick. He had a glass of water at his lips, drinking in large gulps. He said nothing, but he raised his eyebrows at her, then turned back to his dinner.

OUTSIDE, the sky was a luscious cobalt blue, brilliantly lit by stars. Meredith couldn't believe how bright the stars looked, and she found it difficult to look away; the sky looked like it was draped in diamonds. There seemed to be as many stars in the sky as there had been tiny seashells on the shore. She stared upward, entranced. It was so different up here, so serene—so peculiarly, steadfastly beautiful.

She felt a hand on her. Nick's arm was around her shoulder, his fingers stroking her gently.

"So listen," Vince said, rubbing his hands together against the chill. "I know you have to get up early tomorrow, so I'm going to let you go and head home."

"You mean I don't get to see your place?"

"Maybe next time."

Meredith looked at him curiously. He was watching her with an odd expression.

"Okay," she said. "Then I guess I'll see you soon."

"I hope so."

She swallowed back tears. "Come see me again soon, okay?"

They embraced again, holding on for several moments before pulling away. Vince and Nick clapped each other on the back, and Vince wished Nick a good trip. They watched him as he walked up the incline, turning to wave once before disappearing into the crowd.

Nick and Meredith faced each other, then turned and headed back to Nick's truck, hand in hand.

THEY DROVE BACK to Nick's house in silence.

When they arrived, Nick helped her out of the truck and guided her into the house, his hand resting on her back. He closed and locked the door behind them. They stood together in the dark.

Meredith already felt tears welling as she considered that tomorrow could be the last time she saw him.

"Merry," he began.

"Please, Nick," she interrupted pleadingly. "You have one more chance to make this right. Don't leave me." She clung to him, her body pressed to him and her hands stroking his back.

He stood motionless before her, silent except for his breathing, which already was deep and hurried. Meredith pressed her hips to his. She could feel the need in him, could sense the torment of his self-restraint. She was resolved to breaking that restraint.

"I love you," she moaned as she kissed his throat with tenderness, surprised by the sound of tears in her voice. *This is it*, she thought; *no point in holding back now*. She allowed the emotion to rise in her, and she trembled as she embraced him. "Stay with me," she whispered, her voice breaking, "tonight and every night."

She braved a glance at his face. It was wracked with conflict. As her fingers trailed from his temple to his strong jaw, from his thick throat to behind his ear, where they began raking through his golden hair, his eyes closed, and his chest rose with heavy breaths. His jaw tightened as he made his final effort to resist, but Meredith could see that he was not that strong.

"Oh, Nick," she breathed, the joy of being so close to him filling her in spite of her pain. She thought of his gentleness and of and the way he had brought her back to life; she thought of the happiness of their days and the eagerness with which they had greeted each night, of his quiet strength and goodness of heart and of all the magical things she loved about him, and she could not feel sad. "You are so beautiful."

She lifted her face toward his and kissed the underside of his chin, then glided to his neck and behind his ear. He released a long moan as he submitted to her, raising his face toward the ceiling, his eyes closed and lips parted as he cherished the feel of her kisses on his skin. A rush of hope flooded her at the sound, and her tender kisses turned desperate as her hands clutched him, intent on making the most of the last hours they had together.

Suddenly his eyes opened, and he looked at her, surrender and decision in his face. "Merry," he whispered, though his voice was severe. "I'm sorry," he gasped, more to himself than to her. "I can't help it. Oh, God, I just can't help it." Resigned and determined, he grabbed her hips and pulled her back toward his bedroom, finally falling onto the bed beneath her.

Now that he had given in, he held nothing back, and all the need and longing of their recent separation found release. As he lay on his back, his hair falling messily onto the pillow, he took her face in his hands and kissed her, his legs writhing with urgency. She slid her hands under his sweater, where his skin was smooth and taut. She sat straight, her hips spread wide across him and her thighs surrounding him. She pulled her shirt over her head and arms and unclasped her bra behind her back. Throwing it to the floor, she spread her fingers wide and covered his chest and torso with her hands, greedily soaking in the feel of him and grinding into his hips with hers. She felt she would burst with aching.

His hands were on her hips, caressing her; his eyes were open, watching her with excitement. He sat up and met her in a kiss that filled her, drawing from her lungs a long sigh as the heat between them swelled in her chest. His breath warmed her lips in quick pulses, and she deepened her kiss, remembering with hunger what it was like to taste him. She pulled his sweater upward, and he swiftly removed it, exposing the powerful muscles of his chest and shoulders. As he lifted his arms toward the ceiling, Meredith's desire turned primal when she inhaled the musky, masculine scent of him.

She looked at his face. It was tight and serious. His lips were long and straight and slightly parted, and the sound of his deep, rapid breathing made Meredith dizzy. His gaze met hers. He was at the point of no return, pushed beyond the limits of his patience and self-restraint. His jaw was set and his chin lifted as he prepared for the night ahead. Meredith grinned with anticipation. He'd always been passionate and uninhibited with her in the bedroom, but the wild, frenzied look of him told her that this night would be like none she had ever had.

He pushed her onto her back and tumbled on top of her, his

hands folding into hers and lifting them above her shoulders. Meredith closed her eyes and relinquished control, arching her back toward him and panting as his lips traveled over her neck and face. His bare chest and waist were pressed to hers; she spread her legs wide to accommodate him. Her hips were undulating demandingly, and she moaned in desperation, the tender ache tormenting her.

He was frantically fumbling with the button of her jeans, his fingers clumsy and useless in his hastiness. His hair fell in long waves over his face as, frustrated and impatient, with a whispered curse, he lowered his eyes to her waist with the purpose of aiding his fingers. Meredith pushed his fingers out of the way and unclasped the button herself. She replaced her hands above her head as he lifted her hips and undressed her, then straightened and removed the rest of his own clothing, finally sliding naked on top of her with a long, low groan.

Meredith wanted to look at him but could not open her eyes; she was helpless with eagerness and desire, weak and breathless and out of control. His fingers were running through her hair, pulling it backward; she was sweating, and the coolness of the air on her face as he swept her hair away further incited her.

"Nick..." she cried, and her voice was muffled by the crush of his mouth on hers. Her chin lifted toward the ceiling as he wrapped his arms around her tightly and brought his hips to hers.

Enveloping him in her arms, she spread her knees wide apart, throwing her feet on either side of the bed to take him in fully and quickly. He drove into her, and she welcomed and surrounded him, closing her hips around him and bringing her knees together above him, squeezing him into her and melting with him, every movement inviting more fire. Her fingers gripped his back and clutched his hair, pulling him closer—and in the complete silence and darkness of the night, only stars and open field around them, they moved together with perfect understanding, for those moments knowing nothing but each other.

"I love you," he exclaimed in a breathless whisper, his lips at her ear. "Oh, Merry, I love you..."

Her breaths grew short and shallow, and she clung to him, grasping at him and memorizing the feel of him, her heart palpitating almost painfully as she was teased by the first soft shudderings, which sparkled in her blood like the diamonds in the sky. She rose and fell with him, sighing as her senses were filled with him, the fluttering at her center quickening until she was sure she would start flying.

"Oh, Merry...I love you...Oh, God, I love you..."

Her chin lifted into the air, her neck stretching toward the sky as her entire being was consumed with sensation that rippled through her like waves over the shore. She cried out along with him as his hands gripped her, his body tensed, and his face burrowed in her neck; his movement sharpened and then evened and slowed, his hips resting on hers and his lips grazing the small places of her throat. She sighed under his gentle touch, her breathing now calm and deep, and finally they fell motionless, his body pressed to hers, her arms and legs wrapped lovingly around him.

She took a deep breath and smiled, and as he brought his face to hers to look into her eyes, she was surprised to find a sly grin on his face.

"All right, Miss Meredith," he said silkily, his fingers twirling her hair. "Don't think for one second that this night is over." He cupped her face in both hands and firmly kissed her. "You'd better hold on, beautiful. You have no idea what you've started tonight."

"I DON'T THINK I'll ever be able to walk again," Meredith said through a wide grin.

"That's okay. I can carry you around in my arms forever."

They were facing each other in bed, her arm around his neck

and behind his head, pulling him in for endless kisses. His arm was around her waist, pressing her close to him, his thigh nuzzled between her legs and his feet playfully rubbing hers.

"What time is it?" she asked.

"I don't even care."

She kissed him deeply for the millionth time, and sighed.

"Mmm," he breathed. "Please don't get me started again. I don't think I can move."

"We probably were pushing it that last time."

"I think I threw my back out."

They were silent, exchanging kisses.

She snickered. "Remember that night after Framington?"

"Mmm," he said, grinning. "How could I forget?"

"My legs were sore for days."

"Totally worth it, though."

They passed more seconds in silence.

"That was a fun night," he said.

"It was. I'm glad we stopped at that bar."

"You looked so sexy sucking on that cherry."

"You were the sexy one, with those dance moves."

"But you never looked prettier than you did today, holding those seashells."

She smiled. "What? That was nothing."

"It was perfect. You were so happy."

"I was with you. What's not to be happy about?"

He kissed her. His lips lingered.

"Thank you for coming up to see me. It means a lot to me."

Her face grew sad. "I had to. I couldn't let you go."

He touched his forehead to hers. "I love you, Merry."

A wrenching pain pulled deep inside her. She felt tears building. "I love you, Nick. Please don't leave."

"Go to sleep, beautiful. We'll talk about it in the morning."

❀

WHEN SHE AWOKE the next morning, she instantly knew it was too light outside. He was leaving the house at six o'clock. She reached her hand out, knowing she would touch nothing but empty space.

She looked over at the spot where he had fallen asleep next to her. He was gone. In his place was a note.

Meredith sat up slowly, feeling numb. She took the note in her hands and opened it.

MY BEAUTIFUL MEREDITH,

You looked so peaceful sleeping that I couldn't bring myself to wake you. Also, I couldn't bring myself to say goodbye to you a second time. Please know how it pains me to leave you, that I had to force myself to step away from you and walk out that door. But it would be selfish of me to stay. I can't let you sacrifice everything important to you, just for the sake of my own happiness.

Last night was the best night of my life. I will never forget how you loved me and cared for me.

Please drive home carefully. Please be happy.

I love you.

Nick

MEREDITH'S HAND DROPPED, the note falling to the bed. She knew the pain would hit her, but she didn't know when. She looked around the room, Nick's room. It had the practical simplicity of the rest of the apartment, of Nick himself. She didn't want to leave, wondered what he would do if he returned in three months to find her still there. She was tempted to find out. She would have seriously considered it if she wasn't so worried he would never come back.

She stood, resolving to clean up and leave before sorrow incapacitated her. She made the bed neatly and dressed quickly, then took the note in her hands, wondering what to do with it. She wanted to take it, to have a vestige of him to carry with her always, but rather than keep it she left it where she found it, on his bed, not wanting to look back on their relationship and remember this moment.

She packed up her suitcase and looked around one more time. She stood in the doorway and locked the door from the inside. She inhaled deeply, and it was then that the tears came. She wished she could bottle the scent of this room, to take it out and let it surround her when she ached for him at night.

She turned toward the door and walked out, closing it behind her. Then, with her eyes down, she climbed into her car and began the long drive home, wishing Maine a silent goodbye as the road led her far away from the only place she wanted to be.

CHAPTER SIXTEEN

THE SECOND TIME

*M*eredith drove numbly across the causeway, through the winding roads and local highways that had brought her to Nick not even two days earlier. She tried to notice the view as little as possible, not wanting to think about the excitement and hope she had felt the last time she had seen it, and not wanting to see all the beauty that had almost been her home.

She left Maine, following I-95 down through the thick woods of New Hampshire, backtracking through Massachusetts and ending up in Connecticut, once again thinking of Adam as she passed the familiar landmarks of her former life. How ironic it was, this kind of forced nostalgia, rising from the freshly laid grave of the life she'd hoped to have. As she traveled mindlessly down the roads of her past as if her life were a movie flashing before her eyes it occurred to her that maybe there had been some truth in Vince's offhand joke about lanes. Maybe she was better off staying in her own lane after all, going the forged way, staying on the familiar path.

It was a bright, clear spring day. Meredith had driven these roads many times before and drove them now without much thought. She was just getting ready to pass New York City when suddenly, possessed by an urge that she could not deny, she veered off the highway toward the city, annoying several other drivers and receiving more than one rude hand gesture.

She followed the West Side Highway around the city, the Hudson River on her right. She had forgotten how the traffic was so unpredictable here. She turned off the highway and drove several blocks, finally arriving at the bustling campus of NYU.

She parked her car on the street just outside Washington Square and sat there with the car off, staring at the famous arch. She leaned back in her seat, watching people from all walks of life, some rushing and others taking their time, enjoying the day.

Adam had proposed to her in this park. They had had dinner and coffee at a nearby café and were strolling hand in hand toward their apartment in Greenwich Village when, just in front of the arch, he had bent down on one knee and asked her to marry him, to stay with him forever and make him the happiest man in the world. After she had said yes, they had embraced tearfully, looking forward to spending the rest of their lives in perfect bliss, a bliss as eternal and perfect as the sparkling diamond he had given her.

They would have one more year together, three months of it spent in a hospital, engaged in a desperate race against the clock.

Meredith looked around at the familiar buildings of her past. She remembered sitting in some of these buildings, taking classes that would help mold the person she was now, meeting people who would teach her not only about literature but also about life. She envisioned herself walking hand in hand with Adam on these very sidewalks, never in a million years believing the little life they had imagined for themselves was not to be. She had thought they were too insignificant to be touched by tragedy, had blithely lived her life under the assumption that by being a good person, making smart decisions, and planning carefully, she could ensure that she would have a happy, successful future.

She frowned. *Have I really been so naive?* she asked herself. She thought about how little control one had over one's life and wondered what it took for two people who loved each other to actually end up together. No matter which path she took—that which had been prepared for her, or that to which her heart had led her—she was disappointed. What did she have to do—what sacrifice did she have to make—to prove to the universe that she was ready to be happy? At what point was she entitled to some sort of stability? How perfect did her life have to be, in order for it to last?

We are at the mercy of the universe, she thought, *and of other people's whims.*

She pulled away from the park and drove a few blocks until she found the street on which she and Adam had lived. She drove slowly by their old apartment building and stopped. If she concentrated hard enough, she could see herself and Adam returning home on a Sunday morning, their arms laden with grocery bags from the produce market, or with coffee cups and newspapers in their hands.

A loud honk sounded from behind her, and she drove off.

EASTER SUNDAY WAS a few days later. Meredith reluctantly dragged herself to Tara's house, where her friend was hosting her Washington, DC relatives. Meredith had been inclined to stay home and languish in her grief, but Tara had insisted on her presence.

Meredith tried her best to be social, but she often found herself on the brink of tears, having to excuse herself to regain her composure. She appreciated Tara's trying to help her but wished her friend had just let her stay at home. She did not feel ready to make small talk, and it didn't help that Evelyn asked for Uncle Nick, the man who knew the leprechauns.

They were sitting around the dinner table talking. Meredith

made an effort to insert herself into the conversation when she could, but she was having trouble focusing. Her sorrow must have been visible on her face because Tara's kindly aunt, who was sitting next to her, gently placed her hand on Meredith's and asked her whether she was all right.

The older woman's concern touched Meredith, and she was unable to respond with anything other than the truth.

"No, but I will be," she said, and smiled.

"Is there anything I can do to help?"

"I don't think so, but thank you."

"Well, honey, sometimes it helps to get an outside perspective. If you want to talk, you let me know."

"Thank you," Meredith said sincerely. "You're very kind."

The conversation resumed around them. The family chatted happily, exchanging gossipy tidbits and catching up on the news.

"Say, Aunt Grace," Tara said. "Are you and Uncle Frank still planning on driving your RV around the country?"

"Yes," Grace responded, a smile instantly warming her face. "We're very excited."

"When are you leaving?"

"Well, we were supposed to leave next month, but our renter backed out. Now we have to find a new renter."

Meredith's ears perked up.

"How long will you be gone?" Tara asked.

"That's undecided," Grace answered. "Originally we were thinking six months, but we may be gone as long as a year depending on where we end up."

"And you're looking for a renter?" Meredith asked with hesitation.

"Yes, dear. Why?" Grace said, turning to her with interest.

Meredith shrugged. "I don't know. I've been thinking of relocating. I didn't want to rent again, but buying isn't an option right now."

"If you're interested," cut in Grace's husband Frank, "we could make a deal, arrange some sort of rent-to-own situation."

"You're moving?" Tara asked, her face showing her shock. "You've lived in that house forever!"

"We don't need it anymore," Grace said. "We were thinking of moving to a smaller unit in a retirement community somewhere. Nothing is set in stone, though; we've just been tossing some ideas around."

"Where is your house, exactly?" asked Meredith.

"It's in Lovelace, Virginia, about fifteen miles outside Washington."

"My school has a branch in DC," Meredith said thoughtfully. "It's a long shot, but I wonder if they need any teachers next year."

"Find out," said Tara. "Then let me know."

"You won't believe this, Meredith, but sometimes the planets align."

Kevin Williams had called Meredith into his office and was walking toward her after closing the door. He gestured for her to sit. She did, and he took his seat behind his desk.

"What is it?" she asked.

"An English teacher at our Washington location just announced that she isn't coming back from her maternity leave this fall," he said. "The job opening hasn't even been made public yet. I've already spoken to the school board on your behalf."

Meredith stared at Kevin with wide eyes and had to consciously tell herself to close her mouth, which had dropped open with shock.

"The job is yours, pending an interview."

Meredith said nothing.

"I take it you're surprised."

"I am," Meredith said, putting her hand to her heart, which was beating rapidly as she considered the ramifications of what Kevin had told her.

"Are you still interested?"

"Yes," she said tentatively. "Yes, I am." She tried to make her voice sound decisive. "I'm sorry—I'm just so surprised. I wasn't expecting this to work out."

"I guess it was meant to be."

Meredith nodded.

"You don't have to take it, Meredith," Kevin told her, smiling. "We'd love to keep you here."

Meredith shook her head. "I have to go. To stay here—it's just too much."

"I understand."

Meredith wanted to say more, but her mind was blank.

"Meredith," Kevin said, folding his hands together. "I just want to say that I'm truly sorry for what happened. And I'm disappointed in Nick. I thought he was stronger than that."

"He thought he was being strong by leaving," Meredith said, rushing to his defense. "He thought he was doing the right thing."

"I wish it had turned out differently for you. I'd much rather let you go knowing you were leaving us to be happy, rather than to escape."

"Me too," Meredith said, hardly bothering to suppress a sigh. "But maybe this will be the last time I need to escape."

MEREDITH WAS GEARING up for the end of the school year, rushing through her lessons to ensure that she covered all the necessary material in time for finals. Her students were giddy, the prospect of summer on the horizon. The warm weather was making them especially excitable. Meredith had feared that they would be less motivated to sit in a classroom and discuss literature, but in fact the pleasantness of spring cheered them into active participation, and Meredith was delighted to discover that they had actually learned something in her classes that year.

Also on the horizon was her move to Virginia. She was nervous, but mostly she was numb. She found herself not really caring what her house would look like, what her job would be like, what kind of life she'd be living once she fell into her routine. It was all the same to her—another house, another job, another routine. Nothing seemed to matter now that Nick was no longer in her life. He had changed her perspective, had made those details seem insignificant. Now that he was no longer with her, she felt lost.

She wasn't looking forward to the hassle of moving, but every day she remained in her parents' house was another day she was more and more certain that staying there was not an option. She saw Nick at every turn, from her bedroom where she had spent her most blissful nights with him to the garage where she had watched him work on the set for the school play, from the dining room where she, Vince, and Nick had spent so many happy hours to the sidewalk down which she and Nick had strolled on their way to the park. Also difficult was the knowledge that she could never start fresh while living in the house where she had grown up. She needed a change of scenery so she could move on and truly be herself.

To alleviate the stress of moving, Meredith made a difficult decision. She decided to sell the furniture and household items she had stored in her parents' garage, the remnants of her life with Adam. She had been holding on to these things since she had moved from New York, and she felt they were encumbering her, both physically and emotionally. She spent her final months in Philadelphia searching for buyers. With that money, she was able to hire movers to transport the items she had decided to bring with her. She would take with her only her clothing, books, kitchen supplies, and a few random accessories.

Meredith spent her days winding down her classes and planning for her new life. At night she pined for her old one, lying in bed alone with her eyes wide open and willing images of Nick to come to her. She could almost hear his soft laughter, could almost see the kind crinkles in his eyes and the way his lips curved upward just so, with the subtle hint of a smile. She knew these recollections could only upset her, and they did—she cried herself to sleep most every night—but it was worth it to recapture just a tiny part of him.

For the second time, she forced herself to adjust to a new, unknown life, gathering a strength she did not feel and going through the motions of days that held no joy. She wasn't sure which was worse—knowing the man she loved was no longer alive to comfort her, or knowing he was.

HER FINAL MONTHS in Pennsylvania sped by. Before long, it was June, and students excitedly discussed prom dresses and family vacations before college. Also part of the buzz was the school play.

Meredith's role in the play had petered out, and she had stopped attending rehearsals once it became clear that the script was complete. The night of the play, she headed back to school with mixed emotions. She was eager to see the final production and was proud of the efforts of her students, who had expressed themselves sincerely and had worked hard to make the final product perfect. But she knew it would be a difficult night for her as she remembered the role Nick had played in the process. She feared that looking at the set she had watched him create in her garage would be too painful. Her heart ached as she recalled the conversation they had had in the parking lot the day he had first spoken to Kevin, in which she had told him she wanted to move to Maine with him, and how he had been so excited by the prospect.

The auditorium was packed with students, parents, siblings, and teachers who milled about with proud smiles on their faces. She took a program from a grinning usher, a senior for whom she had written a college recommendation, and scanned the room for an empty seat. Her eyes were drawn to a woman standing halfway down the aisle, waving frantically at her. It was Beth Goldberg. Meredith smiled and joined her.

"So you did it," Beth said, patting Meredith's knee as they sat down. "This is all about you!"

"Actually, it's not about me at all," she responded, smiling. "The idea wasn't mine, and none of the writing was mine."

"Sure it is. The whole thing came together because of you."

"I appreciate that, but all I did was supervise. The students did all the work."

They were silent for a few moments as they thumbed through their programs.

"I'm sorry about Nick," Beth said. "I know how much you wanted that to work out."

"It happens," Meredith said dispassionately.

"Have you talked to him since you came home from Maine?"

"No," Meredith said. "I'm not expecting to speak to him again."

The lights dimmed, and everyone grew silent. A student walked in front of the curtain and nervously began his introduction.

"Beloved parents, esteemed teachers, fellow students, and welcomed guests. Epicurus once said, 'We should look for someone to eat and drink with before looking for something to eat and drink.'" He continued his monologue to attentive ears and enraptured faces, and as he concluded, the curtain opened to grand applause. Meredith's eyes scanned the stage. Nick's three-part set had been draped with a mural depicting a cozy dining room. Seated at a table decorated to represent a Thanksgiving meal was a family of four, two students dressed as parents and two as children. Meredith knew this scene would portray a family's first Thanksgiving after the death of a beloved grandparent.

As the students walked across the stage reciting their well-rehearsed lines, as the curtain closed after each scene so other students could change the murals and the props, as the memories of her time with her students filled her, Meredith felt overwhelmed. She was reminded of how special this year had been. She had begun the year gloomily, trying to survive her first year after Adam's passing; the support of Kevin and her colleagues, and the good natures of the students, had guided her through. She was glad she had had the chance to participate in the creation of this play, and she was grateful for the opportunity.

When the final scene came to a close, all the actors lined the stage, held hands, and bowed. The audience rose and clapped with enthusiasm. Amidst the applause, Kevin strolled onto the stage; he was holding a microphone in one hand and a large bouquet of flowers in the other. He handed both to the student in the center of the line, Elaine, a senior Meredith knew well both from class and from their time together as they worked on the play. Elaine took the microphone and the flowers, and the audience hushed to hear what she had to say.

"On behalf of the entire production, I would like to thank Miss Beck for playing such a crucial role in our success tonight. Miss Beck, your caring and hard work have been inspirational to us, both in the classroom and out. Thank you for all you have done for us. We will miss you next year as you embark on your newest endeavor, and we wish you much success and happiness."

Elaine held out the bouquet, indicating that Meredith should join her on stage. Stunned, Meredith remained seated where she was as the audience members cheered and looked around for her. Beth pushed her arm and urged her to stand; Meredith stood in a daze and walked up the aisle to the stage, where Elaine hugged her and handed her the bouquet. Teacher and student looked at each other with mutual respect and admiration, and for a blessed moment Meredith forgot her sadness and smiled, truly smiled, appreciative of the people in her life who had given her memories to cherish forever.

MEREDITH WAS BACKSTAGE, flowers in hand, congratulating and thanking the students with whom she had worked so hard over the course of the last few months. It was a bittersweet day for her, and she resolved to let the happiness engulf her.

As she left the back room to head out toward her car, she was confronted by Ned. His face wore a friendly but somber smile.

"Hi, Meredith."

Meredith stopped but did not meet his gaze. "Ned."

They stood still, facing but not looking at each other.

"What are you doing backstage?" she asked finally.

"I'm sorry, Meredith. I truly am."

Her eyes met his. "It's too little, too late."

"I know. I just had to tell you that before I missed my chance."

"I hope you feel better now."

They stood in silence.

"Look," she said, begrudgingly. "It's not really your fault. He would have come to the same conclusion even without your help."

"He was asinine to leave you. You're probably better off."

"Please stop talking about things you know nothing about."

"I know if I loved a woman who wanted to be with me too, I wouldn't abandon her the way he abandoned you."

"What do you want, Ned?" she asked wearily. "Did you track me down tonight to rub salt in an open wound, or what?"

"No, I'm sorry," he said, backing down. "I just wanted to apologize for what I said to you. About being ungrateful and whatnot."

"Ned, do you want my advice on something?"

"Sure."

"If you stop saying things you have to apologize for, you won't find yourself constantly apologizing."

Ned's face iced over, and he shifted where he stood, but he seemed to accept what she had said. "Got it." He cleared his throat, attempting to recover. "Listen, good luck in Virginia. I hope you get everything you deserve."

Meredith stared at him in silence. She wanted to say, *I hope you do, too*, but she couldn't bring herself to do it. Despite everything, she couldn't wish him harm; it wasn't who she was, and she wouldn't let him change her. She wouldn't let him make her as bitter as he himself was.

"Good luck to you, too," she said instead, meaning it, but unable to keep the irony totally out of her voice. Noting his brow furrow a little, she waved, turned, and left him where he was as she walked down the hallway for the very last time.

Meredith made it through the week of finals. When it was all over, she cleaned out her desk and her classroom and said goodbye. She tried not to focus on the loss, only looking forward to the new chapter in her life.

She and Kevin had a tearful goodbye. She attended graduation and congratulated her students, signing yearbooks and taking pictures with them in their caps and gowns. She spent an extra few moments with Ana and Kim, who had gotten into the colleges of their choices, crediting her with helping them make it happen. Meredith was proud of them, and she chatted joyfully with her study club students and their families about the promising year ahead. Then she went home to prepare for her move.

By the beginning of August, she had sold all her old furniture and was prepared to begin her one way drive to Grace and Frank's home in suburban Lovelace, Virginia. Her parents would be returning two weeks later.

She didn't know what she would find at her new destination. She was harder than before, but no less determined. The people and places she was about to meet would somehow become her new normal. But she would meet them ready to make her own choices, with the confidence to create her own standards in a new future unfettered by the restraints of the past.

She didn't have to shed her optimism; she just had to be careful.

Toward the end of August, the night before her move, Meredith walked the house, making sure everything was where it should be, and letting her memories overcome her. Everywhere she looked, she was reminded of Nick, recalled the happiness of her time with him and Vince. She stood in the kitchen and almost could imagine the sound of the key in the door, could almost recapture the excitement she had felt when Vince and Nick had returned home after work. In her bedroom, she almost saw Nick close the door behind them as they prepared for another joyous night together. Sighing but resigned, knowing she could not languish in a chapter of her life that had already been closed, she climbed the staircase toward her bedroom for the last time, knowing in the morning she'd start anew, once again.

To be continued . . .

MEREDITH AGAINST THE WIND

Loss and heartache brought strength and self-discovery. Now she must stay true to herself as she's pulled back toward the past she's left behind.

Seeking a fresh start, Meredith travels to a Washington, DC suburb of Virginia, where she meets Wes Bickhart, a charismatic attorney recovering from a divorce. Wes sweeps her off her feet with his wit, charm, and amiability, and together they enjoy a passion for intellectual banter and for each other. Meredith feels safe with Wes, who having been burned himself, wants nothing more than to give her a future of comfort and security. She is tempted by the seemingly perfect life Wes offers her. But a change in priorities has her wondering if this is what she wants anymore. And the longer she takes to decide, the more she realizes that this life might require her to sacrifice more of herself than she is willing.

In *Meredith Against the Wind,* Meredith is put to the test as she is forced to stand up for herself, even as she redefines who she really is. Harder now but stronger, and with new perspective, she becomes embroiled in a power struggle as she determines how much is worth surrendering for love.

Meredith Against the Wind **is second in a slow-burn series of cliffhangers ending with a warm and satisfying happily-ever-after.**

ALSO BY AMANDA GALE

Meredith Against the Wind

Meredith Into the Fire

Meredith With the Waves

Love in the Lavender

Strawberry and Sage

Sweet Lavvy

Catherine and the Wind

Gwyneth in the Garden

Maeve in the Morning

The Magic You Bring

Dahlia Almost Drowning

ACKNOWLEDGMENTS

Thank you to Diana, Sue, Heather, Kristin, and Megan. Special thanks to Erin, Katie, Melissa, Andrea, Laura, and Constance. I am especially indebted to my "focus group": Jodi, Anna, Dez, Melissa, Erica, Jessica, Cindy, Bridget, Jennifer, Lasa, and Teresa. Thank you to Gina and editor Jami Nord for feedback on the revisions.

These books are for all the strong women in my life.